A LESSON IN MUSIC AND MURDER

DAVID UNGER, PHD

Cover design by Damonza
ISBN-978-0-9967613-9-0

ALessonInMusicAndMurder.com

THE LESSON SERIES

A Lesson in Sex and Murder
A Lesson in Music and Murder
A Lesson in Therapy and Murder
A Lesson in Mystery and Murder
A Lesson in Baseball and Murder
A Lesson in Cowboys and Murder
A Lesson in Comedy and Murder
A Lesson in Comedy and Murder
Coming soon
A Lesson in Reunions and Murder

THE RELATIONSHIP TRAINING MANUALS

The Relationship Training Manual for Men
The Relationship Training Manual for Men* Women's Edition
Parenting Your Teen: A Relationship Training Manual

If music be the food of love, play on.

William Shakespeare

PROLOGUE

"The best I ever saw? Well, that's an easy one."

"Okay, what is it?"

"Well, I was at Woodstock."

"All right. End of discussion. You win. There's no way I can beat that."

"You can try."

"The best I got is I did see the Beatles at Shea Stadium. I thought that would have been the topper but you got me beat fair and square."

"You dudes left me in the dirt," another guy said. "I was gonna say I saw Janis at the Fillmore. I thought that was pretty cool."

"It is. I saw her with the Who and Jimi Hendrix at the Monterey Pop Festival."

"No way. I saw Hendrix with the Allman Brothers."

Standing in the will call line, listening to these guys one-up each other with their gig credentials, I was quickly put in my place. I hadn't attended any of those concerts. And though my rock-and-roll chops were decent, I knew I was out of my league. That wasn't surprising given where I was, but it still made me feel like someone's younger brother.

"I saw the Allman Brothers in '70 or '71 at the Whisky a Go Go."

"Whoa. That's heavy. The Whisky. I saw the Doors there years ago."

"Wow. The Doors. Very trippy. I saw them in Asbury Park. My good friend broke up with his girlfriend and I got to go with him. They blew my mind."

"I saw them at the Avalon Ballroom. I'd never seen anyone like Morrison before. I almost lost my girlfriend that night."

·I could understand that. Jim Morrison had been a captivating performer.

I wanted to join the conversation but the closest dot I could connect was having seen Bruce Springsteen at the Santa Monica Civic Auditorium. Before I could get up the nerve to speak, they'd moved on to other acts and venues.

I'll take music acts and venues for $20, Alex, I thought about saying, but wasn't sure that was the best entry either. Truth was, I was a bit of an outsider here. While I was looking forward to the weekend of music, I wasn't really here to listen to it. I had another purpose. A client wanted me to help him out if he got into difficulties—a purpose that was both familiar and unfamiliar to me. I'm a shrink after all, and my job is to help people navigate the difficulties they encounter. I see clients in my office, their home, or anywhere they want. When my client asked me if I'd come to the festival and help him out, it took me a couple of nanoseconds to say, *Sure*. If I could go to the festival and get paid, why not?

We never fully know what we're getting into until we get into it. But we usually have a good sense of what to expect. I assumed my client might find himself in some conflicts and want me to facilitate. He might need me to keep an eye on his substance intake. Or he might want to speak with me about life as he was living it.

Some of that happened.

CHAPTER 1

"What You See (Is What You Get)"
Oingo Boingo

Six Months Earlier

RECENTLY I GOT a new client named Drew. I suppose this is as good a time as any to put in this disclaimer—Drew isn't his real name. I need to protect anonymity so I've had to change names and some facts in this book to protect people's privacy. But for the most part, this is a true story and one you might know a thing or two about.

Drew came to me ostensibly because his girlfriend told him if he didn't see a therapist, she would leave him. Not the best motivation for therapy, but I've seen worse. He really liked his girlfriend and didn't want to lose her. He didn't really want to have her either. Well, he wanted to have her, but he also wanted to have some of the other women he was involved with in other cities.

Drew was a musician in a band I'm going to call Magoo. They looked and sounded a bit like the Eagles, except they had a woman in the band and not so many hits. That said, if I mentioned their big hit, you'd hear it playing in the jukebox in your head. They'd been a headliner for some years, and though not in the same league as the bands I heard those guys in the will call line talking about, they were certainly living the dream and knock knock knocking on stardom's door.

I'm not going to get into the nitty-gritty of Drew's therapy, but since he's the reason I was at the music festival I need to share a little. Drew had asked me to come to the four-day festival with him because the band had decided to spend the entire weekend at the event and there'd be plenty of time for him to get into trouble. By that he meant the basics—sex, drugs, and rock and roll, and the consequences thereof.

Drew didn't really need a babysitter. He'd logged in enough years as a rock and roller to know how to monitor himself. This festival would be different because his girlfriend, CeeCee, would be there. While that was a positive thing, he also knew some of his previous one-night stands from the area might be making their presence felt and he thought a steadying hand could be in order. He told me to mostly hang around the stage, food pavilion, and tech tent, and if he needed me he'd find me.

That's how I ended up outside sunny San Bernardino, California, on Labor Day weekend, 1982.

I'm a therapist. I'm also a teacher. A Los Angeleno. A thirty-five-year-old single guy who likes sports, music, time with friends and family, as well as an occasional joint and a shot of Cuervo. A regular guy. Or so I mostly think. I've been told I'm annoying and my "cutesy pushiness" makes some people want to puke. My mother thinks I'll be a late bloomer. My dad is just glad I have a job. My friends think I have redeeming values. You'll have to make your own assessment.

It's one thing to ply your trade. It's another to find anyone who'll pay you for it. Over the years I've been able to build my practice because I started doing something that got me a bit of a local reputation.

Now, I'll apologize in advance for talking about my dissertation, but you'll find it has relevance, not just to how I built my practice but also to your life and what happened over the weekend.

My dissertation was about time. Most therapists see clients for fifty minutes. I'd wondered why. My medical doctor sees me for as long as she needs to see me. Why didn't therapy work the same? I wanted to know what was so special about fifty minutes. Turns out nothing is special about it. Therapists go for fifty minutes because it's convenient for them. It has nothing to do with you.

Once I realized therapy could be fifty minutes long, or an hour and fifty, or ten hours and fifty, it freed me up to see people for varying amounts of time. Most people came to me expecting fifty minutes, but when I explained I was flexible, it wasn't long before I ended up spending afternoons or days with them. In and out of the office. My clients really liked it when I could join them in certain activities—a challenging discussion with their partner, a flight they were too scared to take alone. It really helped me to get an inside view of their life and help them where they needed it most—in their daily life. Therapists usually want you to take what happens in the office and apply it to your life, but I've been able to help clients apply the lessons of therapy on the job, with their partner, with their friends, anywhere they wanted.

When Drew wanted me to attend the US Festival with him it was the first time I'd spent more than a day with a client. It was also the first time that music played while murder happened.

CHAPTER 2

"Good Times Roll"

The Cars

Thursday, September 2, 1982

THE PROBLEM WITH camping is the same as with a lot of things. If you haven't done it in a long time, there's a lot you have to do in order to be able to do it again. Drew warned me that over 500,000 people were expected over Labor Day weekend. The place was going to be a zoo. I'd better come early, get a camping spot, and check in with him. He'd gotten me an all-access pass, and my early entry allowed me to set up my tent in a backstage area sufficiently close but not too close to the stage, food pavilion, and porta-potties.

I was ill-prepared for four days in a hundred degrees. Having grown up on the East Coast, I knew enough to call LL Bean and put myself in their hands. They sent me a tent, sleeping bag, and enough gear to ensure I'd be safe from mosquitoes and any unforeseen thunderstorms—which happens about once every ten years in California but more frequently in Maine. Fortunately, I had my own shorts, T-shirts, loafers, and suntan lotion.

The backstage area was its own city. There were hundreds of mostly young people in the area, some focused and striding with determination, others looking about in awe. I was in the latter group. There were large tents designated for food and hanging out—exclusive areas that barred the hoi polloi. Since I was "with the band" I could get into the areas to which Drew also had access. I could walk through the forested area and stroll by the two lakes that were fishing ponds the rest of the year. It reminded me a bit of summer camp on acid.

Perhaps you're a heat lover, but putting up a tent in a hundred degrees isn't an activity I want to get used to. Especially since I'd neglected to carry out a trial run at home beforehand. With no shade and in the blazing sun, I managed to turn a twenty-minute job into an hour's. Then I rolled out my sleeping bag, unloaded my accessories, and took my sweat-dripping body off to find Drew.

He'd told me to meet him in the round-the-clock food pavilion at seven. By the time I got there he was eating dinner, surrounded by a group of people. Drew and I had spoken about how he'd introduce me. He didn't want people to know I was his therapist and asked if it was okay to say I was a friend. I didn't want to lie and suggested he keep it vague, say I was a consultant who was helping him out with some things. He didn't like it but agreed to it.

Most of the people at the table were his bandmates. There was Josie, the bass player, who looked as good in person as she did on their album covers. Then Michael, the brooding lead guitarist, and Aiden, the drummer, whose long blond hair was tied up in a ponytail. There was one other person at the table, a striking woman named CeeCee, who informed me her name was CC. She gave no further explanation. She had fair skin, long auburn hair that curled around her head, and intense hazel eyes that made you want to look away before she did. She was Drew's girlfriend.

I got some food and ended up sitting next to another new arrival who told me she'd followed the Grateful Dead for years and had seen over fifty shows so far this year. I figured there'd been a lot of acid consumed along the way because her train of thought seemed to have left Terrapin Station some time ago.

Eventually things broke up and I got some time alone with Drew and CC. They took me on a tour of the grounds and gave me some background information on the festival.

"It's funny," Drew told me, "when you think of the sixties and seventies, you think free love and doing your own thing, but Steve Wozniak, or Woz as he prefers to be called, said it was all about me me me. But he wants this festival to be about 'us' and bringing people together. He wants to mix the make-the-world-better vibe of the sixties with technology so we can build more connected communities. He had this whole place constructed. There used to be a little park here with some trees and fishponds, but he moved tons of dirt to create this sloping bowl so people could see the massive stage from everywhere. He cleared out the whole area and brought in all these temporary buildings. It's amazing."

"Yeah," CC said. "He took some of the money he got from Apple and had Bill Graham get all the acts together. It's really something."

"I'll say," I said. "First off, you've got Magoo and the Dead."

"And don't forget Santana and Tom Petty," CC added.

"Personally," Drew said, "I'm really looking forward to Talking Heads and Fleetwood Mac."

"Yeah, they should be great. But my favorite is Jackson Browne."

"How sweet," CC said, which kinda made me feel good. "He's a bit of a fish out of water here. He really is the only singer/songwriter."

"Don't forget Jimmy Buffett," Drew put in. "He's a lightweight singer/songwriter but he's good with a margarita. That's no small thing."

"Yes, dear," CC said. I wasn't sure if she was agreeing or lamenting.

"I have to ask you both something. When I was standing in line, some guys were one-upping each other on what concerts they'd been to. I know guys are competitive but I didn't realize it extended to music. Say it ain't so."

"It's so. Boys compete about everything," CC said. "Guys are always trying to prove their dick is bigger than everyone else's."

"Okay. Good of you to bottom-line it. I have to admit, when one guy said he'd seen the Beatles at Shea Stadium and another said he'd been to Woodstock, I felt kind of limp."

"See…" she said.

"Dave," Drew said, "you know how many people saw the Beatles and were at Woodstock?"

"I don't know—maybe a few hundred thousand at Woodstock and fifty thousand or so at Shea."

"That's about right, but a few million will tell you they went to each. Don't believe everything you hear."

"I hear you. Should I believe that?"

"Dave, come on. You know me."

In case you're not familiar with Southern California, San Bernardino is in the desert. The only reason I could think to live here aside from loving the desert was because it was far enough away from Los Angeles so you could afford to buy a house. You'd have to spend a good portion of your day on the freeway, but you'd get to own (with the bank) a share of the American dream.

While Drew was busy with the band, I spent the evening strolling about the hundred acres that comprised the festival. There were people everywhere, and more coming in each minute. It was visually overstimulating. Everywhere you looked there was something happening. There were rows of food booths, porta-potties, showers, and other structures. A vast parking lot was next to a maze of tents that would make getting lost in the suburbs feel like a day in the park. I didn't know how the people in the middle would ever find their way back to their tents, especially given the condition they'd be in at the end of the evening.

The stage was immense and was surrounded by large screens. There were people scurrying to and fro attending to those things that need attending. The stage was so large it made the people seem small. I was excited to see and hear what was to come.

There was a giant tent that stood out in the grounds. Another was supposed to be springing to life later in the weekend. Evidently, they were air-conditioned and would house small performances and the latest technology. I'd heard there'd be some arcade games, Atari video games, and the movie props from *ET* and *The Empire Strikes Back*. I wasn't really into sci-fi and video games but I was into air-conditioning.

The setting didn't cry out murder, but it did.

CHAPTER 3

"Before the Deluge"
Jackson Browne

Friday, September 3, 1982

IN THE COMPANY of the Dead, Talking Heads, Fleetwood Mac, and the like, Magoo had been relegated to a Friday afternoon slot. They were scheduled to come on at four. Drew had told me to swing by their trailer an hour beforehand so I could hang out with the band for a few minutes before they kicked everyone out.

I wasn't familiar with being backstage at any venue, let alone a place as big as this. Since the festival was within driving distance of LA, many of the bands had planned to arrive a few hours before their performance, do their thing, and take off. Since Woz wanted the festival to be about community, he'd encouraged them to stay for the weekend. Magoo had opted in and brought their regular tour bus which they would sleep in, but they'd be hanging out in a trailer.

I went searching for their trailer, which I imagined served as their own green room. There were rows of trailers with signs on them—for other bands, officials, and functions. Magoo's was about thirty feet long with a door at both ends. I tried one door and it was locked. The other led me into a good-sized living room in which the band members and their partners, friends, and others were hanging out. There was a closed door at the far end which must have led to another room, and a door off to the side I guessed was a bathroom. There was a bar and hors d'oeuvres. Best of all it was air-conditioned.

The trailer had a bit of a cannabis haze. There was a coffee table with some magazines, a couple of full ashtrays, some beer bottles, and a copy of Hunter Thompson's *The Great Shark Hunt*. Drew was talking with a group of guys, and before I could make my way over to him CC was at my side.

"Hey," she said.

"Hi. This is nice. Is it the band's?"

"No, Bill Graham got one for each group."

"Very nice. I like the Persian rug."

"That's Josie's. The lava lamps over there are Drew's. The bonsai belongs to Timothy, Aiden brought the tiki god, and Michael is responsible for the Bob Dylan picture."

"So everyone gets to bring something to decorate the place?"

"Sort of, but it's more of a superstition thing."

"Like baseball players having to readjust themselves before every pitch?"

"I wouldn't know about that. But probably. Like ballplayers, musicians are performers, so they all get nervous and over time discover their own good luck charms."

"So Drew is into lava lamps?"

"Yeah. His dad used to sell them so they had them all over the house and it makes him feel at home."

"That's cool. It sure looks like everybody's having a good time."

"Maybe. There's been a bit of drama but things are back on track."

"Isn't there always a bit of drama in rock and roll?"

"In everything. So how's the therapy going with Drew?"

"You're going to have to ask him. I can't even tell you if he's my client."

"Aren't we're past that? I got your name from a friend and referred him to you."

"And thank you for that. How'd you and Drew meet?"

"He didn't tell you? Oh, never mind. I'll tell you my version and you can see if it matches up with anything you may or may not know."

"Sounds fair."

"I'm a bodyworker. A lot of times, musicians need different adjustments, especially when they play a lot of dates. I was on tour with Crosby, Stills & Nash, and they were playing the No Nukes concerts at Madison Square Garden. I met Drew there. He wasn't playing with Magoo, but sitting in with the house band. We hit it off and the rest is history."

"That must have been a memorable way to meet. I saw the movie, got the album, but being there must have really been something."

"It was terrific. Four nights in a row at the Garden, then a big outdoor concert at Battery Park that was almost as big as this. It really raised my consciousness hearing Ralph Nader speak about the toxicity of the nuclear industry. He said one day nuclear power would be put to rest but it would remain a threat to the environment for thousands of years. Fortunately, he also said one day every house would be run by solar power. I don't know about that, but it put a lot of people, including myself, on the path for getting rid of nuclear power."

"Yeah. That meltdown at Three Mile Island scared a lot of people and put a lot of us on alert. If one of these plants implodes, there could be tremendous harm."

"What could be tremendous harm?" Drew asked as he joined us.

"We were just talking about when you two met and Three Mile Island."

"Yeah. That could have been a lot worse. Not our meeting. That turned out well. I'd be happy to reminisce with you, but the band's going to be meeting now. Let's catch up after the show."

He gave her a quick goodbye kiss. I got a head nod and then everyone but the band left.

CHAPTER 4

"Breakdown"

Tom Petty

Woz HAD WANTED to make this event better than Woodstock. In some ways it was, and in some ways it wasn't. The large, air-conditioned tent was comfortably a step up. The rain of Woodstock had been traded in for the heat, which was pretty much a draw. I'd heard there'd be Diamond Vision screens, the largest anyone had ever seen, which would allow everyone to have a good view of the substantial stage. The sound system was the most sophisticated ever, so maybe there was an edge there. But the performers at Woodstock, in my book, had won the battle of the bands. The anti-war feelings that united people and guided Woodstock wasn't present. The community Woz wanted to build wasn't founded on unrest. It was founded on technology, which he believed would bring us closer together.

While my desire for creature comforts might drive me toward the air conditioned tent, my body decided to get a space in the wings where I could watch Magoo up close. I'd never seen the band perform and I was excited.

I knew lead singer Timothy was a wordsmith because his lyrics read like poetry. Was Drew a great musician? I didn't really know. Seeing and hearing is believing. I'd only heard Magoo's music on my record player or the cassette player in my car, and was never sure which solos were Drew's and which were Michael's. All I knew was, I liked the music and now I'd get to see Drew and the band play on this giant stage in the middle of the desert.

While rock and rollers aren't known for being timely, at a festival things are usually more orderly. If one band starts thirty minutes late, they have to shorten their set or else everyone else gets thrown off their schedule. Rock fans don't mind too much about the schedule but the organizers, as the name implies, like things to be more organized.

The two acts before Magoo had started close to on time. When four fifteen passed and the band was a no-show, it wasn't rock and roll atypical. But it was Bill Graham atypical. He had a reputation for running his shows on time. When four twenty came and went, the audience became a little restless. Standing in the sun without something to distract you aside from the sweating and sunburning bodies wasn't that pleasurable.

At four thirty, someone stepped up to the center stage microphone and said that Magoo would be unable to perform and the B-52's would be up shortly. There was some groaning, booing, and applauding.

I headed for their trailer. There was a cluster of people outside. Security guards and a few police were keeping people out. I asked if anyone knew what was happening.

"Someone said they all had food poisoning," a long-haired guy told me.

"Nah," said his friend with a Yosemite—Go Climb a Rock T-shirt. "I heard they had a big fight and someone got hurt."

"No way," said his friend.

"Yeah, I heard Josie slept with Drew and Michael got jealous."

"I'd sleep with her."

"Dream on."

I moved on to another group.

"Any idea what's going on?" I asked.

"I don't know," a cute blonde said to me. "The police just got here a little while ago."

"Someone's dead," said her blonder friend.

"Yikes. That's horrible. Any idea who?"

"I just heard someone say there was a fight."

I imagined the longer we waited the more versions of what happened would materialize. There were now forty or fifty people milling about. I saw CC talking with an equally striking woman and figured I might as well go over there.

CC introduced me to Lilah. Lilah was my height, slender, blonde, fair skinned, with slate blue eyes and a knowing smile. I tried to balance my eye contact between the two women but I was drawn to Lilah.

"Any idea what's going on?" I asked.

"We haven't heard anything," CC replied.

"I heard some people talking about food poisoning and fighting over Josie, but I don't think they were the most reliable sources."

"It's not like them not to do a show. They've been through a lot but it's always the show must go on."

"That's true," Lilah said. "The bands that last are the ones that take it seriously and have a professional attitude."

"I don't think about rock-and-roll bands being professional but you're probably right," I said.

"She is right," CC said. "She wrote her dissertation about bands and longevity so she knows a thing or two."

"Wow. A rock-and-roll dissertation. That's cool. Where were you in school?"

"UCLA."

"Okay. I did my undergrad there. Go Bruins."

"Before you two break into an eight clap, here comes Drew," CC said, moving to meet him.

I hadn't been paying my usual attention, having been caught

up with Lilah. I turned to face Drew and knew something was very wrong. His eyes were red, his face pale, and his countenance lacked its usual fiber.

"What's the matter?" CC asked.

"It's Timothy. He's dead."

"No," cried CC, and immediately hugged him.

The shock wave Lilah and I experienced hit Drew and CC tenfold. We stood there and watched. Some of the other band members had left the trailer and I imagined the news was being shared and spread.

I sensed the mood in the area shift. I heard some oh-no's, wails, and cries. Soon everyone at the festival would know. It's the commerce of information. People like to be able to tell other people something newsworthy; there's a certain prestige that goes with being the first to know.

Standing there next to Lilah, I had mixed emotions. Minutes ago, I'd met a woman who'd really garnered my attention. I wanted to know more about Lilah. Yet on the heels of that, someone whose songs I'd sung and whose bandmate I'd counseled had died.

Once again, it was the best of times and the worst of times.

I was sad Timothy was no longer alive. Sad he couldn't play, sing, and live more of his life. Selfishly, I wanted to hear more of his music. My thoughts went out to all the people who'd mourn his loss and those closest to him who'd miss his presence.

Truthfully, I wondered what happened to him. I'd just seen him and the band in the trailer. I hadn't spoken to him, but I'd caught a glimpse of him and he'd seemed fine. I'm curious by nature. I've been called annoying more times than I'd like, but usually my annoyance is in the service of my pressing someone because I want to know something. I'm a therapist after all and get paid to encourage and gently nudge people to talk about things they'd prefer to avoid.

What works well enough with my clients doesn't always work so well in other situations.

CHAPTER 5

"Here Today, Gone Tomorrow"
The Ramones

IT WASN'T LONG before someone went on stage and made the announcement Timothy had died unexpectedly. There was a moment of silence, then a pledge that the show would go on in his honor. And that was that.

Of course, that wasn't all of that. But it was all that was said from the stage at that moment. Backstage, groups of people were passing rumors, anecdotes, and joints. There were tears and hugs and a lot of emotion you don't often see at a rock show.

Drew was explaining how it had been the band's custom to leave Timothy alone for a half hour before a show. Everyone but Timothy cleared out of the trailer and the band had gone back to the tour bus to change their clothes and freshen up. I wasn't sure what freshen up meant in rock-and-roll land, but suspected for some it meant more than splashing water on their face.

After forty minutes, Aiden went to find out what was keeping Timothy. He found him unconscious on the floor with a hypodermic in his arm and ran back to the tour bus. The rest of the crew rushed over and Michael took the hypodermic out of Timothy's arm and Josie notified the first aid tent but it was too late. One of the medics confirmed he was dead and brought in the police, who were still in the trailer gathering evidence and information.

Those were the facts.

There was a lot of emotion. The band members were surrounded by different groups of people, and various sounds of distress were reverberating through the crowd.

"Wasn't he off the stuff?" CC asked.

"He was," Drew replied through his tears. "Or at least I thought he was. The fucking asshole. What the hell was he thinking?"

"He wasn't thinking," CC said.

Drew was agitated, his body was heaving, his speech staccato. "I can't fucking believe it. The asshole's dead. Just like that. The fucker shot up and killed himself. Jesus Fucking Christ."

Lilah and I just stood there while CC tried to console him, but she too was quite upset.

"This is horrible. I'm so sorry this happened," I said, more for me so I'd feel I was at least doing something. Neither CC or Drew seemed to hear it. Lilah nodded, which was something.

"My life is fucking ruined. His life is over. The band is over. Everything is over."

"It'll be all right," CC said.

"Fuck you. Nothing will be all right. He's dead. Such a waste. He was something special and now he's just another fucking dead rocker."

One moment Drew was sad, the next angry. Then forlorn. Then back around again.

There wasn't much to do but stand there and feel miserable. We therapists know there are emotional stages to mourning—denial, sadness, negotiation, anger, and acceptance. The thing about these stages is they really don't happen 1-2-3-4-5. It's more like 1-3-5-2-1-4-1-5… until they fade away or you fade away.

Therapists use the stages to offer comfort. When someone gets angry at the person who died, you can console them by saying it's a natural reaction. There's no right or wrong way to deal with death. All ways suck. Which is why a lot of people feel miserable no matter what they do. Death may be a natural part of life, but it tends to be one we'd rather not have to deal with directly.

Watching Drew and CC and the outpouring of emotion, I was swept up in the pain. In my life, a lot of rock-and-roll stars (and non-stars) had died too young. Elvis, Jim Morrison, Buddy Holly, Richie Valens, and the Big Bopper on the day the music died. Gram Parsons, Jim Croce, Bobby Darin, Cass Elliot, Keith Moon, Lowell George, and Harry Chapin. Otis Redding, Jimi Hendrix, Janis Joplin, John Lennon, and Bob Marley. Throw in John Belushi just a few months earlier and you had a lot of great musicians dying before their time.

After a while I heard the B-52's. I could make out their words of tribute to Timothy and dedicating "There's a Moon in the Sky" to him and all the souls among us. Some of the people backstage moved closer to the stage; others drifted off. CC said she and Drew were going to take a walk by the lake and they'd see us later.

That left me with Lilah.

We gazed at each other for a little too long without saying anything. I didn't know what she was thinking, but I was thinking this woman could definitely be a contender.

"Can I ask you something?"

"Sure. What is it?"

"Is it too soon for me to kiss you? I really want to. I know it's too soon and this isn't the moment, but I'm ready. What do you say?"

"I say that's very cute. And it is too soon. We might get there but I'm not as sure as you seem to be."

"I'm mostly sure, but I suppose it would be good to talk a little and get a fuller sense of one another. But I can tell you right now, things look really good to me."

"That's very nice. But, you know, some women like to be courted or at least know a little more before jumping into things."

"Yeah, I've heard that. I do have a tendency to jump in."

"A tendency?"

"Okay, maybe it's more than a tendency. I can slow down now, but I just want to go on record as saying I told you so."

"Now, don't be getting obnoxious on me. Stick with cute and fumbling."

"Okay. I'm good at the fumbling. I'll let you be the judge of cute."

"That's fair. Right now I'd say the judge is in recess."

"So are you interested in the B-52's?"

"Not really. You?"

"Not really."

"Want to go for a shady spot and swap life stories?"

"Not really... How about just talking and seeing what happens?"

"You got it."

We headed for some good-sized tents set up with chairs so people could get out of the sun. I couldn't help but notice she had a long runner's stride to go with her slender physique. I tried to keep my eyes forward but couldn't help but take a sideways glance now and then. Things were certainly looking promising.

We found a spot that caught the breeze of an oscillating fan. I figured I might as well start with the therapist's generic opening question.

"How are you doing?"

"Not that well. I'm not a big fan, but CC is a close friend and I feel bad for her."

"Of course."

"I'd never met Timothy but he'd agreed to let me interview him this weekend. It's strange —he made plans to do something... was about to play his biggest venue and then this happens."

"Yeah. It's hard to understand. He had so much going for him. Maybe he was nervous about the show and needed a crutch but overdid it."

"To hear Drew tell it, he'd kicked the junk."

"Yeah. I heard that too. But, you know, they say relapse is a part of recovery. Sort of two steps forward and one step back."

"I suppose so."

We sat there silently while the fan passed us by. After a while she asked, "How do you know Drew?"

"We met a few months ago. He knows I like rock and roll so he asked me to help out. What about you? How do you know CC?"

Some time ago I'd learned this Aikido-like move to respond to incoming questions. I short-answered Lilah's question and then turned it back on her. Therapists do this all the time. If you ask a therapist what they think about something, a non-Aikido response would be, "It's not important what I think. What do you think?" That response pushes back a little bit and can cause a ripple when you'd rather things be still. An Aikido-minded therapist would say something akin to, "I'm happy to consider that, why not tell me what you think first."

Lilah smiled at me. I hadn't said much about how I knew Drew. I couldn't tell if she'd spotted my sleight of hand or was just being nice. Either way she said, "CC and I met backstage at a Tom Petty concert. She was doing bodywork on a member of the band and I was doing research for my dissertation. We just hit it off."

"Okay. I promise not to get into a long discussion about dissertations, but come on, tell me more about yours."

"I studied the longevity of rock musicians. What are the circumstances that allow a band or musician to have a long career? Needless to say, talent plays a large part, but there are other significant factors that come into play."

"So did you interview a lot of musicians? That must have been fun."

"It was. Mostly. I interviewed them and was often allowed to spend some time with them and observe them. I'm a sociologist so

I was curious about the interactions musicians have with each other and the world they live in."

"That's fascinating. I'm having dissertation envy. What got you interested in that? And how were you able to convince UCLA to allow you to do that?"

"It wasn't hard. Sociologists are interested in all groups and society so my committee members were eager to working on it with me. The rock-and-roll world is written about a lot, but there hasn't been much academic investigatory work. What about you? What was your dissertation about?"

I noticed she'd done a little Aikido of her own and hadn't answered my question about what had gotten her interested in studying musicians.

"I'm happy to tell you but I'm really curious about your work and would like to talk with you more about it. Like, what did you find contributes to longevity and who did you get to interview?"

"Happy to tell all, but don't think that will allow you to skip out on talking about yours."

"Okay, but you know, aside from you and a handful of others, not many people are interested."

"I'll tell you how interested I am once I hear more about it."

"You asked for it."

"I did. But we'll have to do it another time. Right now I need to catch up on some things."

"Very well. I'll see you later. Even though the news about Timothy is upsetting, I have to admit I'm looking forward to seeing Talking Heads later."

"Me too. I'm sure I'll be in the wings for that."

And with that she turned and left. I watched her go until I couldn't see her anymore.

CHAPTER 6

"Spirits in the Material World"
The Police

TALKING HEADS WEREN'T scheduled to play for another hour. Since every step I made was accompanied by a bead of sweat, I needed to drink something to balance out the water that was exiting my body. I'd never been granted backstage access before. I'd had to wait in long lines, pay event prices, and deal with limited food options. Standing in the food pavilion buffet line, I realized the choices were still limited but the fare was considerably better. Bill Graham had hired the best chefs from the Bay Area… sort of compensation for the heat, dust, and sun. I opted for a salad and lasagna complete with garlic bread and a tall glass of water.

Garlic bread is on my list of foods not to eat on a first date along with fried chicken, lobster, and spaghetti. While the neatness factor with garlic bread was greater, the residual olfactory experience would be hard to mitigate. Yet the appeal of eating the bread now outweighed any challenges ahead. An example of choosing short-term gain over future cost. I'm sure you know about that.

There were a lot of circular tables with groups of people sitting around them. I scanned the room but couldn't see Drew, CC, or Lilah. I opted for a table with a high-spirited group and asked if I could join them. One person said, "Sure, we're just leaving." And sure enough, they did.

I don't mind eating alone, although there was a time when I might have felt it reflected poorly on me. Whatever message my being alone might have sent out didn't really bother me anymore. There are advantages to not being a teenager.

I hadn't yet compromised my breath with the garlic bread when I was joined by Michael, Magoo's lead guitarist. He was accompanied by a pale weary-looking yet kinda sexy woman I didn't know and a sunburnt, well-bearded and frazzle-haired man.

"You're Drew's friend," the wild-haired man said. "Mind if we join you?"

"Happy to have you. I was about to start on the garlic bread so you might want to sit a bit aways."

"Hey," he said, gesturing at this plate. "You ain't the only one. We're all brothers here."

I wasn't sure the weary-looking woman agreed, but I considered his statement one of acceptance if not inclusion. I did notice he might be my garlic bigger brother as he had three good-sized pieces and his paper plate was doing all it could to hold its overflowing collection. Michael's plate was modest in contrast. The woman didn't have a plate.

"I'm David," I said.

"Hi. I'm Ross. This is Carol and Michael."

They nodded.

"I'm so sorry about Timothy."

"Thanks," they said in unison.

"I know you, Michael, from the band, and you're the manager, aren't you, Ross? But I don't know you, Carol. Are you connected to the band?"

Ross forked lasagna into his mouth. For someone who seemed to have a large appetite, he wasn't carrying much extra weight. Maybe the bulk eating was due to the free food.

"I'm his wife."

"Do you three want to talk band stuff? If so, I'll just people-watch and focus on the food."

"Nah," Ross replied. "We could use having something else to talk about."

"I have some questions that aren't band related."

"Shoot," said Ross.

"What do you think of this setup? This place is massive. Not long ago it was a desert. I don't know if I want to come back, but I've never seen anything like this before."

"Me either," Michael said. "We've played outdoor venues but nothing like this. Yes, it's blistering hot, but it adds to the other-worldliness of the place. I was out in the tech tent yesterday and they have amazing games. Woz is a genius. They say this year they may sell a million Apple computers."

"That'll never happen," Carol said, and I agreed with her.

"No wonder he can afford to put this together," Ross said. "It must have cost him millions to build this place, and these acts don't come for free. I bet he's going to be out a bundle."

"I don't think he'll come close to recouping his expenses," I said.

"Don't be so quick to judge," Michael said. "You're forgetting the tech tent with the games and computers. He may lose money this weekend but he's getting people interested in technology, and that right there is a money-making industry."

"It's all about money," said Carol, evidently not a glass-half-full person.

"You got it. But I'm loving the sound system," Ross said.

"It's totally radical," Michael added. "The sound in this venue is amazing."

An uncomfortable silence followed. Then Ross said, "Those big-screen TVs. I've never seen anything like that. It's remarkable."

"That's technology," said Michael.

"Technology I get," said Ross. "Use it to make TVs bigger and sound systems sharper, but computers? I'm not so sure."

"I agree with you," I said, trying to make some inroads. "I'm not convinced Apple will survive."

"That's very astute of you," Ross observed. "Frankly, I don't even use my typewriter much. I don't think computers will catch on."

"The truth is," I said, "I'm afraid of computers. First off, they're smarter than me, and I'm scared if I touch the wrong button and do the wrong thing everything will disappear."

"I've heard other people say that but, trust me," Michael said. "There's nothing to be afraid of. Technology is here to make our lives better."

"Your life better, not mine," said Carol.

"Right," Ross said. "Just ask Hal."

"Don't worry," Michael said. "They'll take over the world someday, but we won't know it. We'll end up relying on them so much, we'll no longer need to know how to function the way we do now. Bit by bit, we'll dummy down, but the genius of computers is they'll make you think you're getting smarter. Then one day when we're all complacently living the good life, a robot will interrupt our séance to tell us they've taken over the world and humans will no longer procreate and soon we'll become an extinct species."

"That's grim, though gripping at the same time," I said.

"Yeah, Michael's a fatalist, but a darn smart one so we'd all ought to pay heed," said Ross.

"Fuck you all," said Carol.

"Yeah, it sounds like we're all going to be fucked soon," I said, trying to get on her good side, but not sure there was one.

"I don't know," said Ross. "I'm still back with that fear of making a mistake and erasing something I wrote. It's hard enough for me to type something without worrying about it disappearing."

"Lighten up," said Michael. "We're all going to be destroyed. Don't worry so much about the little stuff."

"Yeah, just worry about the human race being destroyed. That's much more relaxing," Ross said.

"But, you know," said Michael, "some of us will have jobs in zoos and maybe you'll be popular with those robots that have a thing for pets."

"Okay," I said, making my move to go, "while I'm waiting for my possible next job in the zoo, I'm going to go see if I can grab a good spot to watch Talking Heads. It was great, although a bit disturbing, talking with you, and I hope to catch up later on."

"Peace," Michael said.

Carol made a halfhearted attempt at a smile and Ross waved a hand as he munched on his garlic bread.

CHAPTER 7

"Fins"

Jimmy Buffett

I WAS STANDING with a group of people in a designated VIP area at the side of the stage watching the Talking Heads. There was shade, we weren't standing sweating and shirtless right up against each other, and we were a lot closer to the band than most of the crowd. The brave and/or heavily sedated group of fans packed into the area in front of the stage had a head-on view, and if they were fortunate enough to position themselves directly behind someone shorter, they had an unobstructed view. The sound was better up front, and better still if you were further back and in the sweet spot where my audio-engineer client told me is the only place to listen.

Having neither a well-trained nor even a discriminatory ear, I was happy to get a side view of the action and a somewhat off-center mix of the music. Whenever there's music and people together, a communal energy develops. The crowd's energy ebbs and flows, but when a band hits its stride and the audience is swaying/dancing/singing/dreaming/blissing along, it's a special moment.

Sweating in the shade, I was lost in the moment until Drew came up beside me and said, "I have to talk with you."

I could see deep concern on his face as he led me to an area behind the trailer. When we were as alone as we were going to get, he turned to me and said, "You know me. Sure, I've got issues, but for the most part I'm a level-headed person. Yes, I'm worried some of my groupies might show their faces this weekend and make a scene, but I'm not one to yell fire unless there's really a fire."

"Right."

"So, what I'm going to tell you may sound a bit out there, but I want you to take it in the context of knowing who I am."

"Got it."

"The police see this as just another rock-and-roller overdose."

"I can understand that. You said he was found with the needle still in his arm."

"Yeah. That's true. But I don't think he put it there."

"What?"

"Someone shot him up to make it look like he OD'd. I tell you, he's been clean for a while now and I just don't think he put that needle in his arm."

"Did you tell the police what you think?"

"Of course I did. They listened, but that's all. They didn't see any signs of a struggle so they can't figure out how someone would be able to stick a needle in him without some bruises or signs of resistance."

"Makes sense."

"Makes sense, but it doesn't. I'm telling you, he didn't shoot himself up."

"Okay. I get that. You think someone purposefully shot him up. Maybe he asked someone to help him out and they did. When he blanked out they took off."

"No. If he'd wanted to shoot up, he'd have done it himself. As much as we're a band, he was a loner."

"So you think someone came in there and somehow or other got that needle into his arm without leaving any trace?"

"You don't believe me either."

"No, no, no. Don't go there. I'm just trying to figure out what you think happened."

"I don't think anyone could have gotten in there who he didn't know. He must have trusted someone enough to let them in. Then I don't know what happened. But I do know he didn't voluntarily shoot up."

"Okay, let's say you're right. The police will run an autopsy, in which case they'll find evidence that supports your theory."

"It's not a theory. I'm telling you, he didn't shoot up. Jesus Christ, what do I have to do to convince you?"

"I get it. I'm just trying to put the pieces together. Do you think someone wanted to kill him or somehow or other accidentally helped him overdose?"

"That's what I want you to find out."

"What?"

"You heard me. You've told me about how you solved that mystery with the sex doctor. No one else here is going to solve this. Maybe the police will figure it out down the road, but meanwhile you've got all the suspects here. Do your shrink thing and figure it out."

"I'm glad you have faith in me and my sleuthing shrink abilities, but I'm not sure I can be of much help."

"You're my shrink. Your job is to help me. So, help me. My life just got thrown in the toilet. The least you can do is let me know who flushed it away."

"I'm happy to try and help. You know that. Why don't you think about who might have wanted to kill him. Also who he might have let in there that knows how to shoot up. Then you can casually introduce them to me and we can go from there."

"Thanks, Doc. I've been thinking about it... We need to start with the band, Ross, and Carol. I'll see if anyone else comes to mind."

"Well, I've met Ross, Carol, and Michael so at least I've got a step up there. Maybe you can introduce me to Josie and Aiden and anyone else you might think it's worthwhile for me to meet."

"Will do."

"I want to help you out if I can. That sex-therapist thing just sort of happened. I got tied up in it and the next thing I knew I'd figured it out. Well, mostly. The police helped."

"Whatever. Come on. Let's get you working. I'm paying for you being here; earn your money."

Drew had a point. He was paying me to be here and help him out in any way I could. When I first came up with the idea of helping my clients outside of the office and in their daily lives, I'd envisioned spending time in their home, meeting their family, helping them settle some disputes, or maybe going into their workplace and helping them work more effectively. I hadn't envisioned spending four days at a music festival. Not that I minded; it just hadn't occurred to me.

While I had no issue with facilitating during any flare-ups between Drew and CC, as well as any other paramours that might show up, finding out whodunit put the weekend into a different focus.

I had a student who was also a survival-skills instructor at an outward-bound school. He told me to track an animal you basically search their terrain until you find footprints. You have two choices: track it forward or backward. Forward, you face the unexpected. Backward is the safer approach as you can find where it sleeps and set up for its return.

I was thinking about the people Drew suspected. They all had a history with Timothy. I could track their relationships backward and see if I could find any clues in the past that might illuminate the present. I could also track things forward and see how the various people responded to his death. Out in the forest, you'd have to make a choice to go this way or that. In this desert, I figured I could go both ways.

CHAPTER 8

"Around the Dial"

The Kinks

I FOLLOWED DREW to the band's bus in search of Josie or Aiden. I'd never been on a tour bus and I was excited to take a peek behind the curtain. The first thing I noticed was the driver's seat, or more correctly the area surrounding the driver's seat. The area was decorated with streamers that looked left over from a New Year's Eve party, tiki-hut decorations, and pictures of a skinny man with a cowboy hat with all manner of rock-and-roll bands.

"Oh, yeah," Drew said, "Big Bob's been driving bands for a long time. He owns the bus and rents it out to bands year-round, except when he takes it to Key West for some downtime."

"Big Bob doesn't look like Big Bob," I pointed out.

"He got the nickname a long time ago. There are stories about how he got the name, but he's never told us. Says he likes to keep people guessing."

"Well, he sure knows how to brighten up his workspace."

There was an open area with couches and a table where I imagined people ate and hung out. There were tiki gods all over the place, bamboo shades on the windows, and somewhere I imagined was a tape of Jimmy Buffett.

No one was visible.

"Come on, I'll show you the rest," Drew said. It resembled a sleeping car on a train in an old movie. On each side of the center aisle there were curtained bunks. The beds, like the windows, had bamboo privacy shades pulled across them. Then there was a bathroom. And at the end of the bus was a door with *Big Kahuna* written on it. It also had yellow crime-strip tape across it.

"Timothy didn't die there," said Drew, pointing at the door. "But that was where he slept. Bob says every band has a big kahuna."

"I guess he's not an egalitarian."

"Yeah, Bob's more the dictator type. You don't want to cross him. But if you're his people, you're his people."

"I'll try to remember that. But how come the tape?"

"Don't know. The police just want to keep people out."

As we went back down the aisle, the shades on a bunk opened up.

"Hey," Aiden said.

"Sorry to disturb you," Drew said.

"No worries. I was just resting and reading. I needed some time alone."

"I hear you. I want to introduce my friend. This is David."

"Hey, Dave."

"Hi," I said. I wanted to remind Drew we'd talked about him not introducing me as a friend, but figured I'd speak with him later. I also wanted to shake Aiden's hand and say, *It's David not Dave*, but I'm not that guy. Well, in a way I am. I expect a person to call me by the name I've given them, not their version of it. But I'm not going to correct them. Instead, I'll just note it.

"How you doing?" Drew asked.

"Okay... well, truthfully, I feel like shit. How about you?"

"About the same. It's been one fucked-up day."

"You've got that right. I don't know why he did it. This gig could have taken us to the next level. We were all set to move up the chart."

"Yeah. It's fucked."

"What's that you're reading?" I asked.

"Oh, it's one of Timothy's old journals. I was reading some of his entries."

"How is it to read?"

"It's a little eerie. I've read them before. Not sure if anyone else has read them, but I've always valued them."

"How lucky for you to be able to read them."

"Yeah, I guess so. But if you want, I'm happy to lend this one to you as long as I get it back before we leave."

"I'd really like that. Thank you for trusting me," I replied as he handed a leather-bound journal to me. "I know I've lent out a lot of books with assurances they'd be returned and they never made it back, so I really appreciate your letting me borrow it. I'll be sure to get it back to you before the last night."

"Thanks, Aiden, for lending that to Dave."

"No problem. It's good for me to let it go for a while."

"Well, thanks again. If you want it back sooner, just let me or Drew know. I don't mean to pry but can I ask you a question?"

I paused for a nanosecond before saying, "What do you think happened? Drew and I were talking about it and it just doesn't seem to fit. Like you say, things were moving in a positive direction."

"I'll tell you what most people think happened. He freaked. He was always a bit spooked by the fame. He wanted it and yet didn't. Back when he was using regularly, he'd get seriously wasted before he took a step on stage."

"A lot of people get stage fright," I said.

"It was more than that. Sure, he got nervous—heck, we all do—but he also saw our shows as the highlight. Sort of like Saturday night. It's one thing to get wasted once a week, but when you're playing four, five, six nights a week it adds up."

"Yeah, he bottomed out a couple of years ago, though," Drew added. "Since then he's been clean. Sure, he might have had a toke now and then but nothing stronger."

"Yeah, I haven't seen him high in a long time, except that night we all played that rock-and-roll geography game."

"Oh, yeah. I forgot about that. That was a fun night."

"What's rock-and-roll geography?"

"It's a take on the geography game we played as kids. I say *Los Angeles* and then you need to say a place that begins with *S*. Except instead of places, we used musicians, bands, and names of places we'd played."

"Sounds like fun."

"It was," Aiden said. "Except it got weird. We're kind of competitive people so none of us liked it when we couldn't think of something. Timothy was the worst when he couldn't think of something. And, of course, when you couldn't think of something you needed to take a shot of tequila. Things got ugly at the end."

"Yeah?"

I was curious to learn more, but Drew said, "Sorry to bother you, pal, but we're going to take off now. See you later."

And with that he turned and left.

"It was nice meeting you," I said. "I'm sorry for the circumstances. Thanks again for trusting me with the journal."

"No problem."

I couldn't understand Drew's hasty departure. Something was a little off about it. Aiden said Timothy had freaked. It sounded to me like he might have had something else to say, but Drew had gotten us out before I could find out.

Since I was tasked with finding out whodunit, I needed to ask Drew about the awkward goodbye. Not being one to overindulge in foreplay, I got straight to the point.

"Hey," I said as I caught up with him. "What happened back there? How come you cut things off so abruptly?"

"What? No, I didn't end things abruptly. We were interrupting him and out of respect we needed to stop intruding."

"Okay, I get that. But we need to have a little talk."

"About what?"

"About my job description. First off, please don't introduce me as your friend. If you don't want to say I'm a consultant who's helping you out, let's find something else, but calling me a friend is dishonest."

"Sorry. No problem. I forgot. I'm fine with the consultant part. We've had all manner of consultants helping us out so please accept my apologies. It won't happen again."

"Okay. You don't really need to apologize and say it won't happen again, because it could. Just do your best, and if it slips out and you notice, please consider correcting it."

"Got it. Is that the talk?"

"Well, part of it. The rest is this—if you want me to help you out, you need to let me talk with people. Therapy is an intrusive thing. Therapists bore into psychic material. I'm not going to knowingly hurt anyone, but I do want to be able to explore with people."

"So you don't want me to introduce you to people?" he said a bit defensively.

"No, I want you to do that. Just try not to interrupt me when I'm trying to get someone to give me information. I want to know more about what Aiden thinks happened."

"I get it. I need to let you do your thing."

"Exactly. You're welcome to add your two bits, but try not to cut me off."

He looked like a little kid who'd been chastised. He wasn't used to me correcting him that way. It made me realize it might have been a mistake to change my role with him.

Here's the problem. As soon as I'd agreed to figure out what'd happened to Timothy, I'd put myself in a dual role—which is a big no-no in my business. I'm only supposed to be a therapist. Not a therapist and a friend, lover, business associate, or detective. I'd been on shaky enough ground when I'd agreed to see clients outside of the office. I'd run it by my licensing board, who'd basically told me to check with my insurance agent. They'd said I was okay as long as I was working within the "scope of my license." I figured supporting Drew throughout the weekend was within the scope. I wasn't sure if they'd think the same about the detective part.

When I'd told Drew not to interfere with my sleuthing, I was no longer doing the therapy job I'd been hired for. If I'd asked him how he felt about what I'd said and made sure to take the time for him to process his reactions to my evolving role, I'd have stayed closer to the mark.

As it was, I was bending the rules and hoping not to break them too much.

Truth be told, I like the therapy and the detective sides of things. I like trying to help a client figure out why they feel and act the way they do, and I like trying to put the pieces together to solve a murder. But I knew I was prioritizing one role over the other. And that might create complications... if it hadn't already.

CHAPTER 9

"Heartbreaker"

Pat Benatar

As Drew and I walked closer to the stage I noticed I heard him more clearly. Then I realized that was because Talking Heads had quit playing. *Phooey.*

Then I recalled the talk I'd had with myself before I left the house. *David*, I'd said, *the festival isn't about you listening to music and whining about sleeping in a tent. You're working. You can't expect to watch the acts you really want to see. The music will be in the background while you help your client manage his life.*

I'd asked Drew for time off to see Jackson Browne. I wanted that to be my time; the rest of the weekend I'd be available to Drew but hoped to catch some of the other acts. He'd been fine with that, but that didn't stop me from whining about missing the Talking Heads.

The Police were up next and while I was mildly interested, they didn't quite do it for me. That probably meant I'd get to see their whole set. But, truthfully, I was way more interested in meeting Josie.

Before we could find her, CC found us.

"Hey, babe," Drew said as they did some perfunctory kissing. Personally, when it's hot and I'm sweaty I can do with a quick peck on the cheek. That said, I wouldn't have minded some perfunctory kissing of my own.

One of Southern California's claims to fame is it cools off in the evening. Combine that with no humidity and few mosquitoes, and people consider moving here. Unfortunately, the cool evening breeze that might have brought the night to a pleasant close was absent. The winds were off the desert and Vegas-warm, which means you're comfortable as long as you're lying by the pool.

CC looked like she'd been dancing.

"Wow, that was great," she said. "They were even better than I hoped they'd be. He's awesome. What did you think?"

I deferred to Drew. He took a moment to consider his reply. That made me feel good and it also alerted me. In our regular therapy, Drew had told me he had anger issues and he could go from zero to sixty awfully fast. We'd talked about how he'd learned to express his anger and he how he could continue to learn how to monitor it. When he heard or saw something that got a rise out of him, he could take a moment before responding.

CC's question seemed innocent enough to me, but the fact Drew was taking his time to respond told me something.

"Yeah. They were great," Drew said dismissively. "Have you seen Josie?"

Now it was CC's turn to take a moment. I might have seen some irritation in her face.

"No, I haven't. Maybe she's back at the bus."

"Yeah. We were about to check there. Listen, babe, we're on a bit of a mission here so I'll see you later back at the bus."

And with that less-than-warm encounter we went off to find Josie. I could see some couples counseling in the future.

We found Josie at a table in the food pavilion, surrounded by half a dozen guys. She was worth the attention. When guys talked about the best-looking women in rock, she was always on the short-list. She was statuesque, like a runway model, with long straight black hair that came down to her waist and flew in all directions when she played. She had piercing green eyes and a smile that would make any dentist proud. Men, as witnessed in this moment, couldn't stay away from her and, according to what I'd heard, she couldn't stay away from them.

I've had women clients tell me as soon as they're nice to a man, he misinterprets that kindness for romantic interest. It's easier, they tell me, just to act disinterested. Unless they were interested. With Josie, I had a feeling most men thought she was interested because she emitted genuine warmth. Combine that with a healthy degree of sexiness and it was no wonder she had a bunch of men swarming around her.

She was enjoying the attention, although you could tell she wasn't happy. As with the other members of the band, Timothy had played an important role in her life. They'd been an item for a while a couple years ago, and for all I knew the spark they'd shared might have never left. She wasn't crying but it was obvious she had been. While she wasn't looking her best, she was still the best-looking person in the room. Maybe also the loneliest.

Josie had musical skills that would land her in another band, but had she been less good-looking those offers might not have been so forthcoming.

You know the facts. Better-looking people are perceived as smarter, healthier, and more socially skilled. They aren't; we just see them that way. They have a halo effect that's often cashed in for better jobs and better circumstances. Josie seemed to have a lot of talent to go with her looks, and maybe even the reverse was true for her. Maybe because she was so good-looking people considered her less of an artist.

I imagine Josie thought men wanted her for her looks and her rock-and-roll cred, and like someone who is wealthy, she wasn't sure if anyone really liked her for who she was. Of course, I didn't know any of that. It was just a stereotypical response that might very well change if I got to know her. Which, I admit, I was eager to do

Drew hesitated on the outskirts of the table. He seemed unsure as to how to approach her. Would we join the group of admirers or wait for a time when we could be alone with her? I was open to both and it appeared Drew was deliberating along those lines.

After a bit, Josie saw Drew and said, "Hey."

"Hey," said Drew. "When you have a few free minutes, I'd like to speak with you."

"Sure. Happy to," she replied, and smiled at her admirers. "We were finishing up. How about I meet you at the bus in a few minutes?"

"You got it." He smiled at her and that was that.

On the way back to the bus, I realized Josie had done something I liked. She'd shown her care and responsiveness to Drew. Sometimes people are more reserved and don't want you to see their happiness. Her happiness about talking with Drew was overt. She might have felt that way about a lot of people, but when she'd said she'd be happy to talk with him, I'd believed her and she'd earned some points with me. Of course, I could have been ascribing positive attributes to her on account of her looks. Or maybe there was some history there.

Josie showed up about thirty minutes later. That lost her some points. I have a thing about time. I'd written my dissertation about time so, for better or for worse, I'm aware of it. When someone says they'll see you in a few minutes, in my book that doesn't mean thirty. More like five to fifteen. In her book a few could be thirty to ninety. Still, I judge people by my book.

I'm more of a nitpicker than I like to admit.

Still, I was happy when she showed up. Drew seemed to have a grasp on what a few minutes meant in Josie Land and appeared not to mind. I wondered if they'd ever been an item.

"Oh," she said, coming up the steps. "I see you have company. Want to get together another time?"

Add consideration to the plus-points side.

"No. Come on in. I want to introduce you to my friend. I mean my personal consultant, David."

She strode over to me. Gave me a good once-over and a firm handshake. More points.

"Hi," we said in unison.

"What does personal consultant mean?" she asked.

Drew looked at me. I looked at him until he said, "It means he's my shrink and I asked him to come to the festival to help me sort some things out."

"That's cool."

"How's it going?" she asked me. "You able to help him sort anything out?"

"Well, that's kinda why he wanted us to meet."

"Oh? We have some sorting out to do?"

"No, no. We're good. David has some skills that might be able to help us find out what happened to Timothy."

"Whoa. Really? You think we need to bring in somebody to figure out what happened? It's obvious what happened. Timothy freaked out again. Found someone who had a kit and something went wrong. Fucking idiot."

"It sure seems like that and it's upsetting," I said. "You think he found someone with dope and when he shot up something went wrong?"

"Isn't it obvious? I mean maybe he brought the stuff, but he's been clean for some time. Like the rest of us, he must have been going crazy about being here, wanted to chill out, and OD'd. End of fucking story."

"Drew, can I share something you told me about Timothy?"

"Sure."

"You were pretty sure he was clean. That seems to be the one clear point. How and why he died we don't really know. Josie, like the police, you think he OD'd. Which he might very well have done. But we don't know. Since you both think he was clean, I wonder where he got the dope. It doesn't sound like he'd have brought it, although he could have, just to have it nearby if he wanted it. Sort of like packing for a trip and bringing too many clothes just so you cover a lot of options."

"Yeah," Drew said. "I don't think he packed it. We'd have known. My vote is someone gave it to him here."

"I agree," Josie said.

"So maybe I can try to find out who might have gotten it for him. If someone did, they didn't stay. Or if they did and saw him pass out, they took off and don't want to be found. Any ideas about who I might be talking about?"

"Sheridan," they said in unison.

"Okay. Suspect number one. Anyone else you can think of?"

"Jeez," Josie said. "I can't think of too many people in our circle who still shoot up. Maybe Eve now and then. Carol would know how to score even if she isn't still using."

"Yeah. They'd be on my list too. Eve has gone straight but you never can tell with her. She's kind of high on life now. Carol, has been clean for some time but she knows how to score. Maybe Ross. He used to party hearty, although now he too is clean. Heck, all our crowd are over it. We're getting old."

"Maybe you're old," Josie said, "but some of us are just smarter."

"Okay, well that's really helpful. I've met Carol and Ross. Are Eve and Sheridan here for the festival? That would be the easiest place to start."

"Sure, we're all here. This was supposed to be our big blowout."

CHAPTER 10

"What a Day That Was"
Talking Heads

SHERIDAN WAS HOLDING court at a picnic table with a group of people passing a joint. There were some familiar faces. He was regaling them with a story that had something to do with being in a camper in Mexico with another couple. They'd gone for some fresh air and proceeded to get lost. The twelve hours it had taken to find them had been filled with an array of banditos, sheriffs, tourists, magic mushrooms, and a lot of tequila.

He stood while the rest of the group sat. He was in his early forties, and his tall frame and lanky features were captivating. There was a wildness in his eyes that put you on alert, as if you couldn't quite tell what would happen next.

Drew pointed out Eve to me. She was about the same age as Sheridan. I could tell she'd been a beauty, but hard living might have taken its toll. Both Sheridan and she would have benefited from a bit more time outdoors. Their skin had a sallowness to it.

Aiden periodically interrupted Sheridan with a witticism that garnered some good laughs. He and Sheridan seemed to have a rapport. Michael was in attendance but didn't seem to be attending to much.

When Sheridan gave up the stage, Drew introduced me to the group and I got some warm hellos and was passed the joint. Now, I'm no stranger to joints but I usually don't like to smoke before I go to bed. If I do, I tend to spend a fair amount of time lying there daydreaming about wanting to be nightdreaming. While there's nothing wrong with that daydream state, it isn't the most restorative.

I took a hit and passed the joint to Drew. He took it, smoked it, and passed it along. I figured it would be wise to join the group than stand out. Plus, it was a rock-and-roll festival and if you couldn't get stoned here, where could you? In the therapy world we call that a rationalization. Whatever you call it, by the time the joint had made its way around a couple of times, Eve was looking better, I was having trouble attending to what people were saying, and the Police playing in the background sounded better than they ever had.

I felt a new kinship with Drew. This was the first time I'd ever gotten high with a client. I didn't think the licensing board would hold that in the highest regard, but the worry slipped easily from my brain.

"Say, Dave," I heard someone say.

"Yes," I replied, trying to zoom in on who was talking to me.

"Tell us something about yourself that you usually don't tell people."

It was Sheridan.

"Why do I think there's not much you usually don't tell people?"

That got some mixed responses.

"I'm an open book. How about you share a chapter?"

"Okay. Something I don't usually tell people. Pick a category. Sex, drugs, or rock and roll."

Sex was the almost unanimous response.

"Okay, I'll refrain from talking about the things you really want to hear."

That got some boos and a "Who says? We want to hear

everything." I couldn't tell who that heckler was, but as hazy as I was, I could see a clear path to a story… if only I could remember it.

"I went to a conference for sex therapists. I am, among other things, a therapist by trade but not a sex therapist."

"There are sex therapists?" Eve asked.

"Now he tells us," someone said.

"So, that's it? You went to a sex conference. What did you learn?" asked Aiden.

"What did you do?" Eve asked.

"A funny thing, but not a ha-ha funny thing, happened. On the first day of the conference, the keynote speaker was kidnapped and later in the week he was murdered."

"That's horrible!" said Eve.

"It was. Just like Timothy's death is horrible."

I could see mentioning that had taken the levity of the moment and drowned it. I have a way of doing that. I bring up tangential things that throw people off. It's only clear later the tangent was actually connected to the story.

"While that was horrible, a semi-good thing happened. It turns out some of the skills I've developed as a teacher and therapist helped me find out who killed him."

"You found the killer?" Eve asked.

"Yeah. It surprised me too. But, you know, we all have skills in certain areas we don't think to apply in others."

It wasn't as riveting a speech as Sheridan had given, but it was a good way to introduce myself to the group. Maybe now someone would come to me and tell me something about Timothy's death.

Before anyone could tell me anything, I found myself back in my tent, resting in my sleeping bag, and daydreaming about going to sleep.

CHAPTER 11

"Samson and Delilah"

Grateful Dead

Saturday, September 4, 1982

I WOKE UP. Not refreshed but at least not sweating. The sun was up and the sweat would come soon enough. In the meantime, breakfast was on the menu. I took care of my personal business and went over to the food pavilion where I grabbed some orange juice, scrambled eggs, pancakes, and sausage to go with my coffee and cinnamon bun. I'm a sucker for a buffet line. I couldn't remember the last time I'd packed as much on my plate. Hopefully, my eyes would be bigger than my stomach.

I spotted Sheridan with Eve animatedly talking. I hesitated as I approached them. Eve saw me and signaled for me to join them.

"Good morning," I said. "I didn't mean to interrupt your conversation. Please continue."

"Greetings to you, my friend," said Sheridan. "We were just talking about Timothy. After you left us last night, we got into it and there are those among us who think foul play may have been involved. Given your introduction to us, we'd welcome your contributions to the discussion."

"I'm happy to help out. You probably know way more than I do about what might have happened. What do you think?"

Ever the therapist, I knew it was best to get them talking before I jumped in. That said, my mouth sometimes opens before my brain.

"I'll tell you," Eve said. "He wasn't back using. We've all logged in a lot of party years with each other, and if he was hitting it again, we'd have known. He couldn't keep it secret. He's not... he wasn't that type of guy."

"I've heard others say he was clean. So if he wasn't using, what do you think happened?"

"It's possible he was wigging out," Eve said. "Heck, all the cats we've talked with have never played a place like this before. This is big-time. But I don't think his nerves were anymore jangled than everyone else's. I bet someone was talking to him and suggested it, and he just went, *Fuck it*, and did it. A stupid spontaneous thing like we've all done."

"Yeah," said Sheridan. "That could be. But I'm going with foul play. He only would have let someone he knew come in. Someone he trusted did him wrong."

"So someone comes in, they talk, and the other person either shoots up themselves and Timothy decides to join in or they suggest it to him and he shoots up. Then something goes wrong and the other person leaves?" I said, summarizing and asking at the same time. Another therapist thing.

"Yes," replied Eve. "I think so. For some reason we'll never know, he wanted to get high and something went wrong. He might have been twitchy about doing the show and maybe wanted to punch the whole thing up. It was already a high just being here. Doing the show would be on everyone's highlight reel. They're making a movie—it could be Woodstock Two. Maybe he just wanted to blow it up and make it even more fantastic. I can see that. Like the Eagles said, 'Take it to the limit one more time.'"

"One last time," Sheridan said.

"I have a question," I said. "You said there may have been foul play. Did you mean anything involving his death would be foul or were you thinking something else? Possibly there was some misdeed."

"Sheridan thinks," Eve said. Something else happened."

"Something like…"

"Dave, we're talking murder here," said Sheridan, ripping off a piece of my cinnamon bun. "I think, maybe we think, he either purposefully killed himself or someone else was involved. Why hasn't the person who was there come forth? If they aren't showing their face, it means they don't want their face to be seen. Or he committed suicide."

"I get that. I was wondering that myself. Of course, if he brought the stuff with him then there's no one to come forth. Maybe the person that got it for him is in LA. And, truthfully, if I was that person I wouldn't be saying much myself right now."

"My old dealer used to tell me not to blame him if something happened to me," Eve said. "By taking the risk to sell me the stuff, he's doing me a favor. When people started to sue dealers because their partner had OD'd, he said it was time to get out of the business. But before he quit, and I quit, he told me I could never give him up and I had to promise him."

"You both knew that was a promise you wouldn't keep if the police were asking," Sheridan pointed out. "But it made him feel safer in the moment. He also knew you have a good conscience so you'd think twice before you turned him in."

"Yeah, if I was the person that got him the stuff, I'd be sweating," I said. "Of course, we're all sweating so maybe the person's here."

"So, Dave, good food choice," Sheridan said, taking one of the sausages off my plate. "What do you think? You're the shrink. How do you size it up?"

"Happy to share but I really don't have much information. Not that it will stop me from theorizing. At this point all theories are on the table. The police ought to be able to determine if someone stuck that needle in him or he did it himself. Whether it was designed to kill him we won't know until the lap reports are completed and maybe not even then. The one thing I can focus on is the some-one else."

"I like that," Eve said. "How do you suggest we do that?"

I noticed her use of "we." Just like I didn't really want to do my gumshoeing "we" with Drew, I wasn't so sure I wanted to "we" with Eve and Sheridan. While I'd seen westerns where the sheriff talks a bunch of the town folk into being deputized, I couldn't remember any sleuth going down that route. And, of course, there was no way of knowing if either of them was the person of interest. After all, Josie and Drew had said Sheridan was the one most likely to have gotten drugs for Timothy. Yet, like the sheriff, I could use some help.

"I have some ideas but I'm curious what you think. Who do you think that person might be? And how do you think we can find out?" I asked my posse.

"That's a good question," said Eve. "We know Carol's been known to chase the dragon. Ross too. And Michael, Josie, and Drew."

"Let's not forget us," Sheridan added. "We're in that club. How about you, Dave? You in?"

"I can tell you I'm not. But if I were, I'd say I'm not as well. But I'm not. Never been quite tempted enough to take on the risk."

"I get it," said Sheridan.

"So, how about this?" I said pausing to take a mouthful. "Since you're both on the list, how do we find out if you were the person or not?"

In the silence that followed I got in a couple more bites and made sure to include some of the sausage just in case Sheridan had liked the last one enough to want more.

Eve looked down for a bit, then said, "You'd know if I was the person. First off, because if I were I'd say so. Despite what Sheridan thinks, I'm true to my word. I wouldn't have turned my dealer in.

Then you could talk to the people over by my tent where I was hanging out when all this happened. Plus, I have four years sober."

"That's good, Eve. It's better for you this way" said Sheridan rubbing her shoulder. "I, on the other hand, haven't closed the door to anything. While I've not dabbled in some time, had I been in that trailer I might very well have joined him. If the stuff was bad, I might have come to the same end. But, as it was, I wasn't there. I was watching the Ramones and wrapped up in their 'Blitzkrieg Bop.'"

"Thank you both. It's helpful to know where people were and what they were doing. Maybe as you talk with people and think about it, we can all figure out what really happened."

"That would be our gift to Timothy," Eve said.

CHAPTER 12

"Lava"

B-52's

THERE WAS SOME unlisted jam band playing at the side of the stage and a small group of people were dancing and passing a joint. One of the unheralded but significant contributions of the sixties was people no longer needed a partner to get on the dance floor. If you wanted to dance you did.

While I watched, it occurred to me if a person had been involved in Timothy's OD'ing and they weren't coming forth, it meant they wouldn't take kindly to someone trying to out them. I'd just enlisted a posse who were now talking to who knew who about who knew what. One thing they might be talking about could be me.

I can annoy people enough by myself without others submitting my application.

All of a sudden, I was feeling a little paranoid. I knew it wasn't a contact high, or at least I thought it wasn't. Some say paranoids just know the truth.

Then I saw Lilah and my worry about what I'd gotten myself into was displaced by the prospect of what I might get myself into.

"Hey," she said.

"Hey. It's good to see you."

I pointed out the people dancing. "You like to dance?"

"Certainly, although this isn't the kind of music I like to dance to."

"Me too. Not much of a beat. But it doesn't seem to be bothering these guys."

"They seem very much at one with it."

"Maybe later we can find something we can dance to."

She smiled but didn't throw in a "Let's do it."

"So, how are you doing? Enjoying yourself?"

"Yeah. I'm having a good time. I have an interview later this afternoon with one of the Heartbreakers so that should be interesting."

"That's great."

I was really liking being with her. As I peeked at her long tan legs in her white shorts and her French-looking T-shirt, her high cheek bones, and her sparkling eyes, I lost some of my bearings. She didn't intimidate me; she just made me want more of her. And not wanting to blow it, I became overly self-conscious.

Maybe the paranoia was back. Maybe I was having a contact high. This very attractive woman was standing next to me and suddenly my vocabulary had taken the day off. Lilah seemed oblivious to my awkwardness and comfortable with the silence. At least one of us was.

That's when I heard someone talking behind me. It took a moment to realize they were addressing me. I'd missed the first part of the sentence but heard Eve say, "... right away."

I turned and saw the distress on her face. "What?"

"We need to speak to you right away."

"Oh. Wait a minute," I said. I turned to Lilah. "I have to go. It's too bad cause I was really enjoying just being here with you."

"We can catch up later. Who knows? They might still be playing."

"Yeah. That notion also crossed my mind."

Eve directed me to the backstage tent area, and we weaved our way through to a tepee with pictures of buffalo on it.

"Here we are," she said.

"Whoa. What kind of tepee is this?"

"It's a replica of a Cherokee tepee from the southeast region," she said with no small amount of pride. Then she opened the flap.

Sheridan was in there, surrounded by smoke from burning sage. He was wearing yoga pants, no shirt, and glistening with sweat. A scar ran down the center of his chest. Eve wore a short denim skirt and a tie-dye shirt. I had on jeans and a Bruce Springsteen T-shirt, but wished I'd already changed into my shorts.

As soon as I got inside the tent, I started to sweat.

"Been waiting for you," Sheridan said. "We have some heavy stuff to talk about."

"I'm here. You think it might help to open the flap a bit and let some air in? It's very toasty in here."

"That's what we want, brother," Sheridan said. "We need to have a little informal sweat lodge so we can purify ourselves."

"Okay, I'm sure I can use some purifying. Anything in particular we need to be purified for?"

"Sit down," Eve said, and while it wasn't an order it didn't sound like a request.

I sat down and she sat next to me. Sheridan got up and sat on my other side. There we were, three pigs in a blanket, so to speak. Until there was a fourth. Michael stepped in as if he was expected, nodded at us all, and sat down opposite me. His long black hair was hanging freely, but he quickly found a rubber band from his pocket and pulled his hair back. He was a good-looking guy when you could see his face, although he tended to keep it looking down. Maybe that was a carryover from playing guitar and watching his handiwork.

He glared at me and said, "I hear you think I might have something to do with Timothy's death."

"What? Where did you hear that? I never said that or anything even remotely connected to that."

"Sheridan and Eve spoke to me. They told me you wanted them to find out what I had to do with Timothy's OD'ing."

"I'm afraid there's been a misunderstanding. Yes, I did speak with Eve and Sheridan, but I never talked to them about you. We just talked about how he died and were wondering if anyone was involved."

"That's not what they said."

"Well, I don't know what they said to you, but I hope they'll tell you I never asked them to talk with you. I have no reason to suspect you had anything to do with his death. You were bandmates. His death hurts you all."

"You got that right."

I was wondering when Sheridan and Eve were going to speak up. Finally, I just asked, "What exactly did you tell him?"

"You're right," Eve said. "There may have been a misunderstanding. You never said anything about Michael. You just said we ought to talk with anyone who might have gotten him the dope."

"And you thought I did?" Michael barked.

"Well," said Eve, "you all used to shoot up with him. Maybe you did it again. We were just asking. We weren't accusing."

This wasn't going well. Eve was becoming defensive. And Michael's anger wasn't going anyplace.

"You ought to be minding your own business. Timothy hasn't been dead a day and you're already throwing fuel on the fire."

"You're right, brother," Sheridan said. "We're all very upset. Eve and I just wanted to speak with you. Find out what you knew and if you had any ideas. When Aiden came back to the bus and said something was wrong with Timothy, everyone rushed over to the trailer. Do you think everything was kosher? That's all we wanted to talk about. We didn't mean to implicate you. We were just trying to help Dave."

"What the fuck does he have to do with anything?"

"Drew asked him to help find out what happened."

"Fuck Drew. And you guys too."

And with that he left.

I'm not sure if he felt purified, but he'd expressed himself clearly.

Eve offered me an apologetic look. "I guess we weren't that helpful."

"I wouldn't say that," I said.

"I would," said Sheridan.

"Okay, you didn't find out what happened when he went to the trailer and what he thinks might have happened, but you did find out something."

"We did?" asked Eve.

"You might have already known this, but now I do too. He has a temper and he doesn't seem to take kindly to people getting into his space."

"We knew that," Eve said.

"And we know," said Sheridan, "he has his own private hell."

"Well, now we all know. And at this point, all information is good information."

"Thanks for making me feel better," Eve said as she gave me a warm smile. "I can tell why Drew thinks you're a good shrink."

"I'm glad you're feeling better. Maybe the next person you reach out to, you might consider approaching a little more gently."

"Dave, can't you see Eve is a gentle flower? I, on the other hand, am more of the saguaro variety so perhaps I'm to blame."

"No sense blaming. We're all trying to do what we can to find out what happened to Timothy. Was Michael the reason you wanted me to come here?"

"Mostly. We didn't know for sure if he'd come, but we knew when we spoke to him he was upset. We invited him over to talk with you and Eve went to find you while I stayed here."

"Okay. I'm glad we sorted that out. Let me ask you something. You both thought he was the person most likely to have gotten the dope. Was that because you knew they used to shoot up together or something else?"

"Sort of both," said Eve as she wiped the sweat from her face.

"Dave, Michael's a weird cat. Brilliant but not the most sewn-together guy."

"He's been much sweeter the last couple of years since he's been sober. Well, not sober, but off the junk.." She winked at me. "None of us are that sober."

"Dave, there's a lot under the surface there."

"That's for sure," replied Eve. "Ever since he and Timothy started 'writing' together he's been moodier than ever."

"They wrote songs together? I didn't know that. I assumed Timothy wrote all the songs himself. Surely the lyrics. I haven't looked closely at their last album, but I don't remember seeing Michael having any writing credit."

"That's a sore subject," said Eve.

"How so?"

"Timothy was a narcissistic asshole," said Sheridan.

"Okay. He was an asshole. But why would Timothy collaborate with Michael and not give him credit?"

"Timothy won't be able to answer, but let's just say his ego wouldn't allow it," said Eve. "Since Michael has always considered himself the tormented poet, it was just one more way to be exploited and suffer."

CHAPTER 13

"Treat Me Right"

Pat Benatar

SITTING IN THE tepee, I must have lost a good portion of the sixty percent of my body that was water. But I'd gained a next step. Aiden, Drew or Josie? Hmm. Tough choice. Unfortunately, I had no way of knowing where any of them would be. I set off to the food pavilion to see what I could see and replenish some of that lost water.

A lot of people were seeking refuge from the heat. Plus, free food usually draws a crowd. I wasn't the only one with multiple glasses of water, seeking shelter from the sun.

Michael was sitting alone, reading *The Great Shark Hunt*. What the hell? I went over to him.

"Is it okay if I join you?"

"I'm reading."

"Yeah, I noticed. I read that book. I love that story. It's some of his funniest work and quite insightful into the human condition."

He looked up dubiously.

"I'm just starting it. It's radical, all right."

"I'll say no more, but I think you'll like it. Now that I've interrupted you, is it okay if I join you for a while?"

"You're not eating or watching Dave Edmunds?"

"I'm working up to it. I had a good helping of pancakes this morning. I'm not much of a Dave Edmunds fan, though to tell you the truth, I don't think I know any of his music. So maybe I could be a fan."

"He's Welsh. Wall-of-sound guy. I want to check him out, but I'm not in a hurry."

"I get that. The heat sort of cuts into your get-up-and-go."

"I don't mind the heat. I was raised in the desert so I'm used to it."

"What desert?"

"LA. I guess it's more wasteland than desert."

"Thanks to the water we pipe in."

"Yeah. Another shallow story of greed."

"It's pervasive. Although Woz made all that money from Apple and he spent it so we could be here this weekend."

"Another wasteland in the desert."

"Lots of wastelands. So I'm sorry about how Eve and Sheridan approached you. They got overzealous in their wanting to find out what happened to Timothy."

"Overzealous? Is that what you call it?"

"I gather it's not what you'd call it."

"I'd call it fucking imbecilic. They basically accused me of killing him."

"Yeah. That part wasn't good. But can I ask you a question… the question they were supposed to ask. What do you think happened?"

"Can I ask you a question? What are you doing snooping around? Is that your job? You get off on digging in the dirt?"

"I've never considered it quite that way but, yeah, it's true. I do get off on digging in the dirt. I don't like that I'm upsetting you because that's not what I want. I know this is a very trying time for all of Timothy's friends and family, and to have some stranger snooping around isn't a good thing."

"Exactly."

"Well, at least I got something right. But I was asked to do what I could to help. Something horrible happened. I know we can't fix it but maybe we can at least understand it."

"That a shrink thing? That's supposed to do what?"

"Some find it comforting to put things in a clearer perspective. Sort of like those people who prefer their desk tidy. It doesn't guarantee what gets accomplished at that desk is any better, but it gives them peace of mind."

"If their minds weren't so neurotic, they wouldn't need all the tidiness."

"You got it. They have their wounds and they find some peace by organizing. I'm just trying to help people handle things. It doesn't appear you need my help with that."

"He doesn't need your help with what?" Drew asked.

"Hi," I said with some relief. "I don't think Michael needs my help with much. He seems to have a clear if dark view of things."

"Michael is his own man," Drew said. He turned to Michael. "You hear anything from Aiden? I haven't seen him."

"He's lost in his own space."

"No doubt," Drew said. "You two okay if CC and I join you?"

"Suit yourselves," Michael said, standing up. "I'm off to hear the Welshman. Nice chatting with you, Dave. You're not as bad as I made you out to be."

"That door swings both ways."

He smiled at that and took off.

"What was that about?"

"We had a mishap earlier I was trying to clean up. Not your cheeriest of fellows."

"He's a brooding poet," CC said as she sat down next to Drew.

"I gather. It's good to see you both. How you doing?"

"I want to run something by you," Drew said.

"Go for it."

"I've been thinking about how Timothy died. The more I think about it, the more I'm convinced someone stuck that needle in his arm."

"What are you saying?" CC asked. "You think someone purposefully tried to get him high without his consent?"

"Not really," he replied. "Someone tried to kill him and make it look like he'd OD'd."

"That's a big leap," she said. "Why would you think that?"

"He wouldn't go back down that road. Sure, he was nervous. We all were. But if he was thinking about shooting up, he'd have said something."

"What do you think happened? You think someone came in there, got next to him, and stuck the needle in his arm before he could stop them?"

"Yeah, I do. It's possible."

"I don't know if it's possible," I said. "I suppose when the police do the autopsy they might be able to determine the course of events. If someone shot him up without his consent you'd think there'd be some signs of a struggle. But what makes you think someone wanted to kill him?"

"I don't think someone wanted to kill him. Aiden killed him."

"Wait!" CC said. "Aiden? He worshipped Timothy. Why would Aiden want to kill his hero? His meal ticket?"

"Two reasons. First, and I haven't told you this before, Timothy was thinking of kicking him out of the band. Maybe Aiden got wind of it and Aiden figured Timothy was worth more to him dead than alive."

"And second?"

"Aiden had just started writing and was finding out how it felt to have Timothy mess with your work."

"Is that reason enough to kill him?" CC asked. "I'm not so sure. Otherwise everyone would kill him."

"Well, then, where is he?"

The conversation went round and round from there. All I knew for certain was Drew now suspected Aiden. I tried to get him to tell us why he'd changed his mind, but he avoided the issue. Maybe there was something he didn't want to say in front of CC. Or me. I'd need to get him alone to find out more.

Their relationship seemed to be flowing well. Not long ago they were candidates for couples counseling, but I could see they had good rapport, some PDA, and there was that familiarity couples have when they've settled into their relationship. Yet, at the same time I could see there were unspoken elements.

Every relationship has its topics that aren't discussed or are only alluded to. Usually there's some past wound that can flare up so both parties collude and don't discuss it. I knew Drew was worried about other women coming out of the woodwork. Was that the old wound? And did it have anything to do with why he now saw Aiden as Timothy's murderer?

CHAPTER 14

"Too Nice to Talk To"

The Beat

"Hey, how you doing?"

Usually I don't like that question because people say it in passing and don't really want to know. Why not just say *Hi*? I had a friend who moved to Minneapolis who told me when people there ask, "How you doing," they really do want to know and take the time to find out. In California they don't want to know. That said, since Josie was saying it I wasn't minding.

I gave her the stock response. "I'm good. How about you?"

"I'm good. I'm bummed about Timothy, but otherwise okay."

"I'm sure. Where you headed?"

"I'm going to stand in the wings and listen to the music."

"Can I join you?"

"Sure."

After a few steps I stopped and said, "Can I ask you something about him?"

"What do you want to know?"

"Do you think he OD'd or do you think someone might have shoved that needle into him?"

"Huh? You think someone killed him?"

"I'm not sure. I heard someone mention it, and since you were close to him you might have a sense of what happened."

"Well, I don't think anyone would kill him, although I'm sure at one time or another we all wanted to. He could be a prick, but not so much anyone would want to really kill him after they'd cooled down."

"Maybe someone got mad at him and killed him before they cooled down. Do you think he was being more of a prick to anyone recently?"

"Timothy had a temper. It would flare up. He'd shout at you and call you names, and ten minutes later he'd be saying he was sorry. He didn't really hold on to anger. That's not to say someone wouldn't hold on to their anger at him. But I don't think he was being overly pricky to anyone recently. Well, apart from Aiden."

"What about Aiden?"

"Aiden and Timothy are alike in many ways. Both can be nasty assholes. Aiden holds on to his anger longer though. But he really loved Timothy in a way none of the rest of us do, so I can't see him killing him."

"Sounds like those long bus rides could be challenging."

"Yeah, well, we all know how to keep to ourselves. We've had plenty of days when we see each other only at sound check. But I don't think we're much different than most bands. Close quarters aren't easy for anyone."

"Sort of like living in a house with your family."

She stared at me a little closer, maybe thinking I knew more than I did. I didn't mind the look. Especially since there was something else in it. She seemed to be considering something. I didn't know what, but it was the kind of look that made me wonder how things might turn out.

"I don't think you want to talk family to any of us unless we're paying you by the hour. We've all got a story to tell."

"I'd be happy to hear yours," I blurted out before I became embarrassed.

"If you say so."

I paused then said, "I'm sure other people tell you this, but you have an engagingly intriguing look in your eye when you stare at someone."

"I do?" she said without a trace of innocence.

"Yeah. It's as if you're considering something."

"Well, I hope that's a good thing."

"So do I."

We quietly looked at each other. I felt naked. It was an intense, intimate moment. I didn't know what it meant but it left its mark. Like a couple stranded on an island who want to be rescued but realize being stranded is its own treasure, our time together was regrettably/thankfully interrupted.

CC, Drew, and Ross were at our side. Ross seemed worse than when I'd seen him last. Of course, he'd been eating then, which he seemed to do with abandon and delight. This time he was just talking.

"Hey, Josie," he said, giving her an enveloping hug. He had a bit of a big teddy bear presence that could make hugging him akin to cuddling up to your teddy as a child. Of course, it could also suffocate you and creep you out.

Ross hugged me. There were no back slaps and it was considerably shorter than his hug with Josie. I'd never been a hugger, but then I got to grad school and was surrounded by huggers. At first it was uncomfortable and awkward. How much should I lean in or out? How long should I linger? Did I smell okay and where should I put my hands? I used to worry about those things.

As with most things, experience is a great teacher and now hugging is my preferred mode of saying hello to those with whom I'm close. With others I'm usually happy with a hello. With Ross I was glad to be included in his brief hugging group.

"How's everybody doing?" Ross asked, making eye contact with everyone. Maybe he was the cuddly parent bear watching out for his own.

Nobody said anything and the question hung. Then he said, "Josie, I need to speak with you." A moment later he whisked her off.

I seemed to be the only one who found his abruptness unusual, which meant they were used to it. I figured if they were, they wouldn't mind if I followed suit.

"Excuse me," I said. "I just remembered I have to do something. I'll catch you all later. Sorry."

I took off in the direction of my tent, then doubled back. I wanted to catch up to Josie and Ross and find out what was so important he'd needed to speak with her right away. It probably had nothing to do with anything I'd be interested in, but what's the good of being a sleuth if you don't do some sleuthing? It was time to track forward.

I tried to work out where Ross might have taken Josie. We'd been standing in an open area a few hundred feet from the stage. I figured they'd taken off toward the lake to get away from the crowd and noise. Not that you could get away from either, but there'd be less of each in that direction.

I grew up in New York so wending my way through throngs of people has never been an issue. It wasn't as crowded backstage as it was in front, but there were enough people to make it hard to spot them, but easy not to be spotted. They stood at the water's edge. I couldn't get close enough to hear what they were saying, but I know upset when I see it. He was haranguing her and she went from being deferential to getting back in his face. There was some finger-pointing, signs of exasperation, and not a lot of peace-making.

They were going at it for a good ten minutes when she gave him the finger and stormed off. I watched her go and him stay. I was more interested in following her, but since he'd initiated the rift it might be prudent to see what he did next.

When he took off. I followed.

As we passed through the crowds and heat, we were rewarded by rows of spraying mist that, along with the big screens and enhanced sound, were making their world premiere. Aside from the sweltering heat, perusing the festival grounds was very enjoyable. People were dressed in a kaleidoscope of colors and outfits aggrandizing the visual buffet of the event.

Ross kept a fast pace as he aimed toward the giant tent. I was rooting for that destination as our forebears must have hoped the mirage in the distance was actually a real body of water. Every now and then I think about those people who traveled across the country in covered wagons. They had to traverse mountain ranges, rivers, and deserts, all without a map to guide them and lodgings to comfort them. Out of necessity they were a heartier bunch. I imagine if called upon, I could get up to speed, but I was on the verge of whining again about the heat. Then, to my relief, Ross entered the air-conditioned tent.

It was 1982 and less than five percent of the population had a computer. Early adopter isn't a phrase that's often applied to me. I hadn't bought a computer and had no plans to do so. As I've said, I'm afraid of computers. I trust my typewriter. It does what I tell it to do and it doesn't do any thinking on its own. I might push a wrong key, but I now have a typewriter that allows me to erase. Any mistakes are ones I can manage. I have a sense of mastery and control over the machine I know I'd never achieve with a computer. Eventually, I may face my fear just as I encourage my clients to face theirs. But for the time being, my typewriter and I are doing just fine.

I mention this because while I was happy to be in the tent with air-conditioning, being surrounded by the latest in technology made me feel like a stranger in a strange land. I wasn't afraid; I just didn't know one Atari game from another. While I'd seen ads for the Apple Macintosh, I'd yet to see one up close. People were playing arcade games, but Ross hadn't come for that or the AC. He'd come to talk to one of the people by the computers—a just-out-of-adolescence guy wearing a Dead T-shirt.

I was too far away to hear anything but it was clear they were arguing. Ross wasn't as animated as he'd been with Josie, but he was still gesticulating and shuffling his body enough for me to know he was huffing and puffing and wanting to blow the house down. If the other guy had been trying to assuage Ross's concerns, it hadn't worked. If anything, he was adding kindling because Ross seemed to be getting more and more upset and finally stormed off.

Storming off seemed to be the move of the day. I'm not a door-slamming, storming-off kind of guy. I'm more the can't-we-work-this-out type. Dramatic moves play well in movies but don't do much to improve relationships.

I was sad to see Ross leave the tent. I didn't have to follow him; I could have stayed in the tent. But aside from the temperature, there wasn't a lot to keep me there.

CHAPTER 15

"Primera Invasion"

Santana

ROSS STRODE THROUGH the trailer area toward the food pavilion. I was intent on following him when something else caught my interest.

The trailer. AKA the scene of the crime.

There was yellow tape across the two doors that said *Police Investigation—Do Not Cross*. I stopped about fifty feet away and monitored the trailer. I've read enough mysteries to know that sooner or later you need to visit the scene of the crime. This seemed as good a time as any. If I wanted to investigate what had happened, I ought to see where it happened.

That notion was both invigorating and terrifying. It was exciting to think I was actually investigating a murder. To call yourself a psychotherapist there are certain academic and legal hurdles you have to get over. I didn't know what you needed to do to get an investigator's license. Whatever it was, I hadn't done it.

I could be curious and look into what had happened to Timothy, no problem. But I couldn't legally trespass.

If I was caught "investigating" the scene of the crime, the police would have something to say about it. The yellow tape made that perfectly clear.

I could see how if the ribbon accidently fell off, a person wouldn't know not to go in.

Yeah, I could casually amble over there, pull off the tape, and stick it under my shirt. Hurry off, throw it away, come back, and just go in.

I could do that, but would I?

Sure, I bend rules now and then. But this would be a first.

It adds another level of challenge to breaking the law when so many people are milling about Yet nobody was hanging out in the immediate area. It was one of maybe twenty trailers clustered together. If I were quick, I could pull it off unseen.

That scenario was accompanied by a downpour of sweat as my anxiety, adrenaline, and fear spiked. Five minutes ago I'd been following Ross; now I was about to commit a crime. A low-level crime, but one that could easily serve as a gateway to others. If I got away with this, what might I do next? And if I didn't get away with it...

Once I try to be cool, I lose any ability to be cool. I was strolling toward the trailer, trying to effect a hang-loose indifference. I was marginally relieved as I didn't think anyone was paying attention. While I might bemoan that invisibility at times, I wasn't minding it now.

I slinked over to one door and, as nonchalantly as I could manage, checked left and right before ripping off the ribbon and stuffing it into my shirt. Then repeated that on the second door. I was back on my lackadaisical way in a matter of seconds, now trying to manage my overly inflated pride in my accomplishment.

I strolled to the end of one row of trailers. A few people were coming and going but the immediate area didn't seem to be a hanging-out spot. In the next row I found some porta-potties and went into one. I held my breath, lifted my shirt, did my best to wipe my fingerprints off the tape and dropped it into the waste. I covered it up with a lot of toilet paper and made my way back to the one trailer I cared about.

No one was nearby so I ambled up to the door, turned the knob, and stepped in. The front room was much like it had been the last time I'd been there, minus the people—Persian rug, cups, bottles, and full ashtrays. The lava lamp was doing its psychedelic dance, while the tiki god and Bob Dylan looked on. I couldn't see the bonsai plant. I opened the door to the back room, went in, and closed the adjoining door behind me.

I had no idea what I expected to find so had no clue as to whether it was there. The room had a small closet that was open, revealing some empty coat hangers. There was a small couch, two folding chairs, and a coffee table with nothing on it. There were no cushions on the couch where I figured Timothy had died.

I was picturing that scene when I heard the front door open. A jolt of panic zapped me. If someone was coming in I needed to go out. Quickly I tiptoed to the back door and slipped out the back, Jack.

I was even more pleased with myself as I seemed to be making a clean getaway, although I couldn't be sure. I wasted no time getting some fifty yards away so I could watch the trailer without seeming to. Either the person was still in there or they'd opened the door, peeked in, and left while I was making my getaway.

Given the hundred-degree temperature, my options were limited. I angled myself so I could see the trailer out of the corner of my eye, and tried to look like I was waiting for someone. Not being overly familiar with the investigative business, I wasn't sure how long to wait. My fair, freckled skin doesn't take to the sun too well and it wasn't long before I began to feel the burn. As much as I wanted to stand my post, I didn't want to have to make an appointment with a dermatologist when I got back to town.

I couldn't figure out what someone would be doing for this

length of time in the trailer and guessed they'd left. I considered going up to the door, knocking, and going in, as there was no sign to tell me otherwise. But they say the criminal returns to the scene of the crime, and if there happened to be a police officer in there, I didn't think it would be in my best interest to introduce myself. The same applied if the killer was inside.

CHAPTER 16

"Changes in Latitude, Changes in Attitude"
Jimmy Buffett

THERE'S A CAFÉ in Paris where I've heard if you sit there long enough, eventually everyone in the world will walk by. I suspect that's an exaggeration but it has a kernel of truth to it. If I stayed long enough in the food pavilion, maybe eventually everyone would come by and I wouldn't have to worry about getting sunburned.

Some detective I was. Everyone from Hercule Poirot to Miss Marple got shot at and roughed up, and here I was worrying about sunburn.

I saw CC, Drew, and Lilah sitting at a table as I worked the buffet and got a veggie burger and fries—something good to balance out something bad. I'd been taught maintaining balance in life is important. The scales tip one way then the other, so I like to try to even things out when I can. I wasn't sure if a veggie burger and fries did the trick but they beat out a cheeseburger, fries, and a malt.

"Hi. Is it okay if I join you?" I asked as I sat down without giving them time to answer.

"Make yourself at home," CC said. I wasn't sure whether she meant it or there was an edge there.

Drew wasn't doing well. His energy was low and his mood was

synched to it. CC looked concerned about him, but otherwise fine. Lilah looked great.

"How you doing?" I asked Drew. I was his therapist after all. What's the point of having your therapist with you if they don't ask how you're doing?

"Not good."

Before I could find out anything more, Ross came rushing over to the table. He was out of breath.

"I need everyone in the bus right now. I'll meet you there." And with that he was gone.

We all scarfed a quick bite, and made a beeline for the bus.

Michael and Josie were there, summoned by Ross, too. We stood and made uncomfortable conversation. I wanted to get Drew to myself to see what was bothering him, but he was sitting on the couch next to Josie and Michael. CC and Lilah, and I—the outsiders—stayed off to the side.

It wasn't long before Sheridan and Eve joined the group, and soon thereafter Ross came in with Carol. He didn't look good. He must have been running around trying to find everyone. He wasn't the running-around type and it took him a moment to catch his breath.

He viewed each of us as if to register our presence.

"Aiden is dead."

"What?" we chorused.

Eve wailed. Michael sunk his head. Drew looked lost. Josie forlorn. CC hugged Lilah. I stood still.

"I know. It's inconceivable. But it's true. Security found me and told me he was found in a drug dealer's tent. Evidently he OD'd too. It's horrible. I can't believe it. What the fuck is happening here?"

Nobody had an answer. People were in shock. Tears came to one then another. Everyone wanted more information but there was no more to give. We were just stuck in the misery of the moment.

After some time, Ross addressed the group. "I have to go talk with security. I'll see if I can find out anymore. Can we all just meet back at the bus in an hour?"

Everyone agreed and he left. There was a lot of hugging, consoling, and what-the-fucking. Bit by bit the group broke up.

Drew, CC, and I went back to the food pavilion—for comfort, I guess. I re-upped on the veggie burger and fries. We sat there for a few minutes with our own thoughts. Mine included what was I going to do with Timothy's journal that Aiden had given me.

After what I considered a respectful amount of time I spoke up. I'm not the best at treading slowly. Foreplay is something I've never really understood. If you're going to play, why not just play?

"So, Drew, how are you?"

He gave me the finger. Got up and left.

"Well done, Dave," I said, but it could have been CC.

I looked at her, then at Lilah, then at my burger. I grabbed the burger, said goodbye, and followed him. I wanted to make sure he was okay. It wasn't like him to just pick up and go, but then I'd never seen him after two of his bandmates had died.

I decided to follow at a distance. I didn't know which way he'd gone when he left the tent, so I tried a left. Why not right? I tend to trust my instincts. Of course, it's not a flawless system.

I spotted him not too far ahead and followed him past the stage into the main camping area. It was like working my way through a maze. There were tents of all shapes and sizes with banners that proclaimed their owner's value systems. Lots of peace signs and tie-dyed sheets covered the sides of tents. My favorite sign was one of a pirate with the words *The beatings will continue until morale improves*. That touched my funny bone and also seemed to have a ring of truth to it.

It didn't improve my morale when I figured out we were going to the tent where Aiden had died. Drew's steps seemed purposeful and made me think this wasn't the first time he'd passed this way. Aiden, however, would never pass this way again.

Drew went up to one of the police officers standing directly outside the tent. I couldn't hear what they were saying, but I could see his frustration building. There was no ambulance in sight so I imagined Aiden was no longer on the premises. Still, Drew persisted, seemingly trying to get in.

I was glad to see Drew asserting himself. It was an issue we'd been working on, so at least he was putting those skills to use. He went over to a group of people and started talking to an official-looking man with a mustache who wasn't wearing a uniform. The man listened calmly and seemed to be displaying some level of empathy, but Drew remained unable to get in the tent.

After a while, he gave up. I took a few steps into obscurity, and when he went by I took up my position in his wake. There were moments when he walked quickly, others when he ambled. I was guessing there was no comfortable pace or space for him. He seemed to be heading for the trailer, or at least in the vicinity. I picked up my pace and looped in front of him. I scurried to the other side of the trailers, took some deep breaths, and positioned myself so I could intercept him right before he got to the trailer.

When he saw me he appeared surprised, then relieved, then frustrated. He hurried over to me.

"Sorry about the finger."

"No problem. How are you doing?"

"I'm fucked again. I was fucked when Timothy OD'd. Now that Aiden's joined him, I'm doubly fucked. These are the worst days of my life."

"I get that. It's a lot to have to deal with all at once. My heart goes out to you."

"Yeah. Thanks. But that doesn't make anything better."

"I don't think there's much now that can make anything better. The whole thing sucks."

"That actually feels better. Yeah, I hate it when people try to make you feel better. Deal with your own discomfort. Let me feel bad. Don't take it away. It's all I've got."

"I hear you. Spoken like—"

"Yeah, I know. Someone who's been in therapy."

"Well, yeah. That's true. But it isn't what I was going to say. I was going to say spoken like someone who knows a thing or two."

"That too. But, Jesus, Dave, what the fuck is going on? Why are my friends dying?"

"Do you think Aiden killed himself? Do you think his death was connected to Timothy's?"

"I don't know what to think. It's just too much. But I do think they're connected. Don't you?"

"Yeah, I do. But how? Do you think Aiden did a sort of pact thing and killed himself as an act of love?"

"He could have. He was wacko that way. Timothy saved Aiden's life in many ways so I could see him offing himself. But it's just so stupid."

"Stupid, but people do stupid all the time. Love can do that to you."

"Has love done that to you?"

"Stupid? Yeah, I've been stupid about love. I haven't killed myself or anyone else, but I have done some things I'm not so proud of."

"Sometime you can tell me about that. Maybe I can learn from your stupid. In the meantime, I need to talk to Ross."

That's when Michael, Carol, Eve, and Sheridan showed up. Eve looked like she'd been crying as she hugged Drew. Sheridan looked like he'd been drinking as he hugged Drew. Michael didn't hug Drew, but Eve hugged me. Sheridan made some knowing eye contact with Carol and then me, which seemed to say, "And another one bites the dust."

CHAPTER 17

"Stomp"

The Beat

MICHAEL WENT INTO the bus and the others followed. Josie, CC and Lilah were already there. It hadn't been long ago when all these people had been partying, celebrating the band's big-time concert. Now Timothy and Aiden and the bonsai plant were gone. We waited for Ross. We didn't wait long.

He came in wearily. This was a guy who managed the band, took charge, broke down barriers, and pushed and pulled his way through life. No obstacle had been too big, but now he was beaten down.

He scanned the room and made eye contact with everyone. As soon as his eyes met Josie's, he began to cry. His tears filled the room as others joined him. Within that shared space sorrow soared. It was as if the walls that protected us had come down and all that could bind us and protect us was our sorrow.

Everyone was disconsolate. Ross had brought the unspoken truth of the moment into the room and we all were in it together.

"We are Timothy's and Aiden's family," he finally said. "Some of us more than others, but in this room are people that knew these two lovely men as only a sister or brother can. We've shared our lives with these men, and while they're no longer with us in body they'll forever be with us in spirit."

"Amen," said CC.

"Aho," said Eve. I'd never heard that before, but I guessed it was the Cherokee equivalent.

"All right, my friends," Ross continued. "We need to be strong. We need to carry on. We're all deeply shattered and need time to put the pieces back together. But let's not forget, we're a band." He smiled weakly at Lilah, CC, and me and said, "Well, some of us are the band and others are the family and friends. But really, we're all the band. Together we're stronger and together we'll rebuild Magoo. We'll be back on stage and making records better than ever."

Ross was part preacher, part coach, and part salesperson. He almost had us believing the Phoenix would rise again. In the meantime, he got down to brass tacks.

"I don't know any more than I already told you. When I know more, I will let you know. In the meantime, the press is here. The police are here. People are going to want to interview you. Speak your truth and share what you will. But let's put out the word the band will carry on."

People started talking to one another and broke into smaller groups. I observed who was talking to whom and tried to listen to as much as I could. I wasn't sure what to do but I knew enough to observe.

Drew said Aiden might have killed himself as a love tribute for Timothy, but if someone had behaved badly with Timothy, might not the same person have done so with Aiden? If a person had a reason to kill Timothy and Aiden, what would that reason be? And would there be reason to harm others?

I also wondered why Drew had wanted so badly to enter that tent. How come he'd known the way there? And, more importantly, could I find it again?

Lots of questions. But where to start finding answers?

I'm a fan of Ram Dass's book *Be Here Now*. Truthfully, I haven't read the book as I imagined the title pretty well summed up the whole thing. Of course, I wouldn't know that until I read it. But in the therapy world, there are lots of ways to say *Focus on the present because the past is past and the future is yet to come*. They all boil down to—be here now.

I figured that meant I should start right where I was. Now all I needed was some guidance.

Sheridan provided it.

"Dave," he said as he came over to me. "I've had enough of this wake. What do you say you and I grab a smoke and listen to some rock and roll?"

Sheridan and I stepped outside the trailer and he lit up a Marlboro. I'm like a reformed sinner when it comes to smoking. I'd smoked during my adolescence because I thought it was cool. I quit in my early twenties and now I can't stand the smell of it, let alone what it does to you. There was a time I liked going into a smoky nightclub. It was atmospheric. Now, I just don't go.

Being outside, I didn't mind his smoking so much. Santana was still playing and I welcomed the chance to get lost in the music. Unfortunately, Sheridan had another habit I wasn't so fond of. He liked to talk. I was happy just to drift away but he wanted to listen to the music and talk.

"Dave, what do you think happened to Aiden?"

"I dunno. What do you think?"

"I'll tell you. Something stinks here."

"How so?"

"Aiden and Timothy got fucked."

"What do you mean?"

"Someone got some bad dope and it did them in."

"Why do you think that?"

"Dave, you ever buy dope?"

"Yeah."

"Do you ever really know if what you're buying is any good until you try it?"

"Not usually. I mean I can smell it and look at it, but usually the guy I buy from has one kind of dope and that's what I get."

"Precisely. You have to trust your dealer."

"I get that."

"Dave, I've sold more dope to these guys than anyone. I'm their go-to guy. If they wanted to get high this weekend, they'd have spoken to me, but they didn't. Whoever got them that dope is here now and that's the person I want to talk to."

"So, who got it for them?"

"Dave, if I knew that I'd be talking with them instead of you. You're the one playing detective here. I'm just trying to help out."

"Okay, thanks for that. But you know the circle around the band. Who do you think I ought to talk to?"

"Well, everyone will say me, which is why I'm saying CC. I don't think you can make a living doing what she does. She does something on the side. You might start there."

When Santana's set was over, I decided to go over to the tent where Aiden had died. It wasn't as hard to find as I'd worried it might be. That was because it was still daylight and *The beatings will continue till morale improves* was a good beacon. There were still people milling around the tent although not as many as before. There was another police ribbon, but the police had all gone. The uniforms at least. I could have tried to sneak in and find what Drew had been looking for, but would be seen.

I strolled amongst the surrounding tents. Most were empty, the chairs outside them deserted. I found a twenty-something woman close by, sitting in a spot of shade knitting.

"Hi," I said. "Are you Madame Defarge?"

"Huh?" she said.

"Hi. What are you knitting?"

"A scarf, although it seems kind of ludicrous to be doing it in this heat."

"It's ludicrous to do anything in this heat."

"Tell me about it."

"Horrible what happened here," I said, pointing to the tent where Aiden had been found.

"No kidding."

"I'm kind of a friend of a friend of Aiden, the guy who died. I was wondering if you could tell me whose tent it is and anything you saw."

"Like I told the police, it's a popular tent. People have been going in and out since Thursday night. It's apparent the guy who set it up was selling drugs. No one stayed long, although in this heat, sitting in the tent is worse than being outside."

"I guess whoever was selling didn't mind staying inside."

"Yeah, well, he's long gone. I haven't seen him since the guy died."

"You happen to know what he was selling?"

"Somebody said mostly pot and acid, but that guy, Aiden, wasn't shooting up any of that."

"No, I imagine not. When did they discover the body?"

"I'm not sure. When I got up I noticed the commotion, so he could have been discovered any time."

"Any time before...?"

"Eightish."

"What about last night? Were people coming and going when you went to bed?"

"All night. Well, I can't say that for sure either. I don't know when things died down. Oh, sorry. Wrong choice of words. I don't know when the guy finally closed shop."

"Thanks. That's very helpful."

Ross hadn't said anything to us until lunchtime. Was it possible the police had told him earlier? Did his talk with the tech guy and Josie at the lake happen after he'd heard but before he told the rest of us?

I tried to remember how Josie had reacted when Ross told everyone about Aiden's death, but I couldn't remember.

CHAPTER 18

"The Chain"

Fleetwood Mac

THE CARS WERE playing "Let the Good Times Roll." The good times seemed to be rolling for most people. While the death of two members of a band might put a damper on things, that damper was mostly limited to our group.

I debated what to do. I could follow the trail forward or follow it back. I decided to go to the tech tent and talk to the person who'd had the agitated discussion with Ross.

Once again, it was a relief to be in the tent. Though the evening was approaching, the temperature had yet to dip. I took my time going over to the area where they'd met. The same guy was there, answering questions and handing out brochures.

I hoped he'd be able to give me some information.

When the others were done with their questions, I approached him. His name tag read *Hale*.

"Hi, Hale," I said. "Is that your real name or a greeting?"

I could tell he's been asked about his name too many times. "It's my name."

I hadn't gotten off on the best foot; it was time to kiss his ass.

"You look like a guy who knows a thing or two I don't."

"I know a thing or two about music and technology—not sure what else," he said jovially but warily.

"Since I know a little about music and basically nothing about technology, you know way more than I do, and I can see you've helped out some people today."

"Yeah, well, I do what I can."

"I'm hoping you can help me with something. I've got a friend who's very upset. And for good reason."

"That's too bad," he said, warier.

"Yeah, he's been yelling at people because he's all riled up."

"That could be a problem."

"You bet it is. And, even worse, it's been a problem for me, and I suspect it's been a problem for you as well."

Now he was on his guard. "What are you talking about?"

"I'll tell you. I'm not here to complain but he starts the fire and then I have to go put it out. So I'm here to put out the fire he started with you."

"What fire?"

"Well, see, there's the problem and why I'm here. I know he blew off some steam at you but I don't know what steam he blew off. I'd like to try to mend any broken bridges, but I'm not sure what he was upset about when he spoke to you."

"I'm still not getting what you're talking about."

"I'm talking about Ross. I know he came over here and gave you an earful, but I just don't know what he was railing about."

"Oh, Ross. Yeah, I figured that might be where you were going. It was nothing special. He gets that way. There's no damage you need to clean up."

"That's good to hear. Cause I know he can be a bull in a china shop sometimes."

"Yeah, that's him. A bull in a china shop, head shop, chop shop, and hot shop."

"Now I'm the one not getting it. What kind of shops are we talking about?"

"You know Ross. He has his hand in everything. He was just upset about something with one of his enterprises and hoped I could do something about it."

"Can you tell me what enterprise it was?"

"Hold on a minute. You said you were coming here to apologize for him. Not that he shouldn't apologize, but what difference does it make what he was mad at me about?"

"It would just be helpful to me if I knew a bit more so maybe I could help him out."

"Go ask him. If he wants to tell you that's fine by me. I don't have anything to hide. Now I gotta help some of these other people."

"Sure. Thanks for helping me."

I'm sure you've heard about Freudian slips. Therapists joke a Freudian slip is when you say one thing but mean your mother. Nobody ever said therapists are funny. What a Freudian slip really means is that you say something and unconsciously reveal something you didn't intend to. When the guy said Ross was a bull in a china shop, head shop, and hot shop, maybe he'd been referring to the tent where the drugs were being sold. Technically it wasn't a head shop, but it was close enough for me to go, *Hmm.*

I made my way back to the stage area. Once again, I was aware of how much I didn't know. Aiden had been with his bandmates when Timothy died, but disappeared after that, although I'd seen him when Sheridan was telling his story about getting lost in Mexico. If I could find out who'd seen him after that, I could work out when he'd gone to the dealer's tent, probably sometime after midnight. Same with Ross—I might be able to put him at the scene in time to be that raging bull in the head shop.

A few minutes later I was intercepted.

"Hey," said CC.

"Hi. It's good to see you. How's everything."

"Well, everything's fucked if you want to know the truth. But, me personally, I'm fine."

"Yeah, it's weird. I was just over by the tech tent and there are thousands of people having a great time, as well they should. But our little group isn't sharing in that."

"It's really bad. I've never seen Drew this depressed. It's weird to be so down while everyone else is so up."

"I get it. It's also weird as there are some groups here I'd really like to see, but I kind of feel disloyal going to listen to them while Drew is hurting. I know he told me he'd find me if he needed me, but I haven't seen him in a while. Maybe I ought to find him."

"That's a good idea. I'm looking for him too. But I'll tell you, while I'm sure he'd like to talk with you, what he really wants is for you to figure out what happened."

"I'm working on that."

"Any leads?"

"Nothing yet that's worth sharing, but there are some crumbs on the path I'm following."

We entered the VIP tent area. The only difference between it and general admission was density of tents—a few hundred compared to many thousand. Once again, I was impressed by the lengths people went to so their tents were more homelike. Well, if your home had a lot of peace signs, tie-dye, and banners. I saw Camp-A-Lot, Happy Campers, and Camp Get Enuf. Then I saw Drew and Lilah sitting in chairs outside a rectangular beige tent with an awning.

"Hey," CC said as we approached.

"Hey," said Lilah. Drew nodded.

"Okay if we join you?" I asked.

"Sure," said Lilah. "But there are no more chairs. My tent's over there if you want to go get one."

"That's fine. Happy to sit on the earth." CC sat down next to Drew, who didn't offer to get up. I sat closer to Lilah.

I wasn't sure how open Drew wanted to be in front of CC and Lilah, but I asked, "How are you doing?"

"As well as anyone who's had two people close to him die at what was supposed to be the high point of my life." He tried to smile but there wasn't much to it. At least he didn't give me the finger, get up, and leave.

"I'm happy, well, not happy, but wanting to talk with you about it if you're interested. We can talk here or find another place."

"Frankly, Dave, I'm not up for it. I'm beaten down, and right now all I really want to do is get loaded and listen to music."

"You and a couple hundred thousand people," Lilah said.

"Yeah, I'm just a party animal."

"I'm here when you/if you want me."

"Yeah. I know. I've got to talk to CC now. Why don't you go listen to the Kinks and I'll catch up with you later, either at the food pavilion or backstage."

"You're the boss."

I made eye contact with Lilah. She stood and offered me a hand up, which I took as a good sign.

"You up for the Kinks?" I asked.

"Sure, but since they're not playing yet, how about wandering through the wooded area?"

"I'm up for that. Wandering through the woods in the desert. Let's do it."

CHAPTER 19

"Let's Go"

The Cars

"How are things with you?" Lilah asked.

"It's such a trip. People are partying and having a great time, and our group is surrounded by it while we're in our own private hell."

"Yeah. I feel bad listening to the music while at the same time dealing with this."

"I hear you."

We wandered the rest of the way in silence. It was strange to have a little forest in the middle of the desert, but no stranger than having small lakes, a giant stage, and a few hundred thousand people hanging out.

"So how are you doing?" I asked.

"Is that your standard opening line?"

"It seems so. I suppose I ought to come up with a different one."

"It works. Despite the heat and the casualties, I'm having a good time. It's been a while since I just relaxed and hung out."

"How come?"

"Well, Doctor, I'm a bit of a workaholic. I've been getting my feet on the ground at UCLA and I've been offered a chance to write a textbook, so I'm working on that as well."

"I'm impressed. A textbook. For what class?"

"Intro sociology. I've been teaching it since I got out of grad school. It's what they give the new kids on the block. But turns out, I like it. I guess if I write the textbook for it, I'll be continuing with it so I'd better like it."

"That's quite an honor and, I imagine, a workload as well."

"It is. But what about you? What are you doing to fill your time?"

"Right now, I'm trying to find out how Timothy and Aiden died."

"Yeah, that's a mystery. I take it you don't subscribe to them both overdosing with some bad dope," she asked as we watched some people skipping stones across the lake.

"It could be. I found out where they might have gotten the dope. Or at least where Aiden did. But, from what I can tell, unless some other people are overdosing, we have something else at play."

"If someone was selling bad dope we'd have heard about it. The rumors would be flying."

"I'm sure. If foul play was involved, I might have a suspect, but I have only the most circumstantial evidence. The next thing on my to-do list is to figure out timetables. Maybe you can help me with that."

"I'd be glad to."

"Great. Here's what I know. Timothy died between the time the band left the trailer and when he was found. Aiden found him and maybe he stumbled upon something he ought not to have known. No one I've spoken with seemed to have seen Aiden after Sheridan regaled everyone about his Mexico trip last night. So Aiden died sometime between yesterday evening and this morning. Later this morning, Ross told us Aiden was dead."

"That sounds right," she said nodding her head as we continued to stroll through the woods.

"I went to the tent where he died and a woman told me things were busy there until midnight so most likely he died after that."

"You have done some homework."

"Thanks. It's going to be impossible to check everyone's whereabouts between midnight and 8 a.m. It would be nice to know where everyone was during that time but anyone could have snuck out in the middle of the night. I'm curious about when Ross found out and what he did before he told us."

"Not sure I can be of much help but, for what it's worth, CC and I watched the Police, and their show must have ended close to midnight. After that, we came back to the tents and called it a night."

"Well, that takes two people off the list. Not that you were ever on it."

"That's a relief. You'd have a hard time finding a motive for me wanting to kill Timothy and Aiden."

"Yeah, that's a good point. Did they harass you in soc class?"

"We can eliminate that coincidence."

She smiled a little.

"It'll also be important to find out who had a motive."

"Makes sense."

"I'll tell you something you could do. Can you check with CC and see what she did after she left you last night? Maybe she knows about others as well."

"Will do. Drew is a night owl. CC too. Most musicians are. She might have rendezvoused with him after we said goodnight."

"Okay. See what you can find out."

We continued to wander through the woods... well, in circles through the woods because it was maybe a football field's worth of trees that provided some shade. I realized I'd just deputized another person. Of course, any one of my deputies could turn out to be a person of interest. Plus, Eve and Sheridan hadn't done the slickest of jobs.

I've never been good at knowing when to make a move. Nothing Lilah and I'd talked about had a romantic or flirtatious feel to it. And when I'm sweating and hot, I don't feel very amorous. That said, we were in a forest and I did have a strong urge to kiss her. I just wasn't sure how to segue from talking about possible murder suspects.

Some eye contact might help. We'd mostly been walking side by side so I slowed down and faced her. She turned toward me. This seemed like as good a time as any to make my move, but I hadn't done anything that approached foreplay. I have an issue with rushing things, so I was tentative. Feeling clumsy and awkward, I blurted out, "Is it okay if I kiss you?"

"I don't know. Why don't you try and we'll find out?"

That was enough for me. I tried. It wasn't the best kiss I've ever delivered as I could feel the sweat beading on my face, but she was right there with me. Our lips came together tentatively, and gradually the pressure increased. I could feel her body close to mine and put my arm around her back, bringing her closer to me.

That's when I heard, "Get a room, buddy."

That broke the mood. It wasn't much of a forest, and with thousands of people in attendance privacy couldn't be expected. We pulled away from each other, smiled awkwardly but promisingly, and left the forest.

We found a spot on the side of the stage to watch the Kinks. Some people were talking about how Bill Graham liked things to run on time. Evidently, he'd been very upset with the Kinks for lollygagging and told their manager he'd cancel the act. Then he'd arranged for the manager's Mercedes to be forklifted from the VIP parking lot to the outer fringes. The band had gotten the message and come on stage.

Evidently, Bill Graham and I shared some values.

Ray Davies, the band's front man, seemed somewhat taken aback by the vast audience but managed to get everybody up and dancing. At one point, he asked the audience what they'd said and pointed the microphone at them. They yelled back indecipherably, to which he replied, "You don't have to shout," and proceeded to sing:

Cheap is small and not too steep

But best of all, cheap is cheap

Circumstance has forced my hand

To be a cut-priced person

In a low budget land

Times are hard, but we'll all survive

I just gotta learn to economize

I wondered what kind of financial gain would come to Josie, Michael, Drew and Ross. A bigger piece of the pie. Certainly there could be a spike in album sales, but then what? I couldn't see any profit in killing the cash cow.

If money wasn't the motive, what was? Someone could have being jealous or upset with Timothy, and killing him was a crime of passion or revenge. But would that hold true for Aiden as well? Perhaps if sex and drugs were involved. It was rock and roll and from I could tell, more than one member of the band had slept with more than one member of the band.

Could it be Timothy or Aiden's love-interest present or past was involved? In which case, who were their former and recent lovers? That was something I ought to explore. I didn't think Lilah could help me with that, but maybe others could.

It dawned on me I wasn't paying any attention to the music or Lilah. My head was spinning with theories and unanswered questions. When that happens, the best thing for me to do is move.

I leaned over to Lilah. "As much as I'd like to stay here with you, I have to go do some sleuthing. Maybe we can catch up later."

She didn't seem to mind my leaving, which disappointed me, but the quick parting kiss she gave me made up for that.

CHAPTER 20

"Hands Off… She's Mine"
The Beat

I WENT TO the food area and gave myself a little talking to. I'd just been with a woman I had a lot of interest in who seemed to like me. *Why was I going away from her? Was I afraid of getting involved? Afraid of loving and losing?*

I ask a lot of questions I don't always get around to answering.

I spotted Michael alone at a table. He still had *The Great Shark Hunt* keeping him company but it was closed.

"Hey. Is it all right if I join you?" I asked, and when he didn't respond I sat down.

Since it had been pointed out to me that I began every conversation with some version of *How are you doing?* I decided to skip it—in part because I could see he was doing lousy and I didn't want to get into it just then. That's not the best thing for a therapist to admit.

"I've been thinking," I told him, "Timothy and Aiden either died from bad dope or someone had it in for them. If they were killed, why were they? Perhaps for financial gain or jealousy. Of course, there are countless other reasons, but I was wondering what you think."

He stared down at his coffee cup. I knew he'd heard me but I wasn't sure he was listening. I've learned not to interrupt silence and let the burden of breaking it rest on the other. I don't always practice it.

"Any ideas?" I prompted.

"It was the dope."

"That's the most likely reason. But in that case, someone else might have OD'd as well."

"Maybe. Or they brought it themselves." He took a sip of his coffee. "Then there's always killing them because of a woman."

"A tried and true reason. Yet, it's one thing to be jealous of someone and kill them or someone they were cheating with. But unless Timothy and Aiden were both doing someone else's girlfriend, I can't think why anyone would kill them both."

"I wouldn't rule out that third party."

"You wouldn't?"

"I wouldn't. We all do, or have done, a fair amount of sport fucking. It's entirely possible they both did someone, and that someone had a boyfriend who wasn't happy about it."

"Yeah. That works. So do you have a particular woman and her boyfriend in mind?"

"I do."

"Want to share?"

"Not really."

"Any reason you don't want to share that you'd be willing to share?"

"Yeah," he said staring defiantly at me. "I'm that guy."

"You're the jealous guy who killed them because they were messing with your girlfriend?"

"No. I'm the jealous guy who's with the woman that both of them did."

"Oh. Not the killer. Just the jealous guy."

"Right."

"Thanks for letting me know."

"You'd have found out sooner or later. Best you hear it from me."

"So this is public information?"

"To some."

"Like the other band members?"

"Among others."

"Well, I'm sorry you're the jealous one—that sucks. I hate being jealous."

"Join the club."

"So do you want to tell me who the woman is?"

"She can tell you herself."

Josie came to the table and I put two and two together.

She gave him a knowing kiss, then passed behind him, draped her hand on his shoulder, and let it slide off as she sat next to him.

She gave me the kind of smile that would make me jealous and insecure if I were her boyfriend. As it was, I enjoyed it and returned it, but kept an eye on Michael to see if he reacted. The flirtation seemed too customary for him get worked up about, though it hadn't played well with him. Perhaps that's why Timothy and Aiden were no longer here.

"How you doing, Doc?" she said.

"As well as can be expected under the circumstances. How about you?"

"Same."

With that perfunctory greeting out of the way we sat silently. I tried waiting them out. When that didn't work, I said, "Michael and I have been talking about who might have had it in for Timothy and Aiden."

"You mean aside from Michael?" Josie replied, demonstrating a degree of insight into human behavior that must have been born out of experience.

"Yeah, he nominated himself. Why do you think he did that?"

"Because he goes crazy when I flirt with other men. And knowing I have a history, well, he'd prefer he was my first and only."

"Most guys want that. Don't you?"

"Sure. They want us to be slut virgins. Innocent and wild at the same time."

"In the therapy world they call that the Madonna/whore complex. Men want women to be the whore in the bedroom and the virgin queen everywhere else."

"I'd say they want you to be the whore everywhere but when you meet their mother."

"That's probably closer to the truth. Is that how it works with you, Michael?"

"Yeah," Josie asked. "Is that how it works for you, babe?"

"Can we talk about those other suspects? I'm not the only one who might have wanted to kill them."

"Sure. Go for it. Who else do you think might have had a motive?"

He saw something in his coffee cup worthy of his attention. She smiled suggestively at me. I pretended I hadn't noticed. I couldn't tell if she was purposefully trying to pull Michael's chain, but it sure seemed so. My heart went out to him in that moment. It's hard enough to be involved with an attractive woman without her radiating come-hither looks.

A friend once asked his girlfriend if guys hit on her when she went out. She said, "What do you think?" He never asked again because it drove him crazy to think about it.

The flirting may have meant nothing to Josie, but it was obvious Michael didn't enjoy it. Hard being the third or fourth choice after Timothy, Aiden, and maybe Drew.

"Okay, I admit it," he said. "I'm the most likely candidate. I can think of other people who might have had it in for them, but it would be a stretch."

"Do you want to confess now or should I just put you on the suspect list? If you did do it, nominating yourself is a good way to get me to think you didn't do it. If you didn't do it, I'm sorry any suspicion is going to come to you first. But hopefully not last."

"I don't think you need to be concerned about Michael," Josie told me as she snuggled up to him. "His mood is worse than his bite."

"I'll keep that in mind. So who should I be concerned about?"

"I'm not sure it's anyone in our little group," she said. "But if I had to pick someone, I'd opt for Eve."

"Okay. So why her? What makes you think she could be a suspect?"

"I can tell you what Josie's thinking," Michael said. "If I did them in because I was jealous, she did them in because she was the path not taken."

"Honey, don't call her a path. Although not a lot of people have beaten down that path. But yes, she'd have wanted to be the chosen one. Instead, she was always the unchosen one."

It sounded a bit cold the way she said it, but I got it. Being rejected has triggered many tragedies. Watching the male members of the band with other women could have worn on Eve. Killing them would ensure they wouldn't be with anyone else. If that were true, I'd need to keep a closer eye on Michael and Drew.

"All right, I'll follow up on that. But what about you, Michael? Does Eve have her eye on you as well?"

He didn't like that, either because I'd suggested it or because he hadn't, which evidenced her being passed over once again. I've learned to bore in when clients are vulnerable. While that might sound cruel, I have the opposite intent. It's like when you put your feet in the shallow end of the pool. You want to get fully immersed but you're hesitant. As a therapist, you want people to go at their own pace, but you also want to gently nudge them toward the deep end.

"Have you rejected her advances?" I said.

However uncomfortable he'd been before, he was now doubly so. Josie, on the other hand, seemed to be enjoying his squirming.

"Yeah, babe. Did she ever hit on you?"

"Yeah. Maybe. I can't really remember."

I had a hunch he was remembering more than he wanted to say. It was strange. He was jealous of Josie's flirting, but when he had a chance to let her know someone was interested in him, he passed. Maybe he had empathy, but I suspected it was something else.

Josie didn't push him and neither did I.

So I asked again, "Anyone else you think might be worth considering?"

"Yeah, there's one more person you might want to think about," he said.

"Who's that?"

"Sheridan."

"Why him?"

Josie answered. "He and Eve are an on/off item so he could have the same jealous stuff going on. But there's more than that."

"I'll bite."

"He's a wannabe. He's the smartest, most talented of all of us, but he's never made anything of it. While he might be jealous of Eve, he's more jealous of the rest of us."

"That what you think?" I asked Michael.

"He writes a lot of poetry, but Timothy would never use any of it in his songs. He'd sit in with us sometimes but Timothy never wanted him in the band. He's not really that skilled a musician but he's good people. Yeah, he's envious of all of us."

When he said that, something shifted in him. If someone was killing band members out of jealousy, might Michael be next? It was a disquieting thought for someone who seemed to have enough of those already.

Josie didn't seem that concerned. Maybe because she was the killer or maybe because she didn't let her paranoid fantasies get the better of her.

CHAPTER 21

"On the Outside"

Oingo Boingo

I LEFT MICHAEL and Josie and went to find Eve and Sheridan. I felt a bit like a pinball bouncing from one place to the other.

I didn't really like the jealousy angle, though I recognized jealousy did things to you which you'd rather not talk about. Though it was a stretch to kill multiple people out of jealousy, there were plenty of people in jail for just such an offense. And there might be one more joining them.

I didn't know where to find Eve or Sheridan but opted for a circuitous route to their tepee. I might also have been hoping to run into Lilah. I liked strolling through the area. There were lots of colorful displays and people seemed genuinely happy, and as the evening descended things were cooling down.

I found Eve and Sheridan sitting in a couple of chairs outside the tepee, having drinks.

"Hello," I said. "Is it okay if I join you?"

"Why not?" Sheridan said. "We're just taking a little break."

I sat on the ground. I figured being on a lower plane might help them feel comfortable with me.

"How are you two holding up?"

"I can't speak for Sheridan, but I'm not holding up well at all. I'd go home if I didn't feel I needed to be here to support my friends."

"Eve's gotten her emotional bearings unmoored," Sheridan said.

"We all have," I replied. "I don't think any of us are used to having people die around us."

"Well, Dave, that's not entirely true. Some of us have known troubling times. But you're right—sweltering in the desert while your friends die isn't our usual weekend activity."

"I'm sure some of us have had significant troubling times. Anything come to mind you want to share?"

"Dave, you're the therapist, aren't you? None of us have lived a sheltered life."

"Well, I'm here if you want to talk about it, and here if you don't."

With that there was silence.

Eve seemed uncomfortable with the quiet and broke it. "Sheridan's just being dramatic. We're fine. Well, not really, but we're trying to get a little shelter from the storm right now. Sheridan's been writing poetry and I've been meditating."

"Poetry and meditation. Sounds like a winning combo."

"No, Dave, it isn't. Eve mediates. I wax poetic. We try not to mix the two."

"Very well. I'd welcome hearing some poetry. Not sure there's much to share with the meditation."

"I'd be happy to meditate with you. And Sheridan is an exceptional poet."

"Wow. Who knew? Happy to listen and join in. Maybe not right now, but down the line I'd be happy to do both."

"Dave, don't be nice with us. Nice doesn't work."

"I wasn't being nice. Maybe not one hundred percent sincere but close. I'd like to hear your poems. Not so sure about the meditating, but I'm open to it."

"You'd like it," Eve said.

"I'm sure I'd like both. In the meantime, can I ask a question?"

"I don't think we're going to stop you," Sheridan said.

"It really is tragic about Timothy and Aiden and it's entirely possible they just got hold of some bad dope and it did them in. But, if it was foul play who do I focus on?"

"I know you have a special relationship with Drew," Sheridan said, "but if I had to name names, I'd put him at the top of the list."

"You would? I'm surprised. How come?"

"Dave, maybe you don't know him as well as you think you do. You should ask him more about Timothy. I don't know about him killing Aiden aside from we all wanted to kill him at times because he was a jerk, but Drew and Timothy had history."

"He's right."

"Okay, want to tell me that history?"

"You're the one playing detective. Why don't you figure it out? I'm sure if you ask him he'll tell you. It's not like it's a big secret."

"All right. I can do that. But help me out."

"Why don't you talk to him first and then tell us what he said? Then we can let you know how close it is to the truth."

CHAPTER 22

"This Business is Killing Me"
The Ramones

I'M NO PINBALL wizard but I was getting some extra practice. This one was pointing the finger at that one who was pointing it at someone else. Next thing I knew I'd be a suspect. Not entirely unrealistic given someone might have spotted me ripping off the police banner.

If I wanted to find the real perpetrator, I'd need some real information. During my back-and-forthing behind the stage area, I'd passed a trailer with a sign that read The Buck Stops Here. I figured it was as good a place as any to visit.

I went in. No one was there. The buck might have stopped here, but I guessed it had gone out for a smoke. There were a few desks, papers piled up all over the place, and posters of concerts featuring the Rolling Stones, Santana, Janis Joplin, and every big band of the time. One desk was orderly, with a phone and a short stack of papers on it. They were incident reports of people who'd stolen items, gotten into fights, OD'd, or gone to the first-aid tent.

I went over to the cluttered desk. There were stacks of bills, notes scribbled with all manner of indecipherable messages, three phones, and a framed picture of a couple and two teenage boys that looked like it had been taken in the fifties. I was holding the picture in my hand when the door opened.

Two men came in. Leading the way was the fifty-year-old rock promoter Bill Graham. He was angry and yelling at the second man, who was wearing a tan suit with a clip-on tie. He was the only person who didn't seem to know it was a hundred degrees outside.

"Just fucking find the guy!" Graham said. Then he turned to me. "What the fuck are you doing with my family picture?"

"I was admiring it. It speaks of a different time and place."

"Certainly from here," he said.

I put the picture down. Graham was wearing jean shorts and a well-worn polo shirt. I realized he was one of the boys in the picture. I admit, I was a little star-struck. I can't name a single other rock promoter, or any kind of promoter for that matter. Well, other than PT Barnum, who noted there was a sucker born every minute.

I apologize for going off on a tangent, but you'll get a kick out of this, and it does relate to the story. When I was an undergrad at UCLA, I was in a psychology class where the professor had us all take a personality test. We took it one week; he scored it and returned it the next, along with an individual evaluation of our personalities. The professor asked us to rate how well the test described us on a scale of one to five. Most of us answered four or five. He then told us that the evaluations we'd received were identical. We were all wanted to be liked and admired, had unused capacity, prided ourselves on being independent, and a bunch of other generalities. He told us this generic description was called the Barnum effect. Named after PT, who'd once again proved we could all be suckers.

Bill Graham was no sucker. He was a world-class promoter. He'd basically brought rock and roll to the West Coast. Among other things, he was known for his temper.

"Want to tell me what you're doing here?"

"Sure," I said carefully. "I was hoping I could get some help."

"The first-aid tent is on the other side. The quack doctor is a couple trailers down, as is the drug gal. The non-sanctioned drug guy is out in the tents."

"That's very helpful to know. But that isn't the kind of help I'm wanting. I'm with Magoo's Drew."

"Yeah. That's a horrible mess."

The other guy sat down at the neat desk and got on the phone.

"Drew actually asked me to look into it. While no one I've talked with knows for sure, there seems to be a consensus that either some bad dope was involved or, more likely, someone murdered them."

He was sorting through the papers on his desk, seemingly unaffected by what I'd said.

"No one's ever accused Elsa or Hank of selling bad shit."

"I'm guessing one of those two hasn't been seen for a while, which doesn't bode well for their reputation."

"Elsa's been talking with Sully over here who's in charge of security so maybe he can help you."

Sully nodded. I nodded back. He was talking on the phone and I was having trouble overhearing what he was saying—something about some stuff being stolen from one of the trailers.

"I spoke with someone whose tent was close to the dealer's, and they said the dealer's been scarce ever since Aiden's body was found."

"That was Hank. The police haven't found him. But I don't think he had bad dope, just bad luck."

"Yeah, not good for business to have people dying on your premises."

"Tell me about it. Elsa's been in here, and according to Sully the dope she sold is fine. We've had no other ODs with her dope or Hank's. They've both been selling a lot so Sully told her it was okay to go back and deal the rest."

"So do you think foul play was involved?"

"Of course. Sully here is on it. I've got way too many things to do, and as much as I'd like to chat about this, I have to go scream at some people." And with that he grabbed some papers and left.

Sully appraised me. I had on my jean shorts and a Bruce

Springsteen T-shirt. The going-over he gave me let me know his opinion of my attire and investigative prowess.

"What exactly is your role here?" he said.

"One of the members of Magoo asked me to look into the deaths of his bandmates."

"And what exactly qualifies you for that distinction?"

I was feeling a bit defensive and didn't have a star-studded résumé to show off. "Let's just say, like you, I was hired to do a job. And, like you, I want to do a good one. Since it seems we're both of a mind these deaths weren't accidental, I was hoping we could help each other out so maybe we could figure out whodunit."

"I've got my hands full here. I got Bill screaming at me and people fucking up left and right, so maybe the best way for us to help each other is for you to stay out of my hair."

My attempt to get us on the same page didn't seem to be working.

"Fair enough. With all that's going on you don't need me bugging you. So I'll be happy to get out of your way," I said, not moving. "Before I go, can I ask you one question?" Before he could answer, I said, "Since you got to see both victims, did they both have the needle in the same arm?"

I was trying to sound smart and not ask something that would immediately show him I didn't know what I was doing. I'd let him figure that out later.

He had to think a moment before he answered, which I took as a good sign. Then he said, "Yeah. Now get out of here."

Not the best sign but at least it confirmed the same person might have done them in.

"Just one more question. Left or right arm?"

"Let me ask you one, friend of the band. Who gets their drugs for them?"

"I don't think I know."

"You don't think you know? That means you know something. What do you know?"

I now knew he was sharper than I'd thought.

"Well, I met someone who gets the band drugs now and then."

"Name please."

"I don't know it."

I didn't want to share Sheridan's name with him, but if I helped him maybe he'd help me. And if it helped him find out whodunit that would be a good thing. Not as good as if I could figure it out, but still… we weren't exactly on the same team but we were trying to solve the same mystery.

"I only know his first name—Sheridan."

"Got it."

"Okay, but you don't need to tell him you got that from me."

"You should have asked for that first. I'll consider it."

Okay, he was definitely smarter than me. Hopefully he'd think the smart thing to do would be not to tell Sheridan I'd ratted on him.

"Okay, so tell me. Left arm or right."

"Left. Now go."

So I did.

If the person were right-handed, and ninety percent of us are, and they came at the person from the front, they'd most likely stab the left arm. But how could someone approach you with a needle and get it in your vein without some level of cooperation? If they came at you from behind, and they were right-handed, they'd need to have awfully good aim.

I wasn't sure if left- or right-handedness made any difference because the more I pictured it the more it seemed to me the needle must have gone in voluntarily.

It was time to talk to the drug dealer. Evidently having a drug dealer and quack doctor were two rock-and-roll backstage perks. Sully and Bill didn't seem interested in stopping them from doing their business just as long as their business wasn't stopping anyone.

CHAPTER 23

"Every Little Thing She Does is Magic"
The Police

DRUGS—WELL, THE ONES being consumed at the festival—were illegal. That didn't stop the organizers from designating a trailer for the VIPs and looking the other way for the rest of the throng. Rock and roll had created its own culture and norms—why fight it when you could join it?

There was a short line outside Elsa's trailer. I got in the queue. There were two high-school-aged girls in front of me talking about the summer issue of *Teen Beat* and whether Ralph Macchio or Matt Dillon was more attractive. Thankfully, the line moved quickly.

Inside, I was surprised to see an arrangement of drugs laid out on a coffee table covered by a Navajo rug. Evidently, Elsa wasn't worried about leaving the goods out in the open.

"Hi. How can I help you?" she asked.

"Hi. Actually, I just want to ask you a question. I was talking with Bill Graham and Sully." I name-dropped to give me some credibility. "They mentioned you spent part of the day with them because they were worried about whether any junk you sold to Timothy and Aiden might have been bad."

"That's such bullshit. I've got a reputation to uphold. If they say I sold bad shit I'm fucked."

"Actually, they said you sold good shit."

"Well, that's a relief."

"I'm curious. Did you sell stuff to Timothy and Aiden together or separately?"

"Actually, I didn't sell them anything. They must have come with some bad shit or gotten it from Hank. But, truthfully, his stuff is just as good as mine. Aiden did come here to get some ludes and windowpane. I sold him the ludes, but I only have blotter acid. That's about it."

"Any idea how Aiden ended up in Hank's tent?

"Yeah, I told this to Sully so I guess it's okay to tell you. Hank came by here in the middle of the night totally freaked out. He told me Aiden had dropped by his tent, looking for windowpane. He didn't have any, either, but he asked Aiden if he'd hold down the fort while he got something to eat. With all the deadheads here, we've been working 24 hours a day. Aiden used to be a dealer and we both trusted him, so that wasn't an issue. When he got back Aiden was dead. Hank was afraid the police would think he did it. I told him to tell Sully but he just took off."

"Okay, that's good to know. I don't think the police have found him."

"Yeah, well, his alibi kind of sucks, but he'd never kill a fly. He's a total vegetarian. Won't wear a leather belt or shoes. He's all about saving the whales. I don't think the police will pin it on him."

"Sounds like it. They won't like that he ran from the scene, but that's a slap on the wrist."

"Well, he made sure to take all his drugs with him so they won't have that to use against him."

"Just as long as he makes sure to stash them somewhere safe."

"You don't need to worry about that. He's a safety freak as well."

"All right. So do you think Aiden OD'd, and if so, why there?"

"Who knows? Maybe Aiden just got horny being around all of Hank's shit and shot himself up."

"It's possible. Temptation can be hard to resist. Any other ideas?"

"The only other thing I can think of is maybe he got some bad shit from the quack and went over to Hank's tent to say hello and shoot up."

"The quack?"

"You know, the woo-woo doctor."

"I heard Sully say quack doctor, but I figured he just had a bad opinion of him. What's the woo-woo doctor?"

"He's a licensed doctor but, you know, he's also a rock-and-roll doctor. He gives out a lot of B-12 shots, an assortment of vitamins that don't come from the drug store. And if that doesn't work, he has all sorts of lotions and salves he can use to cure your hangover, broken heart, and lovesick blues."

"Maybe I ought to see him. Where is he?"

"He's got his own trailer. Can't miss it. It's over by the Grateful Dead's."

I decided to go see the quack doctor. Maybe they'd have something for the sunburn I figured I'd eventually get.

I asked someone and they said to look for a bus with *Sugar Magnolia* written on the side. I didn't find that, but did find a nondescript trailer with a simple Grateful Dead sign on it. Just like Magoo's. Close by was another trailer with a Doctor sign on it. I went up the steps and knocked on the door. There was no answer. I knocked again. Someone behind me suggested I open the door.

We went in. It didn't entirely resemble my doctor's office. There were beanbag chairs, large pillows, and a small sofa sitting on Moroccan rugs. A few people were relaxing or possibly tripping on the sofas. Incense wafted through the air. There were some Buddhas, dream catchers, and peace signs decorating the place, and a long table cluttered with jars filled with various unknown substances, piles of herbs, and a mortar and pestle. There was also a refrigerator, massage table, an examining table, a small desk, a couple of metal folding chairs, and a person who must have been the doctor, although his shorts, tie-dye shirt, ponytail, and bare feet threw me off. What didn't throw me off was when the guy who suggested I open the door said, "Hey, Doc. How's about a pick-me-up?"

"Sure thing, Phil," he replied, and went to get something while Phil flopped down on one of the pillows. I guessed Phil was a returning patient. The doc gave him a shot and soon Phil was perking up.

"How can I help you?" the doc asked me.

"Hi. Actually, right now I'm feeling mostly good. I'm friends with members of Magoo and they asked me to look into what happened to Aiden and Timothy."

"That's such a tragedy."

"Indeed. What do you think might have happened?"

"I haven't heard anything to the contrary so I'll just go with they got hold of some bad dope. It happens."

"You have any idea where they might have gotten the dope?"

"I haven't heard any other stories, so they likely brought it with them. I take it you already checked with Elsa. If you haven't, she might know something. She's good people so I don't think she sold them any bad shit."

"What about air bubbles? I've heard if air bubbles get in a needle it can kill you. Is that true?"

"You'd have a heart attack or stroke. I don't think you can attribute their deaths to that."

"Okay. Well, if you think of something, please let Drew of Magoo know. Or Sully if you know him."

"Sure, we go back. If I do think of something I'll leave a message."

"Thanks. And if I need a little pick-me-up or something for a sunburn, is it okay if I swing by later?"

"I'm here to serve you."

Isn't it nice to know there's actually someone who wants to serve you? Of course, levels of service vary and slogans don't often carry their weight, but his words did no harm and it seemed as though his services, like the food, were on the house. Or maybe Phil was running a bill.

CHAPTER 24

"A Gallon of Gas"
The Kinks

I WASN'T SURE what to do with myself. Pat Benatar was hitting it with her best shot and I was happy enough just to listen without watching her. When in doubt, head for the food pavilion, so I took the scenic route via the lake. I saw Sheridan standing alone, looking off into the distance. A cloud of smog hung in the air so he wasn't looking very far.

I came up from behind but didn't want to startle him, so when I was a few feet away I said, "Hey, Sheridan. Is that you?"

He sighed and said in an Eeyore way, "I suppose so."

"I'm sorry to break up your reverie. Can I join you."

"It's a very lonely place. I don't think you'd want to."

"Maybe if we're in it together it won't be so lonely."

"Perhaps."

"So how come the lonely?"

"Dave, I've lost two friends, well, two almost-friends. There aren't many people I like so losing any I'm partial to, well, it makes me lonely."

"I get that. Friendship isn't a numbers game, unless you're in junior high. It's not easy to have close friends."

"It isn't hard either. But it's not my style. I have a disturbed way of seeing the world that precludes a lot of entry."

"I'll take your word on that and try not to trespass."

"So far, Dave, you've managed not to get on my bad side."

"I'll endeavor to retain that position. But I want to ask you a question. If it compromises my position you can tell me and I'll leave you to your loneliness."

"Go on."

"I talked with the designated drug dealer and she said she didn't sell them any dope."

"Yeah. Elsa would tell you if she had. She's a straight shooter."

"I got that impression. Now, I know you've supplied the band with various drugs over the years, but I imagine whatever you've passed along has not been laced with anything that would cause anyone to OD."

"Dave, you're treading on thin ice here."

"I'm not pointing a finger at you. I don't want you to think that. I just figure you have a certain expertise in this area that I'd like to tap into."

"Proceed."

"Thanks. The way I see it, either they both shot up some bad dope and maybe the police will be able to trace it and figure out where they got it. Or someone shot them up. But if that happened, they either said, 'Okay, let's shoot up,' or someone got them to do it."

"Right."

"I don't think anyone could have snuck up behind them with a needle, aimed for a vein, and been able to make a direct hit. Nor could they have done it facing them. It's just too sloppy. Maybe someone put a gun to their heads and told them to shoot up. That's a possibility. What I want to ask you is, what else is a possibility? How did somebody get them to shoot up?"

"Dave, you've been doing some thinking."

"It's a bad habit, I know."

"There are worse."

"So, any ideas?"

"The gun thing sounds possible, as does some other threatening tactic, but off the top of my head I can't think of anything else."

"If you do, let me know."

"I can do that. In the meantime, Eve is planning a little something at the tepee later if you want to swing on by."

"Before or after the Heartbreakers?"

"That would be after. If you're up, come on by."

"You know us therapist types don't keep rock-and-roll hours."

"I can help you with that if you want."

I'd taken a few steps away when he called out to me, "Dave, have you talked to Johnny Romano?"

"Who's Johnny Romano?"

"He drives the equipment truck for the band. Kind of a strange fellow, but interesting. You know how these union guys have strict rules they have to follow. He drives the band's instruments and equipment from place to place, but he can't lift anything in or out of the truck. That's someone else's job. So he drives and then he does nothing. Well, in his case, nothing is sleeping, eating, and being nosy. He might be a good person for you to talk to."

"Okay. Where can I find him?"

"Well, there's the tricky part. He might be over where all the equipment trucks are parked. His truck has a picture of some horses running on the plains. If he isn't there try the food pavilion. Or he might just be hanging out. He doesn't sit still for long. He's kind of a speed freak, though he tries to come off it when he isn't driving."

"Even speed freaks need some sleep. A colleague once told me he loved speed freaks. He'd invite them over to his place because they were twitchy and needed something to do; he'd get them to help clean up his place."

"Sounds like Ross, though I don't think you'd want him cleaning up your place. Maybe he could wash your car."

"Well, it's gathering dust now so that might work. Want to tell me how to recognize Johnny Romano?"

"He's very pale and he'll be wearing a Hawaiian shirt and shorts."

"That makes it easy. There are only a few thousand of those guys here."

"He'll also be wearing a Mets baseball cap. He's close to six foot with a good beer belly. You wouldn't peg a speed freak for a beer belly, but he eats a lot of fast food and confines his exercise to the cab. He's from Jersey so you'll hear some of *dese* and some of *dose*."

"I got it. Anything else?"

"He drives fast, talks fast, and is connected."

"Connected like…"

"Precisely, so tread lightly."

I treaded lightly over to where the trucks were parked. There were easily fifty lined up next to each other. Most were nondescript but some had extra lights and reflectors, and a few had scenes of mountains and rivers painted on their sides. I wondered why some people painted scenes on their trucks but very few ever did on their car. The canvas was smaller, but still.

I saw the truck with the running horses, but no Johnny Romano.

There were some chairs spread out and men chatting but no one with a Mets cap. I asked a few people if they knew Johnny, but just got a lot of shrugs. I legged it over to the food pavilion. The time of day or night didn't seem to matter; the place had a steady flow. I guess if you're serving rock and roll and 24-hour free food you can expect that.

I saw one Mets cap, which wasn't surprising since this was mostly a Dodger town, although LA has as many people from New York and Chicago as it does native Californians.

I zeroed in on the guy with the hat. In front of him was a

collection of desserts. People heading to the buffet and piling on the desserts is a phenomenon I've only seen in Vegas. I guess if you're paying for all you can eat or not paying, why not dose yourself with sweets—though you'd pay for that down the line.

He was working on some chocolate pudding when I came up to him.

"Hi. Are you Johnny Romano?"

He gave me a good looking-over.

"Yeah?" he answered and questioned all at once.

"Hi. My name's David. Sheridan suggested I talk with you. I'm a therapist and friend of the band's and he thought you might be able to help me with something."

He took a good-sized spoonful of the pudding.

"Waddaya want?"

"Good question. I'm not entirely sure. Is it all right if I sit down?"

"Suit yourself,."

"Thanks. So here's the situation. As you know, the band's hurting. They asked me if I could try to find out what happened to Timothy and Aiden."

"I'll tell you what fuckin' happened. The fuckheads OD'd. That's what fuckin' happened."

"Yeah. That's what it looks like. Maybe they got hold of some bad shit and paid for it. But, you know, things ain't always what they seem."

He stopped spooning the pudding and gave me a close stare.

"What the fuck are you saying?"

"Some of us think maybe someone had it in for them."

"What the fuck you talking to me for? I didn't do nuthin'."

"I'm sure you didn't. But I was hoping you might have an idea who might have. Sheridan said you keep your eye on things. Maybe you saw something that would be useful. Any ideas?"

"Those boys were knuckleheads. I'm not going to say anything bad about the departed, but they were no saints."

"What do you mean?"

"I mean they're like all the rest of the rock and rollers here. They fuck around and they don't give a shit about anybody but themselves."

I could sense that Johnny's blood pressure was rising as fast as the heat had earlier. As a therapist, I like to bore in when emotions are triggered, but I value my life and have no compelling interest in upsetting someone who's connected.

I tried to tiptoe.

"Yeah, they're not always the best citizens," I said, figuring agreeing with him was a good way to go. "And I suppose any number of people might have issues with them."

"That's right."

It was good to know I'd got something right. I just wasn't sure if being right was helping.

He went back to his desserts. Done with the pudding, he moved over to a piece of pie.

"Want to tell me who you think some of those people would be?"

"Excuse me? Do I look like a snitch? End of discussion. I'm going to eat in peace now."

That was a good idea. I thanked him and got out while the going was good, noting he'd told me nothing about anything. All I knew was, he liked desserts, didn't think highly of rock musicians, and had a temper that could flare.

CHAPTER 25

"Once in a Lifetime"
Talking Heads

I SURVEYED THE food pavilion. I couldn't see anyone I knew so I moseyed over to a table with four people who were more dressed up than the rest of us—three guys and one woman. She was wearing a suit and was very coiffed. She seemed the most out of place.

"Hi," I said. "Okay if I join you?"

"Sure," said one of the men.

"Pardon me for asking," I said, "but I couldn't help but notice you four seem a bit out of place. There's nary a band T-shirt among you."

"Don't rub it in," said the guy who'd welcomed me.

"What's the occasion?"

"We're working," said the woman.

"Oh. Me, too, though I have a different dress code. What are you working on?"

"The news. We're newscasters."

"Ah," I said. "You do look familiar. Channel 9, right?"

"Yes. I'm Christine Lund. This is Harry Silkes, Bob Andrews, and George Francis."

"Hi. So are you doing remotes from here?"

"Yes," said Harry. "Interviews. Human interest. This is quite the event. Getting a lot of good ratings."

"Good for you. I'm sure the deaths must have heightened the interest."

"It's so sad," Christine said. "I did an interview with Timothy Durant Friday afternoon and he was so excited about doing the show."

"It's horrible. I'm with one of his bandmates and it's really been upsetting for them."

"You are?" she asked, her interest piqued. "Are you with Josie?"

Christine had assumed I'd meant "with" in a romantic sense. Before I could clear things up, she said, "I've been trying to interview her, but she hasn't wanted to talk with me. Do you think you could convince her? I really just want her to tell her story."

"I don't think I can do that. I could ask her, but I'm not that close to her. I work for one of the other members of the band."

"Oh. Who?"

"I'm afraid I can't share that. But let me ask you something. When you interviewed Timothy was there anything he said that might have been out of place?"

"There was one very chilling prophetic and weird thing."

"Want to tell me?"

"Tune in at eleven," she smiled. "Just kidding—it's already been on the news. You just haven't caught it out here."

"Oh, what did he say?"

"He prophesied his death. In the interview, he told me, 'It's all downhill from here.'"

"Yeah," said one of the guys whose name I'd already forgotten. "We've been playing that clip all day. It's eerie."

"It is that. Although it's downhill attendance-wise for anyone doing a festival this large."

"Yeah," said another guy—I'd also managed to forget his name.

"They say Woz is losing millions so I don't think too many people are going to rush to do another large-scale event."

"Especially in the desert," said a third guy whose name had also slipped my mind.

"Not that you'd ask," I said to Christine, whose name I still remembered, "but did you talk with him about drugs? I'm curious if he gave any indication he might be taking any this weekend."

"I didn't ask and he didn't say."

"But," said the first guy, "he did reference that line from the Stones' *Brown Sugar* about how he was doing all right.

"I don't get what that has to do with anything," Christine said with a bit of an I-know-better attitude. "He was just tooting his horn."

"Could be," he replied. "But that song is about brown sugar."

"He's just talking about a woman that's caught his eye."

"Could be," he replied smugly. "But brown sugar is heroin."

When they'd left, I wondered if there was something to the brown sugar comment or if I was creating connections where they didn't exist. That's the thing about mysteries, you don't know what's what until you do, or you don't.

I tried to focus on my barbecued chicken and potato salad. I might have had some sauce on my face and hands when Lilah sat down next to me. I didn't get a hello kiss. Since we'd finished on a kiss that last time we'd parted, I'd been hoping we'd pick up where we'd left off. Of course, we hadn't been in the food pavilion then and I might have been less messy.

"Hey, I said. "It's good to see you."

"You too. Who were those people that just left?"

I couldn't tell if she was just curious or jealous of Christine, which could be a good or a bad sign. I opted for the safer route.

"Yeah. I noticed their out-of-place dress as well. Turns out they're from Channel 9 and broadcasting live updates."

"Did they come when they heard about the deaths?"

"No. They were here before. The woman sitting next to me told me she'd interviewed Timothy right before he died."

"How eerie."

"That's what they said. They told me Timothy sort of prophesied his own death."

"Like when Hendrix wrote "The Ballad of Jimi" and predicted he'd be dead within five years."

"Is that fact or urban myth?"

"Not sure, but it's something a lot of people who really know his music think."

"Sort of like when John Lennon wrote he was living on borrowed time and got killed before the song came out."

"Very creepy. What do you think, Doc? Can people predict their deaths?"

"Could be. I do believe we're way more capable than we know ourselves to be. Some people might be more tuned in on that wavelength while the rest of us try to stay more focused on the moment. We tend to remember when things fall into place or a certain woo-woo happens."

"Like when I catch all the green lights."

"Yeah, you forget all those times you had to stop and go. But Timothy said something like 'It's downhill from here.' And then he died. Maybe he foretold his death, but I think he was really alluding to how many more times he'd play in front of a couple of hundred thousand people. It's a once-in-a-lifetime thing. Well, of course, so is everything really, but playing here is especially so."

"This is as big an event as I've ever been to in my life."

"They say there are three hundred thousand here today, two hundred yesterday. Where else do you go in life where you're doing something with that many other people all at once?"

"In LA that would be the freeway."

"That's true. But it doesn't quite feel the same."

"This is a peak experience. That's more business as usual."

"I'll say."

"You'll say what?" Sheridan asked.

"Hi," said Lilah. "Have a seat."

"What are you kids up to?" Eve asked.

"Just talking about prophesying death and seeing into the future."

"You mean Lynard Skynard's 'That Smell,'" Eve added, and then sang:

Oooh, that smell
Can't you smell that smell?
Oooh, that smell
That smell of death surrounds you

"And then they had the plane crash."

"Yeah, like that," I said.

"Good. We will join you then," Sheridan said, sitting down beside me.

"We were also talking about how we've never been to an event the size of this before," I said, trying to hide my disappointment about their joining us. "I did a Renaissance Fair that had maybe ten thousand, and a baseball game with fifty. Last year, I did see the Rolling Stones at the Coliseum so that's my personal best."

Suddenly, I sounded like those guys at the will call line who'd been trying to one-up each other.

"Nice," said Lilah. That felt good although I'd had to brag to get it.

"Dave," Sheridan said. I noticed how he often started his talks with my name. "We have to talk."

"Why's that?"

"Earlier, I had a visit from someone sent by you. A security person, a certain tight-assed, would-be cop called Sully."

While I'd hoped Sully would keep his source to himself, it made sense he'd tell Sheridan how he'd got his name—mix things up and see what happened.

Sheridan was upset. I couldn't blame him. I'd be if things had been reversed. But he also had a bemused look on his face.

"Yeah. I'm sorry. I wasn't sure it was a good idea to tell him that occasionally you provided the band with drugs but, in my defense, I could tell he wasn't out to bust your chops. He just wants to make sure what happened to Timothy and Aiden doesn't happen to anyone else."

I blanched a little when I said that. I didn't want to be prophesying someone else's death. I just hoped it was one of those things you say that you don't remember because, like ninety-nine percent of what you say, it doesn't mean much.

"It was an asshole thing to do, Dave. I can understand why you threw me under the bus—well, almost—but I can't condone it. But, then, you probably don't condone a lot of what I do. So even though you're an asshole, I trust you more."

"I hope I haven't harmed our relationship."

"I wouldn't say you've helped it, but I wouldn't say you've harmed it. You've just made me more aware of the possibilities."

"Well, awareness is a big deal in my world. The more you're aware of the forces within and without you, the freer you are to make your own choices."

"Spoken like a true therapist," said Lilah, which helped to break the tension.

"Guilty as charged. So, Sheridan, Eve, aside from that Sully visit, how are things?"

"We're trying to have a good time," Eve said. "But the dark cloud surrounding us is bearing down."

That was either a very profound or a very stoned-out thing to say.

"Yeah, there's that cloud," I said, because that's what therapists do—we acknowledge what people think, feel, and do. We don't always support and encourage, but we're good at acknowledging what you said is what you said.

I could join Sheridan and Eve in the darkness of it all. Empathizing with and encouraging them to share their pain might eventually lead to their sharing some profoundly insightful information. But, not being a fan of foreplay, I was keen to skip first and second base, and slide into third.

"So, Sheridan," I began...

Here's another thing I've learned. If you want to connect with someone, use the language they use. Language makes for borders. We all belong to groups that have words that mostly only the people in that group know. Be it doctors or plumbers, rockers, or shipyard dockers, each group's language lets members know who's in and who's not in their group. I'm not a sociologist but I know if I want to connect with someone when they say *potato*, I say *potato*. Since Sheridan began sentences with my name, I'd do the same.

"So, Sheridan, how come you wanted me to talk to Johnny Romano? I met him. He didn't seem pleased to meet me. Aside from knowing he likes desserts and dislikes musicians, was there something else you wanted me to know?"

"Dave, I told you he was connected right?"

"Right."

"He drives everywhere in a big truck. What else do you think he has in that truck aside from the band's instruments and equipment?"

"Fast-food wrappers?"

"Decidedly. Anything else?"

"Medicinal supplies."

"You're getting warmer."

"Maybe more than just a personal supply."

"Warmer, but what kind of medicinal aids do you think he transports?"

"Heroin?"

"And?"

"Coke?"

"And?"

"Weed?"

"Too stinky."

"Uppers, downers, in-betweeners?"

"Mostly, but there's one thing he carries most of us in the profession don't."

"Chocolate?"

"For personal consumption. But given he travels a lot, he's known as the go-to person if you want something esoteric and off the beaten path."

"Okay, that's interesting. You think he might have gotten the bad dope for Timothy and Aiden?"

"Possibly. He is connected."

"I don't think he's going to want to be forthcoming about any of that."

"I imagine so. I'm not suggesting you poke about because if he finds out, you'll be trading in your loafers for some nicely fitted cement shoes."

"So I don't want to poke about. Do I want to buy from him?"

"That's your choice. I'm just saying there might be more there for you to find out."

"What Sheridan is hinting at," Eve added, "is whatever you do, don't get caught."

CHAPTER 26

"Truckin'"

Grateful Dead

I RELUCTANTLY SAID goodbye to Lilah and less reluctantly to Eve and Sheridan. I told them I'd meet up with them in Eve's tepee after Tom Petty's set.

I got my flashlight from my tent and went looking for trouble.

As I passed the backstage area, Tom Petty started playing. He was the day's headliner and closing the show for the night. His music had only really come to the public's attention in the late seventies, but here he was a few years later playing in front of a couple hundred thousand cheering and exhausted music fans. I caught a glimpse of him and he appeared to be savoring the moment.

I wanted to savor the moment. But I needed to seize it.

I needed to talk with Johnny about drugs. While Johnny was no big fan of rockers, I figured if he'd watch any show, this would be a good one. If he was there, I'd talk with him. If he wasn't, I'd have to consider getting out of my comfort zone.

You might have already grasped the fact I'm not the bravest fellow and don't overly enjoy breaking the law. Sure, I can exceed the speed limit and smoke a joint now and then, but breaking and entering isn't high on my list of desired ways to endanger my life.

My mother told me if I was going to steal to steal big. I don't think she wanted me to become a major player in the underworld. But if I was going to do something stupid, I might as well do something really stupid.

Breaking into a connected driver's truck, searching for clues to a murder, would have qualified in my mother's eyes. I didn't think she'd condone my actions; I wasn't even sure I could. But I had a job to do, and while I didn't think it would earn me any points with a judge, crime boss, or my mother, it did hold its own with me.

I approached the truck. There were a few people in the truck area but no Johnny, and the area next to his truck was deserted. I took that as a bad and a good sign. I'd have taken it as a better sign if his truck had been gone and I could've watched Tom Petty. Instead I heard him singing "Don't Do Me Like That" in the distance.

Then he said, you better watch your step

You're gonna get hurt yourself

Someone's gonna tell you lies

Cut you down to size

Ugh. Not quite the encouragement I needed. But I knew what I had to do.

I tried to adapt a carefree gait as I walked directly to the passenger side of the cabin. My plan was to open the door and casually hop in. If Johnny was there, I'd just say hi and ask if we could talk some more. If it didn't open, well, I hadn't gotten that far ahead in my contingency planning.

I approached the cabin, stepped up onto the step, and tried the door. Bingo. I opened it, jumped in, and closed it as quietly as I could. Johnny wasn't there and I urged the interior light to hurry up and go off. Before it did, I scanned about. Behind the seat was a sleeping area that was pretty funky. There were some magazines on the rumpled bed covers that might have provided some free-time stimulation. Before I could see more the light went out.

I took out my flashlight, opened the glove compartment, and found some papers, chewing gum, and life savers... nothing you couldn't find in my car. Well, except the gun.

I don't know a lot about guns but I know one when I see one.

I closed the compartment and turned my attention to the compartment by the bed. Kleenex, KY jelly, condoms, some loose change, and a black notebook that caught my interest. That could be informative. I was flipping pages when the driver's-side door opened and Johnny came in.

"What the fuck?" was his greeting.

My stomach moved to my chest and my blood pressure attained a new high. I did the best I could.

"Hey," I said. "I came looking to find you."

"You did?" he said, reaching into the glove compartment. He took out the gun and pointed it at me. "You know, if I killed you right now I wouldn't go to jail. I'm just protecting my property. But even though I'd like to shoot you and be done with it, we need to talk first."

"That's fine by me. I'm all about the talking."

"You stay there."

He closed the door and quickly scurried in the front of the truck and opened the side door.

It dawned on me I could've jumped over to the driver's side and made a run for it. So much for that escape plan. If I got another opportunity, I'd need to be a little faster with my reaction time.

He waved the gun at me and told me to get out. I did. He escorted me to the back of the truck, opened the roll-up door, and told me to get in. I did. He came in after me and shut the door. A light came on.

Oh boy, this wasn't good. A profound realization hit me—I was alone with an armed, connected fella who'd just caught me rifling through his stuff. I hoped I could find my A game. I wasn't sure if my A game would make a difference. I wasn't even sure what my A game was or if I had one.

Things didn't improve when he took me to the side of the cargo space and used a rope-like binding to tie my hands to some iron rings on the wall—one hand over my head to the right, the other to the left. Classic torture-chamber pose. Well, at least my A game wouldn't need any sleight of hand.

On the positive side, he put the gun on a shelf close enough to me I could reach it… if my hand wasn't otherwise detained. He went over to a cabinet in the corner and took out a bottle of Seagram's Seven and a glass. He put the glass on the shelf and poured himself a decent shot, which he proceeded to drown. *More power to you* I said to myself. *Keep drinking.* Unless, of course, he was a nasty drunk, in which case, maybe he'd share.

"I guess you're not a Petty fan," I said.

"I like some of his stuff but not enough to stand next to all those people. I can hear fine from here. I'm thinking you were thinking the same thing."

"Kind of. You're very intuitive."

"Yeah, well, I fuckin' figured you might be trying to do some bullshit thing. I got a bad vibe about you earlier and knew you'd be up to no good."

"You're good. I actually got that same vibe from you. Great minds, huh?"

My nervous babbling sounded as bad to me as it likely did to him. I don't always do my best thinking or verbalizing when I'm tied up.

"You can fuck around as much as you want," Johnny said. "I ain't going nowhere. And before I go anywhere, you're gonna have to fork it over."

"Fork over what? You want my wallet? It's got about sixty-five dollars in it."

"Forgeddaboudit. Well, wait a minute," he said as he reached in my back pocket and took it.

Reading out loud he said, "David Unger, 3392 Laurelwood Drive. You don't look five eleven to me."

"I may have lied a little about that, but the weight is still holding."

"When we're done here, you might find you've lost some more."

While people who live in Southern California are always happy to lose a few pounds, his weight-loss approach didn't hold much appeal for me.

Maybe if I could help him, he'd be less inclined to shoot me. But how? Thinking gave me some hope, which is a good thing. But I knew I was doing what therapists call wishful thinking. I prefer that term to its opposite—catastrophic thinking. Which is what I'd be doing soon enough.

"We're on a similar wavelength. You know where I live and I know where you spend a good deal of your time. Maybe we can help each other out."

"How's that? I dunno, I don't see a lot of ways you can help me, and I'm not in a very helping-out mood."

"Nor should you be. Let's face it, you caught me red-handed doing something I ought not to be doing."

"Decidedly."

"But you don't know what I was doing there. You didn't get a good vibe off of me when we met and I didn't get the best off you. So, right there, we're thinking alike. I figure once we get more lined up, we really will be able to help each other."

"You're cracking me up. I'm still not hearing anything that would make me want to do anything other than shoot you."

"I'll grant you, there's always that option. But you wouldn't be maximizing the situation. Plus, you'd have to get rid of the body and worry about someone finding out. Who else knows I'm here, what time I'm expected back—you know, that stuff."

He poured himself another drink. I had a hunch he didn't

believe anything I said. I didn't either; I was just making it up as I went along. Like many who get caught up in perilous situations, I was trying to raise my GPA.

While it was possible Johnny had killed Timothy and Aiden, it was more likely he hadn't. Why not approach him like I had everyone else? Give or take an exaggerated truth or two.

While letting the client break the silence is a valued therapeutic technique, my nervousness wouldn't allow me to be quiet. I might as well try to take the evening's activities in a direction that was preferable to me.

"Okay, let me tell you what I was doing in your cab and why we can help each other out."

He picked up the gun. Not a good sign. My catastrophic thinking kicked right in—*if he shoots me I'm not going to be able to see Jackson Browne tomorrow.* That prompted me to pick up the pace.

"Johnny—is it okay if I call you that?" He didn't answer so I continued. "The reason I'm here is because I was told you have a side specialty in exotic drugs. If that's true, and, come on, we know it is, I was hoping you could help me figure out what happened to Timothy and Aiden."

"What the fuck are you talking about?" he said, waving the gun. Another bad sign. I could be getting an *F* any moment now.

"The common conclusion is they both OD'd from bad junk. Now, no one is suggesting you provided that sugar, but sooner or later someone is going to come to talk to you. I figure if we can work together, we can clear your name and figure out who did give them the bad stuff."

"What makes you think there was any bad shit? Those guys could have died from any number of things."

"What are you saying?"

"I'm saying, don't go pinning this on me. I've been selling dope for years and no one has ever died. A few complaints here and there but I took care of those."

I had a hunch how he might have taken care of those complaints. I decided not to complain.

"I'm sure you did. I'm not complaining about anything. Well, maybe the heat, but I'm not holding you responsible for that. Unless I should. Were you the one that turned up the heat?"

I was trying to shift the focus and inject some humor. I vaguely recollected a technique to use when someone's mad. You ask them a specific non-related question that requires them to shift their thinking. I'd never tried it but was happy I'd been able to reach into the archives of my mind and come up with something.

"Fuck you. I don't have nuthin' to do with the fucking heat. If you were smart, you'd realize the truck is air-conditioned and heated twenty-four seven, so anytime you put something in here you don't need to worry about it."

"You're right. I missed that. It's very comfortable. Nothing would spoil in here. You're smart to have it. So maybe you can help us out. Did you observe anything unusual that might relate to the deaths?"

"You know, I didn't like you when we first met and I'm not feeling any different about you now. You're full of shit. You were trying to steal from me and now you want to distract me and help you out. Forgeddaboudit."

"Okay, I forgot it. But you're not seeing the bigger picture here. The police are going to find out you know a thing or two about drugs and are connected to Timothy and Aiden. Maybe that was a poor choice of words. You know what I mean—you drive their truck. The cops are likely on their way to come talk with you. You're much better off dealing with me. You might not like me or trust me, but if you can avoid having to deal with the police it might make life easier for you."

"I don't worry about the police."

"Of course you don't. And I don't want you to worry about

them. But why not spend a few minutes with me so we can figure this out and you can avoid the hassle of dealing with them and me?"

"You got a point there. Though I'm not sure I wouldn't prefer dealing with them."

"There's that too. But, you know, as annoying as I can be, I'm not serving you bad coffee and having you wait endlessly in a small room that smells."

That wasn't the whole truth; the truck was a little stinky. The air-conditioning wasn't an air freshener. But Johnny didn't seem to care.

I could tell he didn't know what to do with me. He wasn't alone in that.

CHAPTER 27

"Twist and Crawl"

The Beat

"I GOTTA FUCK you over, you know that. I caught you stealing from me. If I let you go without roughing you up, it ain't gonna look good."

Good news and bad news. He was thinking about letting me go, but not without exacting a price. While I was happy with one out of two going my way, I wanted to see if I could reduce the bodily harm.

People like it when you agree with them even if you don't. I've found it's good to start a potentially dicey conversation with agreement so the person doesn't get defensive right away.

"I get it. You have a reputation to uphold, and you caught me legitimately. Roughing me up is a good way to handle the situation."

He probably wasn't used to people agreeing with him on that subject unless they were the ones handing out the punches.

"You're right." I said trying to take advantage of his confusion. "I do need to be put in my place, but there's a problem. Fortunately, we can solve it." Notice how I said we. I was working the team approach here. I wasn't getting very far with it, but if at first you don't succeed… "Tomorrow night the festival is over and people will be heading out. You don't know if Magoo is going to finish up their tour or cancel it. Who knows what'll happen? What we do know is the people involved with Timothy and Aiden's deaths are here now and I'm getting close to figuring out whodunit," I lied. "But if you rough me up it's going to make it hard for me to do my job. Why not just let me give you an IOU? I'll spend the next twenty-four hours trying to solve this and if I do, you don't beat me up. If I don't, well, I owe you the face-saving opportunity to rough me up. You have my address in case I don't hold up my end of the deal. How does that sound?"

"It sounds like bullshit."

"It's only bullshit if I don't figure things out or if I don't come back here and let you kick my ass. I'm not going to tell anyone you caught me and let me go. That wouldn't be good for your reputation or mine. Let's just work together to solve this thing. I'm happy to tell people you were instrumental in solving the mystery. Who knows, you could be a hero."

He kinda liked that. Who doesn't want to be a hero?

I could see him wavering. I wasn't sure what I could do to seal the deal but needed to do something. I tend to babble in hopes I'll stumble upon something. I didn't think babbling would be the best approach, so I remained quiet.

As a therapist, I've learned to be comfortable with silence. Well, that's not entirely true. I've become more comfortable as I've learned the silence isn't an indicator of my lack of ability. I see the silence as time to quietly reflect. Of course, if it goes on too long, my own discomfort rises and causes me to speak. Evidently Johnny, as fast-talking as he was, was more comfortable with the silence.

"Let's say there was no bad dope and someone wanted to kill them both. How would they do it and make it appear to be an overdose? That's the thing I can't figure out. Any ideas?"

"You really are a piece of work," he said as he put the gun down and poured himself another drink. "First it was bad dope and then it's murder. Make up your mind. There ain't no way to shoot someone up without their approval unless you put a gun to their head or knock them out first."

"That makes sense. I guess if someone put a gun to my head I'd opt for the needle. But if they knocked me out, wouldn't the police be able to see a bump or some sign?"

"Maybe. But there's more than one way to knock a person out. You don't have to be Muhammad Ali to sting them like a bee."

"What are you saying?"

"I'm saying I could knock you out right now and no one would ever know unless they did some serious blood work."

"Okay. Please don't show me how you'd do that, but tell me. How would you do that?"

"Normally I'd just hit you over the head," he said and pointed out a baseball bat I hadn't seen. "But I've got a little something extra on this trip that would do the trick."

"Oh, yeah? What have you got?"

"Ibogaine."

"Ibogaine? What's that?"

"You ever read Hunter Thompson?"

"Sure. 'We were somewhere around Barstow on the edge of the desert when the drugs began to take hold.'"

That earned me some points. Maybe we actually were a team. Although it was hard to fully embrace that with my arms tied over my head.

"That was the Las Vegas book. Ibogaine was from another one."

"*The Great Shark Hunt?*"

"No, the one he wrote about the election. *Fear and Loathing: On the Campaign Trail '72.*"

"I did read his dispatches in *Rolling Stone.*"

"Yeah, well, if you remember, that was the drug he said Edmund Muskie took."

"Oh yeah. Wasn't that because he said he was sort of frozen?"

"Right. Hunters in some African tribe took it so they could stand still for days, waiting for prey."

"Wait, are you telling me you got some of that for someone here at the festival?"

"I'm not saying nothin'," he said putting his hands up. "I'm just saying if someone took a drug like that they might freeze up."

"That was a joke. Does that drug really freeze you? Thompson was just saying Muskie had no personality."

"Well, he didn't. I don't know if the drug had anything to do with it. I'm just saying if someone took a drug like that it might do something to their system."

"Okay, let me see if I understand. You travel a lot. Know a lot of people. And maybe if in your travels someone asked you to get hold of some ibogaine you might be able to score some. That about right."

"About."

"So, did you get that for someone who's here at the festival?"

"That is what you call privileged information."

"Wait. I understand it's not good for business for you to be outing your clients. But, just so I'm clear, if this person got that drug and gave it to Timothy and Aiden, they might have frozen up. Then the person could have shot them up so it looked like they OD'd."

"Could be."

"So come on, help me here. Let me know who bought it from you. I won't say where I found out. Call it a professional courtesy. I can focus more closely on that person and see if I can find some other evidence that would incriminate them. You really could be a hero."

"If I sold the killer ibogaine, you think they're going to make me a hero because of that?"

"Okay, well, that makes it a bit more difficult. Let's keep that between us. If we catch the guy, I'm happy to give you credit but leave out the details."

He was thinking about it.

I was thinking about it.

It seemed far-fetched someone would read about ibogaine from Hunter Thompson and know someone who could get it. If that were true, they'd planned this out for some time.

"Can you tell me when the person asked you to get the drug?"

"It was months ago. I've hauled for Magoo on a couple of tours, but when they ain't touring I'm still driving for someone."

"So, wait, was the person who asked about the drugs not connected to Magoo?"

"I didn't say that."

"Okay, we can play twenty questions all night. But why not just release me and let me get to work on this. It would help a lot if you'd just let me know who it was."

He was considering.

I was listening.

I could barely hear Tom Petty singing in the background.

> *Somewhere, somehow, somebody must*
> *have kicked you around some*
>
> *Who knows? Maybe you were kidnapped, tied up*
>
> *Taken away and held for ransom*
>
> *Honey, it don't really matter to me, baby*
>
> *Everybody's had to fight to be free*

In a lot of mystery and suspense books, the protagonist gets in fights, shoots a gun, and otherwise lives a life vastly different than my own. My weapon of choice is words. They say, "Sticks and stones may break my bones, but words will never break me." Whoever came up with that had never been in therapy. I've seen many people still bruised by words they heard as children.

That said, I wasn't planning on using my words to hurt Johnny and get my release. I was hoping my words would make enough sense to him and give him a good way out of a potentially troubling situation. If Johnny had sold the ibogaine to the killer, he might be an accessory and need to hire a real mouthpiece to help him out.

"Here's the deal," Johnny said. "I'm gonna let you go. I'm gonna hold you to your word on that IOU. If you don't find out who did this to Timothy, I'm going to come after you. I don't really give a shit about Aiden. He was an asshole. But Timothy, for a rocker, was good people."

With that, he undid the ties that bound me.

"I didn't know Aiden was such an asshole," I said as I massaged my hands to get some circulation moving.

"He was to me. That's all that counts in my book."

"So do you want to tell me who ordered the ibogaine?"

"No, I don't want to, but I don't feel good about it. Come on back tomorrow afternoon and we can talk about it some more. I got some things I gotta do."

I left just about the time Tom Petty was winding up his set by singing about how even the losers get lucky sometimes.

It was Bob Dylan who said he couldn't help it if he was lucky. I felt lucky with my upgraded GPA. I hoped my luck would hold out long enough for Johnny not to want to collect on the IOU.

CHAPTER 28

"In the Heat of the Night"
Pat Benatar

WHILE I SHOULDER the responsibility for not putting more energy into remembering things, I attribute some of the blame to my schooling. Throughout my school years I had to memorize things. I'd cram for a test, remember enough to get through, then forget the bulk of it. You'd think a system that depends so much on memorization would have offered at least one course on how to memorize things. Not that I'd have put much energy into such a class, but it might have helped.

Some say it's not so much we're forgetting but with each day there's more and more incoming material our brains need to manage in addition to all the old information. All that analysis and filing is a lot of work. The brain wants a rest now and then. None of us run in fourth gear all day; we shift from first to second, to third, back to second, over to first and into fourth now and then. We also spend a fair amount of time in park.

What I'm trying to say is, despite my shortcomings, I focused and remembered where I'd seen *The Great Shark Hunt*. It took a little while but maybe putting more energy into something does help.

It was with Michael. In the food pavilion. Hmm. If he read one

Hunter Thompson book he might have read another and he'd had access to Johnny.

He could have had any number of simmering resentments against Timothy and Aiden, and the time to plan this whole thing out.

He could have gotten hurt, frustrated, angry, and upset, and let his revenge be a dish best served cold.

He could have waited to take Timothy's and Aiden's lives at their apex.

Something awfully bad would have had to trigger that kind of vengefulness.

I entered Eve's tepee as the group was standing in a circle passing around some sage and smudging themselves. Sheridan waved me over and I stood between him and Drew. CC, Lilah, Ross, Josie, and Eve completed the circle. The group had a peaceful, easy feeling among themselves.

As people passed the smoking sage and gently waved it about their bodies, I felt the closeness of the group. I can't speak for the others, but my soul lifted a little.

Soon we were all seated on a Navajo rug and after a moment of silence Eve said, "I wanted us all to be together. You're my family. My family of choice." She slowly looked everyone in the eye. "We've lost members of our family and I know we're all grieving. I want us to have time to mourn together and honor those we loved and still love."

Countenances shifted. Sadness filled the room. Eve gave it a moment, but before it could settle in she said, "There'll be a time for words to be spoken and memories shared, but this is not that time. I know if Aiden and Timothy were here, they'd want us to get good and fucked up and celebrate their lives. The times for mourning and loneliness will come. The time for celebrating the lives of those we love is here."

With that, she turned, touched the play button on her Panasonic boom box, and out blared the Rolling Stones' *It's Only Rock 'n' Roll.*

That was a mood changer. With sadness mixed with joy, everyone sang along, stood up, hugged, and talked.

We splintered into smaller groups. I went over to Lilah, CC, and Drew. First things first.

"Hey, how's everyone doing?" I said in my customary way.

Drew shrugged. "It's a mixed bag. We're all depressed but Timothy would want us partying and rockin'. Aiden would have liked a wake."

"So it's a little of both," CC said. "We're also all worn out and ready to crash."

"How about you?" I asked Lilah.

"I'm still rockin' but ready to get rolling off to bed as well."

"I hear you," CC said.

"I have a question for you all. Think back six months or so ago. Can you think of anything happening with the band that might have caused bad blood?"

"You onto something?" Drew asked me.

"Perhaps. I have a person of interest but I need a motive. Anyone got one?"

"Six months ago, that was March or April. We were on the East Coast. Nothing stands out. We had the usual squabbles but off the top of my head I can't think of anything. But give me some time."

"Will do. I'm going to ask others and see what people remember. When you say usual squabbles, can you give me an idea of what those were about? In marriages they say people have at least one perpetual issue they're always arguing about. Got any perpetuals?"

"You might have noticed," CC said, "Drew is always early and considers everyone else late. He and I are always squabbling about that. And, just so you know, it bugs the rest of the band."

"Guilty as charged. But with an explanation. I don't consider other people late if they're on time. I consider them late if they're late. But, truthfully, as soon as they're five minutes late I get crabby."

"Get crabby?" CC said.

"See? It's perpetual. Anymore examples?"

"Some of us are tidier than others and that gets annoying," Drew said, glaring at CC.

I hadn't meant to open up a can of worms, but he was my client and it was good to see him in action. We'd have a lot to talk about when we got to actually talking.

"Aren't you always arguing over the music?" Lilah asked.

"That's a given," Drew said. "Timothy always wanted total control, and at any given time one or more of us had our own ideas about how things should go."

"Didn't some of you fight with him over which songs would be included on the albums?" CC asked, knowing the answer. "As I recall, none of you ever got credit on any of the songs."

"Yeah, that's a sore point."

"What's a sore point?" asked Josie, joining our group.

"Timothy wouldn't let us play any of our songs or credit us on any of the albums."

"Don't get me started. He was a total control freak. We all shouted at him and tried to get him to let us each have at least one song on an album or writing credits that we were due, but he was adamant."

"Once," said Drew, "I told him we should write a song like Loggins and Messina did with 'Watching the River Run.' Loggins would write one line and Messina the next. It seemed to work out well for them. That was one of their hits."

"I didn't know that," said Lilah. "That's cool."

"It is," replied Drew. "But Timothy didn't care. It was his way or the highway. We had big fights about it."

"Didn't he threaten to leave the band?" said CC.

"Only every other day," Josie said, having lost any noticeable degree of sadness.

"Whenever we pushed back, he'd threaten to leave," Drew said, now getting into some of his frustration. He knew we knew he was irreplaceable and we weren't. He'd pull those power plays all the time."

"Ouch," I said. "I hate it when that happens. I've had parents threaten to leave their children when the kids got angry at them. I've had people in relationships threaten to leave whenever the other person got upset. It can shut down the other person, but those threats leave them resentful and simmering."

Josie nodded. "Don't I know it."

"Can I ask you something?" I said to Josie. "Can you think back to six months ago when you were on the East Coast tour? Did anything unusual happen?"

"You mean aside from the frat guys that streaked the stage?"

"A bit dated, but well within fraternity partying boundaries," I said.

"That must have been fun," Lilah said.

"Maybe to the audience. For us it was distracting and Timothy stormed off the stage. We had to convince him to come back and finish the show."

"I forgot about that," said CC. "I remember you were all upset at him for making such a big deal of it. You told me you all had road fatigue."

"Yeah, we did, but he was being an artiste," Drew said. "With a capital asshole."

"Anything else stand out?"

"We did have that gorging dinner at Ross's parents' house on Long Island. I don't think any of us needed to eat for another week."

"Yeah, his parents are dyed-in-the-wool hippies in a million-dollar beach house full of books and art. It was a trip. They started feeding us at lunch and didn't stop till after midnight. It was a memorable day."

"Sounds great. Anything else?"

"That's it for me," Josie said.

"I'm tapped out myself. But if something comes to mind, I'll let you know."

"Thanks. It's helpful for me to get a sense of the band and your life together. I've got another question. Where are Michael and Carol? How come they're not here?"

"They're not into the kumbaya stuff," Josie said matter-of-factly.

"Oh. Anything else?"

"You say anything else a lot?" said Josie.

"Occupational hazard. I'm sorry. I'm just curious by nature."

"And annoying," Drew said. "But helpful."

"There you have it," I said.

No one seemed to want to add anything else about Michael and Carol, so I said, "One more question. It's about Johnny Romano. Anything I ought to know about him?"

"Johnny's connected," CC said. "Did you know that?"

"I'd heard that, and from meeting him it might be true."

"You met him?" Drew said. "How come?"

"Sheridan said it might be helpful. And it was. Just curious if there's anything else I need to know."

"Connected says what you need to know," Drew said. "He's the only person Timothy didn't control. He does what he wants when he wants."

I was tired and ready to call it a night but wanted to walk Lilah back to her sleeping quarters, and see if I could sleep there as well. One could hope. To be truthful, even though there was lust in my heart, I was grimy and sweaty from the day and being tied up in the truck, albeit an air-conditioned one. While I knew my lust would overcome my desire for cleanliness, I preferred the idea of our love-making, should it occur, to take place when there was more than a tent flap and ten feet between us and her neighbors.

That said, I wouldn't have minded making out for a bit and

letting nature take its course. That's the thing about nature. Like it nor not, it's going to take its course.

When the gathering broke up, CC came over to me and said, "I know it's Saturday night and you want to see if you can get lucky with Lilah. And, frankly, you've got a good chance. But I want you to go talk with Drew. I can tell he's distressed. Lilah and I will head off to our tent and I'll make sure to put in a good word about you."

"That's very kind of you. I'm mostly happy to go talk with Drew. As for the good word, feel free to put in more than one."

Drew and I headed back to the bus.

"How you doing? You seemed quite upset in there talking about Timothy."

"I'm a roller coaster. One minute missing him and remembering how wonderful he was and the next hating the fucker."

"Death can trigger the emotional range. Mad, sad, glad, and scared. They all come into play."

"Well, I haven't gotten to the glad yet, but I've spent time with sad and scared. I guess it's time for the mad."

"Feel free to let it loose."

"I don't think I've got much more. He was just so controlling about the music. I told you before, we all tried to credit for our contributions and some our songs on the albums, but he was having none of it. I get it on one level. He really is, was, in a different league. He was the show. But he told us if we wanted the recognition we could leave the band." He let out a big sigh. "It was just so unnecessary."

"Yeah. I hear that. It's hard when someone dies. You can remember all the drama and see how little it meant."

"No, you're wrong. It meant a lot. To me. To Josie, Michael, and Aiden. We're not just assembly-line workers. We're creative people who want to be able to express ourselves. He blackmailed us into staying. It really was imprisoning."

"Yeah. It sounds like a dictatorship."

"One you want to overthrow but know you can't."

"I'm sorry to hear all this. I knew you were unhappy with aspects of being in the band but I didn't know it was this pervasive."

"I didn't harp on about it because there was nothing I could do. But I have to tell you, as scared as I am about the future, I feel a certain freedom. It's like we all got a get-out-of-jail-free card."

"Glad you feel that way."

"Yeah. But I feel shitty talking this way about him. Is guilt one of those feelings too?"

"Guilt manages to find its way into most things. If you want to, you can usually find something to feel guilty about."

"I'm sorry, Timothy, for calling you such an asshole, but you know it's true."

We stood outside the band's bus for a moment. Given what he'd said, maybe he'd killed Timothy. But, if he had, why kill Aiden too? Aiden seemed to have been an adjunct. I hadn't heard anyone speak that badly about him, except Johnny. There'd been squabbles and arguments, but the vehemence that had been evident toward Timothy seemed absent. While I could see motives for killing Timothy, I hadn't come close to finding one for Aiden.

"I have a left-field question. When you're on tour, or even at home, what do you like to read?"

"You mean like magazines, books?"

"Yeah, like that."

"I don't know. I'm not a big reader. The last book I read was *Fools Die* by Mario Puzo."

"Ever read any Hunter Thompson?"

"Oh sure. We passed around *Fear and Loathing in Las Vegas* a couple of years ago. That was fun."

So much for that lead. Of course, knowing they'd all read one of his books didn't tell me who'd read the campaign-trail one.

"You ever read his book about the presidential campaign?"

"No. Was it any good?"

"I actually think it was his best work. Any idea who started you all reading the Las Vegas book?"

"What's all the interest in Hunter Thompson? You starting a book club?"

"That's a good idea. I don't know if there's a Hunter Thompson one but it wouldn't be boring. No, I'm just curious—maybe there's a connection."

"I can't remember who had it first. I know Josie passed it along to me and I gave it to Aiden."

"That's okay. Maybe Josie knows."

"Could be. She has an excellent memory."

It was late. I was tired. Various groups of people were still up and hanging out. Some had brought their instruments and I could hear snippets of various songs people seemed to remember the chorus to and not much else.

By the time I crawled into my sleeping bag someone nearby was attempting "While my Guitar Gently Weeps." I was hoping for While my Guitar Gently Sleeps.

I pulled out Timothy's journal and opened it up. The first entry was dated January 1, 1978. I couldn't be sure but it read like he'd been under the influence. The writing was sloppy, sentences ran on and on, and he seemed concerned about the shallowness of his life. I skipped to other entries; things didn't improve. While there might have been some profound insights into the human condition, there was a lot of attention given to the amount of sex and drugs he'd taken and the subsequent consequences. Not that I didn't have some prurient interest, but the answers I sought weren't there. The journal had little of the magic of his songs.

CHAPTER 29

"Oye Como Va"

Santana

Sunday, September 5, 1982

I WOKE UP surprisingly refreshed and eager for the final day of the festival to begin. I was hoping to solve the mystery before the day was out, but first I needed to attend to morning matters, get over to the food pavilion and gather some clues.

Ross was sitting alone, working on some waffles. I got my own, along with some scrambled eggs and coffee, and joined him.

"How are you this morning?" I asked.

"I'm fine. I don't have much time to talk."

"I've noticed you're a busy guy. What's on the list for today?"

"You name it. In some ways it's a relief to be here this weekend. I know when I get back to the office I'm going to have calls from every venue about canceling the tour. It's gonna be a shit storm."

"I bet. Do the remaining members want to continue the tour?"

"One minute yes, the next no. I don't blame them, but this is a business and this is the time to capitalize on it. Next year, no one is gonna care. But right now, people being the fucks they are, they will turn out to see the car wreck."

"I suppose so. I know Timothy was the heart and soul of the band, although from what I hear maybe to fans only. I gather the other members would have liked more credit and a say in things."

"We all want more of a say, but that ain't how it works. The way I see it, the songs are written. The fans know them and will want to see how the rest of the gang carries on."

"I'm not sure I'd want to go see them without Timothy and Aiden, but you're right—there will be those that do. It's sort of a way for everyone to share in the loss and to close one chapter and open another."

"That's it. Will you talk with the band? You can do this bullshit better than I can."

"I'll take that as a compliment. Yeah, I do think it's a good idea for them to carry on. Play Magoo's hits, slip in one each of theirs, and maybe get some guest artists to help out in the bigger venues. Yeah, I can see it happening."

"You sure you're not a promoter?"

"Well, I do want to promote one thing and maybe you can help me with it."

"Let's hear it."

"Who killed these guys and why? The way I see it, someone had it in for them. But what I can't figure out is, why Aiden? Evidently Timothy wasn't all heart and soul offstage, but Aiden didn't seem to ruffle anyone's feathers more than usual. Although I did hear he was an asshole."

"Aiden was an ass-kisser. You ever want to kill one of them? Don't answer. I know. But would someone really kill him for that? Perhaps. If someone wanted to kill Timothy that badly they might throw in Aiden. He stabbed a few people in the back by squealing to Timothy."

"Wait, you sort of said yes and no all at once. Most people don't like ass-kissers, although we all do it. It's just that some are more obvious about it. But, like you say, ass-kissing isn't usually punishable by death. But stabbing someone in the back—you did say stabbing, didn't you? That could be a different story."

"Doc, don't tell me I have to watch myself with you. It sounds like you're actually listening to me. I'm not used to that. People tell me what to do all day long. Now, I'm not really a friend of Bill Graham's, but we've done business together and he's often screamed, 'What about me?' I can relate. I'm used to talking, having people interrupt and tell me what they want. All day long."

"I'm happy to listen to you. I actually like listening closely to what people say. You're right—most people don't really listen. If they do, they're hearing what they want or don't want, and just the headlines. They don't want to hear the rest of the story."

"You don't have to tell me. I know all about it."

"So who did it? I'm listening."

"Truthfully, it could have been any number of people and it could have been bad dope. Sheridan's a straight shooter so if it was his dope it was good. Bill brought the babe in who sells the stuff, so she's solid. Unless they got the dope someplace else, it wasn't that."

"Not that you can trust everything you hear, but I've spoken to Sheridan and Elsa, the babe drug dealer, and as far as I can tell they didn't sell them any bad junk. Maybe some ludes and acid."

"I thought Aiden was off the acid. Oh, well. So then you got Josie, Michael, and your boy Drew. They've all had their moments with Timothy. I don't know of any recent hassles that would have pushed things over the line."

"Anything happen on the East Coast tour that could have pissed someone off?"

"There was some whining about eating too much at my parents' house, but that ain't news. I've been whining about it for years."

"I heard about that. It sounded like, aside from the belt-loosening, everyone had a good time. That was a nice thing for you to do."

"My parents get a kick out of it, and since I rarely see them it's the right thing to do."

"So, aside from that, everything was copacetic?"

"You ever been on tour? There's always something to be pissed off about. The band is just starting to get big enough to tour in greater style, but even then you're in each other's hair too much. Timothy liked to practice all the time. Everyone felt he was unrealistic in his demands but, hey, it's show business."

"Anyone outside of the band I should know about?"

"Well, you know Sheridan and Eve. I suppose they could have had reasons. I like Sheridan and don't want to think ill of him, but he has a vague, distorted past I've never been able to figure out. He knows people everywhere and has had more day jobs than I've had hand jobs."

"Okay, he's a man of mystery who has unknown ties."

"Yeah, and, you know, he'd be a lot richer if he didn't use so much of his product."

"I can see that. Sort of like the person who works at a clothing store spending all their money on clothes."

"Right. Or the person who works at a record store."

"And Eve?"

"You fuck her yet? Just kidding. But she has the hots for everyone she can't get. She's not a bad-looking woman, a bit clingy and too New Agey for me, but she's got a good heart."

"A good heart and therefore..."

"And therefore it can be broken. Hell hath no fury like a woman scorned."

"Was she scorned?"

"Depends what that means. She was never really involved with either Timothy or Aiden, or even Sheridan. Although they usually end up together, but its more by default. She's like the woman you see right before the bar closes. Do you want to go home alone or do you want to go with her? A lot of guys make that late-night call, especially when they're driving their train high on cocaine."

"Speaking of which, even though we're having breakfast, I'm

excited to be having another one with the Grateful Dead. That ought to be a good way to kick off the last day."

"Yeah, I'm sure there'll be a lot of day tripping today."

"I have one tangential question for you. You ever read Hunter Thompson?"

"Sure. Hasn't everyone?"

"He does appeal to a certain demographic. So, what have you read?"

"I read the Las Vegas one, *The Great Shark Hunt...*" Then he added, "And, of course, all his dispatches in *Rolling Stone*."

"Yeah. He's prolific. Hard to grasp how someone who imbibes so much can write so productively and so well."

"Hello. Take a look around you. He's got some competition here this weekend. They're called musicians."

"Yeah, I'm sure. Anything else I ought to know?"

"Just that I got to go. I enjoyed this and if I wasn't up to my ass in things to do I'd stay and chat." He picked up his tray and was about to head out. "And make sure you talk to the band about carrying on."

CHAPTER 30

"Touch and Go"

The Cars

I'D SPENT MUCH of my time bouncing from one person to another, picking up bits and pieces of seemingly non-related information. Now I needed to put together those disparate pieces so I could explain who, what, when, and why. At least, I knew where.

Everyone seemed to have a why. While one person's motive might be more or less viable than another's, I'd no way of determining whose won out.

I've seen *Assume* written on more than one blackboard as *Ass U Me*: to assume is to make an ass of you and me. It's a handy way of reminding yourself not to make too many assumptions. But I'd made one—Timothy's killer was also Aiden's killer. I could be wrong. If I was, the police could figure it out. I can't do everything. I'd go with the odds, despite the writing on the board.

If they had been killed, how? I had no idea about the specifics, but that didn't stop me from considering the ibogaine theory. I figured anyone so motivated could figure out how to get someone to ingest the paralyzing agent and what to put in a needle with heroin to deliver a last ride. Getting the ibogaine or another paralyzing agent would have been difficult, but Johnny had scored some. But who had he given it to and what was he doing about that no? He'd said he had some things he had to do. What were they?

Ross had read Hunter Thompson in *Rolling Stone*. That got me thinking he might be the one, but then it occurred to me that *Rolling Stone* would be routinely shared on the bus so anyone could have read about ibogaine. Or any other knock-out drug.

A recording of George Harrison's "Here Comes the Sun" started playing over the sound system. Likely a cue that the Dead were about to play. I overheard someone say the show was so early the Dead had just decided to stay up all night. I didn't have the drugs or the youth to do that.

The program said *Breakfast with the Grateful Dead*. Having already eaten mine, I was happy just to listen. I noticed a lot of people were toking and tripping. I guess that constitutes breakfast with the Dead. While I could see the joy on their faces as they danced and swayed to the music, it was a little too early for me to alter my reality. I was having a good enough time listening and watching. Plus, I was working. I'm no saint when it comes to my work ethic, but I don't always do my best work when I've imbibed. Of course, that's not what I think in those moments.

I listened as the Dead sang:

> *Driving that train, high on cocaine,*
>
> *Casey Jones, you better watch your speed.*
>
> *Trouble ahead, trouble behind,*
>
> *And you know that notion just crossed my mind.*

Sometimes you hear, see, smell, taste, or touch something and it creates a spark. Listening to the lyrics, it crossed my mind there was trouble behind and there could very well be trouble ahead.

I saw Lilah, and my worries about what I'd gotten myself into were displaced by thoughts of what I might be getting myself into.

"Hey," she said. "Everything all right? You seem a little off-kilter."

"You've got good perception. I was tripping out on some trouble I might have gotten myself into, though that suddenly feels far away."

"That's good and not so good to hear. I hope you didn't get yourself into too much trouble. Hopefully just a little."

"We both know a little trouble can be a good thing. But my new duties may have brought with them some additional proclivity for distress. Or I could just be overreacting after listening to the Dead repeat *Trouble ahead, trouble behind* for the last umpteen minutes."

"Yeah, the Dead can do that to you. They put the jam in jamming."

"That's cute. You just think of that?"

"I did. Of course, every time I have an original thought I find out someone else had it before me."

"I've had that same experience. It's both humbling and affirming."

"I guess the fact that others have had the same idea makes for a more universal theme. Yet it still rains a little on your parade when you find out your original thought wasn't all you'd stacked it up to be."

"That's like when you first meet someone. You think they're all that, but that's before you get to really know them. As you get to know more, all that can become not all that."

She gave me a quizzical look. "Are you telling me something I ought to listen to?"

"I'm not sure why I said that as I'm hoping the opposite is true."

She smiled but I could tell there'd been some damage. She seemed a little warier, which made me warier. Had I said something she should be listening to or something I ought to be listening to?

I sure hoped Lilah wouldn't disappoint. She hadn't done anything to dissuade me and yet those words had come out of my mouth. Everyone was becoming a suspect.

I needed to get back on track.

"Who was it that said there's nothing new in the world?"

"It was 'Nothing new under the sun' from Ecclesiastes."

She definitely knew things I didn't. While it can be intimidating to be with someone smarter than you it wasn't an entirely new experience for me. Wariness aside, I was becoming more and more attracted to her.

I watched her swaying to the music, looking peaceful and beautiful. She was a smooth cruiser for sure. When she glanced at me, I felt connected to her, like I knew her. It was exciting, comforting, and disconcerting all at once. She was smart, had a sense of humor, and was very easy on the eyes. I didn't want to suspect her.

I too was swaying away when Lilah and I got a tap on the shoulder. It was Drew and he was pointing at someone. It didn't take long to work out who. When you're six foot eleven you stand out. Bill Walton was dancing along to the Dead in his tie-dye shirt with a peace symbol. Drew knew I was a UCLA grad and basketball fan.

"Cool," I said.

"Just another Dead head," said Lilah.

"Indeed."

"If you get a chance," Drew said, "you ought to touch base with Carol."

"Who's Carol? I can't remember."

"Ross's wife."

"Oh, yeah. Not a very cheery soul. But kinda sexy too."

"Ross would agree with you. She's hot, but hard to take. She's a rescue project that went too far and now he feels stuck in it."

"And why do you want me to speak with her?"

"A couple of reasons. One, she's making his life miserable and it's already miserable enough."

"Okay, and I'm supposed to—"

"Well, you can't cheer her up so forget that. See if you can get her to keep her act together so Ross doesn't have to take care of her and can figure out our next step."

"And you want me to do that by talking with her?"

"Don't sell yourself short. But you're right—I don't really think you'll be able to make much difference. But just meet with her and get to know her because…"

"I'll bite. Because…"

"Because when I'm thinking about who could have killed Timothy and Aiden, she's always lurking on the edge of my most-likely list."

"Okay. You want to tell me why?"

"Talk with her. You'll find out."

"That's vague but I'm getting used to that. Is Ross also on your list? Do you think they did this together?"

"If they did, it would be the first thing they've done together aside from bicker."

"She sounds delightful. I'll see if I can find her."

"Thanks."

"You're the boss. I have to tell you, I'm hoping I can figure out whodunit by the time Fleetwood Mac plays 'Go Your Own Way' to close out the show tonight."

"Right on. Want to tell me anything?"

"It's too soon, but hopefully it'll all come together tonight."

I wanted what I'd said to be true. But it was more wish than reality. All I had was a lot of loose strands that might have nothing to do with Timothy and Aiden's deaths.

If you've ever been in therapy, you might have noticed something about the process. The vast majority of sessions run fifty minutes. After a few sessions, most clients adjust to the timing. Clients often wait till the last few minutes to get into the really important, emotional stuff. There are a few theories about why they wait. One is the anxiety of not addressing something builds up until they have to let off some steam. We all can relate to holding back until we just have to blurt something out. It's hard to keep a secret. It can weigh on you.

You might be wondering what this has to do with the festival. If the killer(s) had kept their cool so far, wouldn't they just clam up more? Heck, it was the end of the weekend; they only needed to hang on a little longer. Not that the police investigation wouldn't continue, but they'd be away from the scene of the crime and could either take off for parts unknown or head home, act innocent, and cover their tracks.

All good reasons to keep a low profile, which is why I was hopeful and not certain. But perhaps with some prompting and a little sleight of hand I might be able to tip the scales in therapy's favor.

CHAPTER 31

"Grey Matter"
Oingo Boingo

WITH REGRET, I said goodbye to Lilah and went in search of Carol. I still needed to find something to shed light on the situation so I could focus more on target. In the meantime I was letting the forces of nature move me where they would. While there's nothing wrong with that, at some point I'd need to get in the driver's seat. First, though, I had to find the car.

What was I missing? I've learned as a therapist when a client gets stuck you can either just ride it out or you can get back to basics. I was already mostly riding the wave so I decided to go back to basics.

Motive, means, and opportunity—they're the keys to whodunit. Everyone had some degree of motive. Everyone's boiling point is different. Something that wouldn't be motive enough for me could drive someone else over the speed limit. I could search for motives and still not know I'd found the right one.

It dawned on me I hadn't really investigated opportunity. I couldn't clearly remember the sequence of events but, as best as I could recall, everyone I'd met had been in close proximity to Timothy until the last half hour of his life when he'd asked to be alone. Everyone had left. But if he had been murdered, somebody had come back.

The band members had left the trailer and gone to the tour bus and hung out until Timothy would join them. Where had Lilah, CC, Eve, Sheridan, Carol and Ross gone? Had someone slipped back in the trailer for a few minutes? I could at least eliminate those with a solid alibi. Of course, Carol might say she was with Ross when Timothy died. And Ross might say he was with Carol, which could be true—they could have been killing Timothy together.

Given Aiden's death in the middle of the night, everyone would have had opportunity and whatever motive they'd had for killing Timothy could spill over to Aiden. There could be other reasons why Aiden was killed that weren't connected to Timothy, but I was even more in the dark about those.

If the killer had rendered Timothy and Aiden quickly immobile or unconscious, they'd have needed something to help them. If they used a gun, there might have been some resistance and there would be signs of a struggle, but everything had been in order in the trailer when I snuck in. I'd seen movies in which the bad guy put a chloroformed cloth over someone's face and they slipped into dreamland. But that left a smell. Ibogaine didn't.

I was going all in on it being ibogaine. Why not? It was the '80s. It was a drug. These were rock and rollers.

CHAPTER 32

"Don't Stand So Close to Me"
The Police

I WASN'T OVERLY eager to speak with Carol. I was basically procrastinating as I slowly made my way toward where I hoped she'd be spending her morning.

She was in the food pavilion with Michael.

She ate with the kind of interest my students show when I veer off into talking about my dissertation. She slowly gathered up some cereal from a bowl and lifted the spoon to her mouth, moving in slow motion.

I usually bring a cheery countenance to my greetings but it's often best to match another's mood. I toned it down a few notches, said "Hi," and sat.

Michael nodded. Carol didn't bother. I'd have to carry the ball.

"I haven't seen either of you in a while and wanted to catch up," I said. When that elicited no response, I forged on. "How's the book coming along?"

"Book?"

"You know. Hunter Thompson."

"Oh, yeah. My head isn't really into it. I like it, but..." He shrugged.

"I get it."

I was guessing they both were loaded.

I've never really understood why those who are depressed opt for downers while those who tend to be speedy go for uppers. People seem to double down on their mood rather than using a drug to balance things out.

Michael and Carol were operating in first gear. I wasn't sure how that would affect my ability to learn anything from them, but I figured they weren't going anywhere fast.

"I have a question for you," I said. "From what I gather, it was a regular thing for the band to leave Timothy alone for about a half an hour before each show. Was it also a regular thing for one of you to get him, or did you rotate, or did he come when he was ready?"

"Everything was when he was ready," said Carol without lifting her head.

"That so?"

"Yeah," said Michael. "He always joined us when he was ready. He'd say, 'Play time,' and we'd go."

"So how come you didn't wait for him to show up?"

"He never kept us waiting that long. We agreed someone should go knock on his door. Aiden volunteered, ass-kisser that he was."

"Why didn't you volunteer?" I said to Michael.

"Because he's the most talented person in the group and Timothy resented him the most," Carol said.

"Really? I didn't know that."

"Well, while that might be true," Michael acknowledged, "nobody really wanted to disturb him. Finally Aiden got up and went."

"Wouldn't Aiden have wanted to do that?"

"Not if Timothy would be mad at him," Carol said.

"I get that. If it were me, and I was concerned he'd get mad, I'd take my time, hoping he'd come out of the trailer."

"Yeah, he wasn't in a hurry. But it's not that far away."

"So he ambles over there and knocks on the door. When there's no answer he goes in and finds Timothy slumped over. Something like that?"

"Yeah, I guess."

"Was it just you, Josie, Aiden, and Drew on the bus? No lovers, spouses, friends?"

"Just the band. That was our ritual."

"So where were you, Carol? Were you with Ross, Sheridan or Eve?"

"Used to be we'd all hang out together during that time, but things ain't what they used to be."

"How's that?"

"Drew got into it with Carol a while back.," Michael said. "Since then, the group's been cold to her."

"I'm sorry to hear that. Must be rough to feel excluded."

"Fuck 'em. This whole band thing is bullshit." As her voice rose, I saw how easily her motor got running even in low gear.

"What do you mean?"

"Timothy fucked them all over."

Michael stared at her as if to say, *That's enough*, but she seemed intent.

"He was an ungrateful control freak and everyone let him get away with his bullshit. Michael has more talent than Timothy could ever have hoped to have. That's why Timothy kept them all in their places. He was afraid they'd leave him."

"What? You think Timothy was so controlling because he was afraid of the talent they all had, especially Michael?"

"Obviously. Josie and Drew too. All the time I told them to leave. But mostly I told Michael coz he's really the talented one. Like it or not, Michael's going to go out and prove who's the real star."

I couldn't tell where her artistic appreciation left off and her attraction to Michael started. There was something between them.

I didn't know if Ross knew, if it mattered to him, or whether he was for it, against it, or both.

Michael seemed a little embarrassed, ashamed, and proud all at once. At least that's how it seemed to me.

I left their merry confines. Drew had wanted me to help Carol keep her act together and check her out as a suspect. I hadn't achieved the former and knew little more in relation to the latter, other than she had no qualms about expressing herself.

I added talking to Drew about his blowout with Carol to my to-do list.

For some reason, I'd been reluctant to ask Carol about why she and Drew had gotten into it. Perhaps I'd picked up a No Trespassing sign coming from her, or maybe I was hesitant to go there. I didn't want to spark a flashpoint. I wasn't afraid of her getting angry but didn't want to estrange her. Of course, with people who like to argue, conflict can serve as a means of intimacy.

Carol hadn't said where she was during that half hour, but it seemed she hadn't been in the company of anyone else in the group. If that were the case, she didn't really have an alibi, which moved her up a step on the suspect list. I still needed to find out the others' whereabouts and work out whether anyone else had moved up or down the list.

The police could ask anyone questions and not worry about the consequences to their relationships. I, however, needed people to be cooperative with me and so far I'd elected not to confront anyone directly. There certainly could be more to learn from Carol, which might require my stepping things up.

CHAPTER 33

"Psycho Killer"
Talking Heads

Johnny Romano wasn't lounging outside his truck. Of course, the last time I hadn't see him, he'd seen me. I made sure to take a second look. Last time I'd climbed into the cab, but that hadn't worked out so well. I went to the back of the truck. *What the hell. Let's go in.*

Unfortunately, what I found wasn't what I'd come for. I wanted to think he was just taking a nap on the floor, but as I got closer I knew better. I sometimes drool in my sleep but I don't bleed.

I bent over him to make sure he was dead and wasn't pleased to have it confirmed. I knew not to touch anything. I needed to get out of there as fast as I could, but I was also curious to see if I could discover anything that would help me figure out what had happened.

Things were as I'd left them. An empty space with ropes, blankets, and not much else. If he had a space where he stashed stuff, I couldn't find it. I made sure to wipe off any fingerprints I might have left behind and made my exit. I hadn't seen anyone, but that didn't mean someone couldn't see me.

In for a penny, in for a pound. I opened up the passenger's door and hopped in. No gun. No notebook. No hidden stash. No sense staying.

My first impulse was to tell Sully. I knew that was the right thing to do. I didn't want someone else telling him they'd seen someone fitting my description going into the truck. I was wearing my Jackson Browne *Late for the Sky* T-shirt and I'd spotted only a few other people with the shirt. If someone remembered, there would be trouble ahead.

That said, I didn't really want to tell Sully, wait for the police, and spend a good portion of the day explaining myself. Johnny wasn't going anywhere; maybe I could wait a little while before I said anything. It wasn't the most civic-minded thing I've ever done and I don't think my parents would have been proud of me, but it did have an upside. I was still free to do what I wanted to do. I wasn't yet late for the sky.

I don't run into a lot of dead bodies. In fact, this was my first. I've seen movies and newscasts, but this was very different. I'd talked with Johnny. Heck, I'd been tied up by him. It wasn't like we'd been buddies, but I'd shared a memorable experience with him, and seeing him dead on the floor made me nauseous, frightened, and mad.

While I'd liked Timothy's music and sung along to it, I was mostly sad he wasn't going to make any more. I hadn't even paid Aiden's death much attention. I ought to have felt bad about that but, truthfully, I didn't.

I felt shallow and disconnected from my feelings on the one hand but physically upset and angry on the other. I was mad at the person who'd killed Johnny. Being mad wouldn't help me, but it did kick my motivation up a notch.

I'd assumed all the people close to Magoo had known Johnny could score whatever they wanted. But it was Sheridan who'd sent me his way. If Sheridan had known Johnny, Eve likely did as well. As the manager, Ross would have known him best, and Carol, the not-so-loving wife, could have had her own relationship with him.

I quickly made another assumption—not necessarily a good

thing, but it's what I do. Johnny's killer was also Aiden and Timothy's. That thinking suited me as it would be easier to find one or two people than three—I was motivated, but not that motivated.

If the same person was responsible, their reasons were probably different for each murder. Even if the person who'd killed Timothy and Aiden had done so for basically the same reason, it was hard to see how that would fit with Johnny. No, there needed to be different reasons. The most obvious was the person who'd bought the ibogaine had killed Johnny so he wouldn't tell me or anyone else.

But if you were going to buy an obscure drug from someone and then use it to kill others, wouldn't you know from the start the person might out you? In that case, wouldn't you kill them when they gave you the drug? There'd have to have been some assurances given, something good enough at one point if not another. Eve said her word to her drug dealer would be her bond, but Sheridan wasn't so sure.

After you'd killed someone using the drug you might start to worry about the dealer outing you. You'd be a bit jumpy, paranoid, and invested in covering your ass. So I could see that being an impetus.

Maybe Johnny had confronted the person or I'd said something about Johnny, and when someone heard me talking, their blood pressure jumped the fence and they went and took care of things before it was too late. If they were willing to kill Johnny, they might also be willing to kill me. Fear bolted through me like lightning.

My nausea and anger quickly morphed into paranoia. While I was seeking out the killer, the killer could be seeking me.

I felt a sudden urge to be with people. It wasn't a good time to be alone.

My mind has a mind of its own. I remember this but forget that. I've purposefully told myself to remember something and then forgotten it. I've not done something for years and it pops into my head. All of which is to say the only people I remembered talking to about Johnny were Sheridan, Drew, and CC.

Sheridan had told me to talk to Johnny. Since Sheridan had sent me, I suspected him the least. But maybe he had wanted me to think that?

I'd seen Drew and CC right after I was untied and had asked them what they knew about Johnny. CC had said he was connected. Drew had said something, too, but I couldn't recall what.

CHAPTER 34

"Come On Now"

Ramones

"Hey, Dave."

I flinched.

"Sorry. I didn't mean to startle you," Drew said.

"You didn't really. I'm just a bit jumpy."

"Everything okay?" CC asked.

"I think so. I just got a little off track, but I'm glad to see you. I've got some more questions for you."

"Well, I hope we have answers. What have you got?"

"I've been thinking about the time between when you all left Timothy in the trailer and when Aiden found him. As far as I can tell, the band went to the bus and everyone else went somewhere. Want to help fill me in?"

"You're right; the band went to the bus. I'm not sure where you went, CC. Where did you go?"

"Let me think ... I went off with Lilah to the food pavilion to get something and we stayed there and chatted."

"Okay. How did you know to come back to the trailer?"

"Well, usually Timothy took about thirty minutes to himself. Then the band gathered for a bit before going on stage. So after about thirty minutes, Lilah and I came back to the trailer and that's when we saw the commotion."

"Yeah. That must have been off-putting. Knowing something was wrong but not sure what it was."

"I was relieved when I saw Drew."

"I'm sure. Drew, when you went back to the bus did you all stay in the common area for the whole time? Did anybody leave for a bit?"

"We mostly were just hanging out. I was noodling on my guitar. Aiden went out for his smoke; Timothy didn't like us smoking on the bus. That was it mostly."

"Did anyone leave to go to the bathroom or anything?"

"Like go over and kill Timothy while they peed? Maybe. How long does that take? Yes, we all took a pee break. Usually we just go in the bus, but when we don't have to, we prefer not to."

"So each of you was gone for a few minutes during that time?"

"I guess that makes all of us suspects."

"Well, you all had opportunity. It would take motive and means to really make you suspects."

"They've all got that," CC pointed out.

"We could all have gotten hold of some bad dope, but I don't think any of us could have made Timothy shoot up. And I'm not sure we all had motive."

"I've been thinking about motive," I said. "Everyone has motive. What I mean is, what would drive you to want to kill is different than what would drive me. We all have different boiling points and issues. It might be hard to detect whose simmering resentments drove them to act."

"I can see that," he replied. "But if someone was so mad they wanted to kill Timothy, we'd know. Sure, we've all griped about a lot of things but that's not breaking news."

"I heard there was some extra tension on the East Coast tour. That could have boiled over."

"Maybe. But it would have to be someone who simmers to themselves."

I was listening, but in my increased hyper-vigilant state, I noticed Ross out of the corner of my eye. He was fast-footing it behind the stage. I decided to follow him, talk with him, and see what more I could learn from him.

"I'm sorry to run out on you but I've got a mystery to solve. And while I'd like to chat, my boss put me on task and I need to get back to work."

They smiled at that. I wanted to ask Drew about his flare-up with Carol, but I needed to seize the moment. Plus, I rationalized, it might be advisable to ask when CC wasn't there.

I took off after Ross. He was fifty yards ahead of me and in a hurry—although he always seemed to be in a hurry so maybe this was his usual pace. All I knew was I had to double-time it to close the gap. Before long I knew where he was going and slowed down, but my heart rate picked up. He strode right up to Johnny's truck, peered in the cab and circled it.

I inhaled. Exhaled. Held my breath to settle myself.

Then he hustled away. I thankfully followed.

As Ross headed back, I hastily swung ahead of him so it would appear I was coming from another direction.

"Hey, Ross," I said when I got close enough.

He seemed startled. "Oh, it's you."

"Yeah, me. Can I accompany you and ask you some questions?"

"Seems like you already are."

I wasn't sure if that meant *Sure* or if he'd spotted me following him. Either way, I got in stride with him.

"I've been asking people about the half hour when everyone left Timothy alone, before Aiden found him. I gather the band was in the bus and some people were in the food pavilion. Do you remember where you were?"

"Sure. We were all in the trailer, and when it was time to leave, Carol and I went with Eve and Sheridan back to their tepee."

"You all went directly from the trailer to the tepee?"

"I went off to the men's room, if you can call a porta-potty that, and then joined them."

"And when did you come back to the trailer?"

"We passed a joint around. Then Eve needed to do some New Age chanting stuff to bless the band. You see how well that turned out. When we got to the trailer, everyone was outside and we knew right away something was wrong."

"Yeah. Such a tragedy. Do you know if Carol, Eve and Sheridan were together when you went to the men's room?"

"You'd have to ask them. Everyone goes to the bathroom before a show starts."

"Is that one of those superstitions things?"

"It's more a mom thing. Clean up before going out. Remember to go to the bathroom and brush your teeth kind of thing."

"I get that."

I'd expected him to go to the band's bus, but instead we ended up at Bill Graham's. He stopped and said, "Work to do," and went in.

Here was my opportunity to go in after him and tell Sully I'd just seen a dead body. Ross might be surprised I'd been with him and not said anything.

One thing I've learned about people charged with law enforcement is they tend to notice things that are out of the ordinary. While those things could be completely innocent, there's no upside in bringing extra attention to yourself unless you want it.

No, I rationalized; this wasn't a good time to tell Sully. Plus, my original rationalizations were still valid. Telling him would take up a lot of time and lead to possible unforeseen consequences. Of course, so could not telling him.

CHAPTER 35

"Message in a Bottle"
The Police

WITH NO PARTICULAR place to go I found myself at the food pavilion. I opted for a veggie burger, fries, and a Coke. Neither healthy nor totally unhealthy. I spotted Eve and Sheridan and sat down next to them. Sheridan had gone for the hamburger and a Corona. Eve had a salad and lemonade.

I skipped the foreplay and got on task.

"I've been asking people where they were and what they were doing in the half hour Timothy wanted to be alone before Aiden found him. Want to fill in the blanks?"

"Let's see," said Eve. "We were all at the trailer and then what? Hmm, what did we do? I guess we went back to our tent to freshen up before the show."

"Makes sense. Was there anyone with you?

"Ross and Carol were with us."

"Oh, were you all together the whole time?"

"Mostly, Dave," Sheridan said. "These days I don't slip into the bathroom with Eve as much as I used to."

"Yeah, now it's mostly for blow, not blow jobs," Eve said.

Sheridan gave me a *whatever* look and I said, "I get the distinction. One might take longer than the other."

"One hopes."

"And, of course, there's nothing that says you can't do both."

"Without question."

While informative I didn't know if it was an actual recounting of events. Slipping into the bathroom for a line could qualify as freshening up, but they didn't need to go to the porta-potty for that.

"So there may have been some minutes when you don't know what others were doing."

"Dave, you found us out. We have no witnesses to vouch for our whereabouts during that whole period."

"That's basically the same for everyone. You each had enough time to go over to the trailer, see Timothy, and do whatever it is that was done."

"Okay, so that about closes that end of the investigation," Sheridan said.

"Let me move on. I have a question for you, Eve. Want to tell me about your relationship with Hunter Thompson?"

"Here? In front of Sheridan? I don't think so."

"What? There's a story I don't know?"

"It's just a rumor. I never really slept with him."

"You slept with him?" Sheridan asked with surprise and maybe a degree of admiration.

"No, I never really slept with him, unless you call passing out together sleeping together. You know I know him."

"Yeah," Sheridan said. Then he turned to me. "Eve was working on the set of *Where the Buffalo Roam* and got quite chummy with the lot of them."

"Very nice. Did you happen to read *Fear and Loathing: On the Campaign Trail '72* while you worked on the movie?"

"No, I haven't read that one. Is it good?"

"It's the best thing he's written."

"Better than *Las Vegas*?" she asked.

"It's close. I like politics. Not that I don't like sex, drugs, and gambling. Part of the reason I like it more is I read it week by week in *Rolling Stone* as the campaign unfolded."

"That's the way Dickens did it," Sheridan said.

"It got me hooked. I had to wait for each installment to come out."

"Sort of like *Roots* and *Rich Man, Poor Man*," Eve said.

"You got it."

"What have you got?" CC wanted to know as she and Lilah sat down with us.

I wasn't happy about the interruption, but then again, I wasn't getting a trunk full of information and seeing Lilah did raise my spirits. Each time I saw her I noticed something else about her I liked. This time it was her poise. She seemed well contained and content within herself.

"We're talking about our favorite Hunter Thompson book. You have one?" Sheridan asked.

"I've only read the Vegas one," CC said. "And, truthfully, I don't think I finished it."

"I don't think anyone remembers how it ended," Sheridan said. "But we all remember how it started."

"We were somewhere around Barstow on the edge of the desert when the drugs began to take hold," we all said, almost in unison.

We shared that bonding moment with smiles, then Lilah said, "My mom got me a lifetime subscription to *Rolling Stone* for my eighteenth birthday so I've been reading his dispatches. Well, I did buy the Vegas book. I figured it was like the Beatles' *White Album*. Something you just needed to have."

Another reason to like her. I wondered what else was in her collection.

It also meant she might know about ibogaine. I didn't like that, but knew I needed to heed it.

"It seems everyone has similar literary interests. What else has the book club read? Anyone read *Great Shark Hunt* or *Fear and Loathing: On the Campaign Trail '72?*"

That got some shrugs but no takers. I'd exhausted that line of inquiry. There were other questions I could ask, but all I could come up with was, "Anyone know where I can find Josie?"

It was one of those things that comes out of your mouth and before you're through you know it was a mistake. I was trying avoid Lilah's stare, but could tell something in her countenance had shifted.

"She was back by the trailer the last time I saw her," said Eve.

"Thanks. I'm going to find out if she has the same literary tastes."

"You want to tell us why you're so interested in our having read Hunter?" CC asked. "Aside from just wanting us to discover our mutual interests?"

"Yeah," Sheridan said. "Aside from that bullshit."

"How about I talk with Josie and then I get back to you on that. You might find it very revealing."

I wasn't sure if I'd made a bigger mistake. I'd been trying to keep my suspicions about Hunter Thompson and ibogaine to myself until I had more information. No one would blurt out, "I read the political-campaign book and got the idea about killing Timothy with the drug Hunter said Muskie took." But I might have told the killer I was on to them, and if they were going to kill me they ought to do it soon.

I'm not the kind of person to deliberately put a target on my back and encourage a killer to take their best shot. I'd just got caught up in the action. It's sort of like when you gamble and lose money. The smart thing to do is to step away and suffer your losses. The riskier thing to do is to double down so maybe you can win back what you lost, even though it's more likely you'll suffer more. You play long shots when you're desperate.

I didn't think I was desperate but time was running out. My dissertation had been about the task expanding to fit the time available. If I had a week to solve the mystery it would take a week. If I had a few hours, well, I hoped that was all it would take.

CHAPTER 36

"So You Want to be a Rock 'n' Roll Star"
Tom Petty

I WAS ON my way to the trailer area with a kick-me sign on my back, except it said—kill me.

What's going on here, David? I asked myself.

Drew had paid me to protect him from any former paramours who might kick up a fuss but none of that had happened. Or at least nothing I knew about. Well, if Carol was a former dalliance maybe it had already happened.

Now that the tape had been removed, there seemed no reason not to go into the trailer. I went in. No one was there. Things seemed the same except I could hear a guitar strumming. I inched quietly over to the door that led to the room where Timothy had played his last song. Someone was singing but I couldn't quite decipher the words.

My mother raised me with a certain attention to etiquette and propriety. I was taught to knock before entering. Experience has taught me it's often more illuminating to enter before knocking.

Josie was sitting on a chair playing her guitar. I'd startled her.

"I'm sorry. I didn't mean to scare you. That was lovely. What were you playing?"

"It's okay. I'm not supposed to be here but I wanted to come in and play something for him."

"Oh. I'm sorry to interrupt that. Would you prefer I leave?"

"No, it's fine. I was just finishing up."

"Was that one of the band's songs? I didn't recognize it. Of course, I just heard a snippet. I don't think anyone would have guessed it on *Name That Tune*."

While I'd hoped my referencing the TV show might elicit a bit of a smile, her face held more of a grimace.

"No, that wasn't one of the band's songs."

"Well, the part I heard sounded lovely. I'm sure if Timothy were here, he'd be thankful you played it."

"I doubt that. He'd rather I'd have played one of his."

"Well, I liked it. If you want to continue I'd be happy to sit and listen."

"Thanks but no thanks. I'm done here."

"Can I ask you something?" I didn't wait for her response. "I've been talking with the other band members as well as Ross, Carol, Sheridan, and Eve about a few things, and wanted to hear what you have to say."

"Okay," she said, but got up and walked past me out of the room. I followed her outside.

"When Timothy had everybody leave, people went out for a smoke, used the bathroom, whatever. Were you with anyone the whole time in the bus?"

"I was in the bus with the guys. We were all nervous and excited so there was a lot more up, down, in and out than usual."

"Yeah, that's kind of what I'm getting. I'm sure you all were antsy."

"Very."

"I have an unrelated question about Hunter Thompson. Have you read any of his stuff?"

"We passed around *Fear and Loathing in Las Vegas* a couple of years ago. And, of course, we all read *Rolling Stone* so I've caught some of his stuff. I like him. He's a rebel."

"He is that. I have another question. How are you holding up? I know this has been a trying time for all of you."

"I'm good in a weird way. Losing them has freed me up. I'm missing them and the band, but I'm ready to head out on my own."

"Was that one of your songs?"

"Yeah. I'll play it for you sometime. You can let me know if you like it once you get to hear it all."

"I'd like that."

"Good. Now I have to go."

"Before you do, there's something else I want you to know. I was talking earlier with Sheridan, Eve, Drew, CC, and her friend Lilah. I'm not sure if you know her."

"I've seen her. I know who you're talking about."

"Anyway, I told them I'd learned something regarding Hunter Thompson that I'll share when everyone's together. It'll be very revealing."

She was half-listening, said okay, and left.

While it wasn't comforting, I did need to let everyone know I knew about the ibogaine. I stood there alone and considered what she'd said. She too had no alibi and could have read about ibogaine. Talking with her wasn't reducing my suspect list, but it did get me to thinking. Everyone had opportunity, motive, and access to the means, and so far that was a draw. But who'd profit from the deaths was an avenue I hadn't explored.

I wasn't sure if Josie would profit, but she hadn't seemed very broken up and had expressed her readiness to head out on her own. Her bandmates' deaths might help launch her solo career. Even if she went on a memorial tour with the band she'd get to showcase herself, which would give her a head start.

On my follow-the-money/who-profits list she was my first entry. I could add Drew and Michael but I'd need to explore more.

I couldn't see how Ross would profit from losing the band when it was on the possible verge of stepping it up a notch. Of course, they might have also been on the verge of stepping down a notch. It's not like rock bands have longevity. They're right up there with professional athletes and restaurant owners in terms of the percentage who stay in business long enough to successfully retire.

The only way I could see Carol benefiting was if Ross was at home more. I wasn't sure which side of the ledger to put that on.

I couldn't see Sheridan and Eve profiting directly. Though if killing someone would profit me, I wouldn't be overt about it.

One thing was for sure: I'd broken one of my own safety guidelines. Right after I'd told myself not to be alone with someone, I'd done just that. It wouldn't be wise to take that risk again.

CHAPTER 37

"Go Your Own Way"
Fleetwood Mac

IT WAS TIME to revisit Michael and Drew.

Of course, Drew wasn't where I'd left him. That's the thing about the world; it just doesn't stand still and wait for you. The only time it does is when you live alone and come home—the place is just like you left it.

I went back to the food pavilion. Michael was not far from where I'd seen him before, again with Carol next to him. Not sure what that meant, but it was a pattern of sorts.

"Okay if I join you?"

"It's a free country," said Michael. "Or at least it used to be."

"Thanks. I have something I want to ask you. I've been think-ing about the band and going forward with the tour. I know some people are all for it. Others less so. What are your thoughts?"

"I'll tell you what I think," Carol said, perking up. "They should give it up. It's time. The Beatles could have stayed together, sold out stadiums, and continued on their insipid ways. But once they separated they were free to explore new dimensions. Their fame oppressed them."

She seemed very adamant for someone who'd barely mustered

any energy before. Maybe she'd taken a hit on something. Or I'd hit a nerve. I wasn't sure I agreed with her assessment, but Michael seemed to.

"I'm ready. I know Ross thinks we ought to cash in and finish the tour. If we want to launch solo careers he's happy to help us out, but I'm over it."

"The disappointment of not being able to have your biggest show has to be wearing you all down. I'll tell you something I've learned as a therapist. A crisis is usually not the best time to be making major decisions. That said, that's when a lot of them are made. There's some big upheaval and you say, 'What the hell? I might as well just go for it.' A lot of people leave their jobs, partners, and homes all at the same time."

"What are you saying?"

"Just that when there's upheaval people often choose to make other changes. Nothing wrong with it, but statistically things turn out better if you wait a bit."

"You're saying he shouldn't head out on his own?" Carol asked a little too confrontationally.

"No, I'm not saying that. You should do whatever you think is best. I'm just saying you might want to sleep on things for a bit before you decide."

"That sounds very wimpy."

"Perhaps it is. People basically need to trust themselves and if it feels right, do it. For my peace of mind, I like something to feel right for a bit longer before I make significant shifts. But you need to do what's best for you. What works best for me may not work best for you."

Michael seemed to like that. Carol didn't seem to like anything I was saying. While her reaction wasn't a first for me, it did seem a little too much.

Of course, her too much and my too much might differ. If you're comfortable with something and I do it more or less than you, that's probably too much for you. Doesn't mean either of us is right. It just means we tend to accept our own behavior and measure others' accordingly.

I could sense why people might have issues with Carol. At the moment though, it didn't seem Michael was one of them. She was good-looking and sexy in a way, but like Drew said—she was hard to take. Michael, however, seemed to enjoy her pushing back at me.

I didn't feel any need to push back with her, but felt I could probe a little deeper with him.

"Have you considered putting together a band, making an album, touring, that kind of stuff?"

"Only since I was fourteen."

"So heading off on your own isn't an overnight whim."

"I've not really given it much energy recently. I know some guys I'd want to play with, but that's about it."

"I've thought about it," said Carol. "I've got it all figured out."

I glanced to see if Michael had rolled his eyes, but he seemed rather stoic. I wasn't sure if he was just tuning her out or surrendering. I decided to find out.

"Sounds like she has it all figured out," I said.

My saying "Sounds like she has it all figured out" gave Michael a chance to confirm or deny. Instead he said, "She always has it figured out for me. She just can't figure it out for her."

"Why don't you go fuck yourself!" was Carol's response.

There was a cold silence that didn't improve the scorching temperature. The more I talked with them, the more they fell into contention for the most-likely-to-be-at-fault prize. Even if they hadn't killed Timothy and Aiden, it sure looked like they were killing time together. Again, I wondered how Ross felt about that. Maybe relief.

I wondered whether the killings had been a group effort. Everyone had motive, means, and opportunity, and may have seen a way they could profit, or at least take a shot at it. I recalled an

Agatha Christie story in which everyone had been complicit. Still, I didn't think that was at play here, though I couldn't entirely rule it out. I needed to stick with the percentages; and if the long shot was the answer, well, I didn't want to think about that.

I needed something to sway the tide—something that would force the person to show their hand. Either that or I'd have to dig somewhere I'd yet to go. I'd already put the word out to Sheridan, Eve, Drew, CC, Lilah, and Josie about having a hunch. I might as well throw in Michael and Carol so everyone would have a clear shot at the target.

"I'm going to leave; but before I go, I wanted to let you know I have a good hunch about something to do with the deaths and Hunter Thompson."

"What?"

"Yeah. I'm close to figuring it all out, but I have to run now. See you later."

Of course, that was a lie. But they didn't need to know that.

Now the only person I hadn't told about having something of value to share was Ross. I needed to find him, watch my back, and see who came calling.

CHAPTER 38

"Coconut Telegraph"
Jimmy Buffett

ROSS WASN'T AT the food pavilion or the trailer or bus. I went to the side of the stage. Jerry Jeff Walker was playing but I didn't know any of his stuff so I was happy to head for the tech tent.

Sweet relief came over me as I entered the air-conditioned tent. I felt doubly good when I spotted Ross talking animatedly with the guy in the Grateful Dead T-shirt. He seemed highly aggravated. I figured I might as well stick my neck in. If Ross were going to kill me, he'd need to find a way to do it surrounded by people.

"Hey," I said, acting surprised to see him.

He wasn't happy to see me.

He managed a *Hey* of his own.

"I remember you," the guy told me.

"Good to see you again, Hale."

"Ross," he said. "This is the guy I was telling you about."

Ross glared intently. I nodded my head and tried to look innocent. "Some really interesting things in this tent. Not that I know what much of it is or how to use it."

"You will," said Hale while Ross glared.

"Maybe. I'm not so sure this technology stuff is going to take root. Sure, there'll always be a segment of society—scientists, artists, creative types, and explorers—who are into it, but I don't think it'll ever catch on mainstream."

"Plastics," said Ross. "You remember how in *The Graduate* he was told *plastic*? I'm telling you *tech*."

"Okay, if you say so."

"He does," said Hale with a little disgust. "There are kids in here playing games instead of being out there listening to music."

"Well, it's country music and there's AC in here."

"We'll see."

"Ross," I said, trying to restore some degree of ease between us, "I have a question for you, if I can interrupt for a minute."

"What?"

"Is it okay if I ask you in front of Hale?"

"I don't know. I'll tell you after you ask. Does it have something to do with what you were talking about before with Hale?"

"No, not that. That was just me snooping around. Let me ask you. Who do you think would most profit from Timothy and Aiden's deaths?"

"I don't see anyone profiting. It's a big loss for all of us."

"Their record sales went up this weekend," Hale said. "I called Discount Records and they were sold out."

"Yeah," said Ross." People love you more when you're dead. Heck, Elvis just had one of his best years. But the band's sales would have gone up anyway when the festival was over. Everyone goes home, visits their local record shop and buys the album."

"So no one really profits?"

"I didn't say that. Of course they all want to go off on solo careers and be the star, but it ain't gonna happen. They'll each get their fifteen minutes, but then it'll be back to waiting tables and selling cars."

"Who waited tables and sold cars?"

"Josie and Drew. Didn't he tell you about those days?"

"We haven't gotten there yet."

"I'll tell you who won't be selling cars and waiting tables," Hale said. "Michael is already getting into the tech stuff. He'll catch the wave. Just wait and see."

"How about you, Ross? You going to ride this wave?"

"I tell you, it's before the gold rush and a lot of people are going to make a lot of money. Take Woz—he was living at his parents' house a few years ago. You bet I'm on board."

"I'm feeling like I might actually have to listen to you. I'm still not sure though."

"If you want to be an ostrich, so be it."

"Thank you, Ross, for your heartfelt acceptance."

"My pleasure. Now, if you don't mind, we have work to do."

Since I didn't mind, and it wouldn't have mattered if I had, I left. I wondered what work they had to do.

CHAPTER 39

"Shakedown Street"

Grateful Dead

I DECIDED TO amble over to the trucks and see how Johnny Romano was doing. I wasn't expecting him to be doing differently, but wanted to see if others had discovered what I and the killer knew. It struck me I had a secret just like somebody else had a secret and now they knew I knew it.

If anyone else knew about Johnny's condition they weren't making a lot of noise about it. There was no police tape or lingering crowd. Noting the absence of those things, I absented myself. No sense being places where I'd prefer not to be found. Preferable to see if I could find Lilah, or at least someone who hadn't spent the weekend killing others.

I was cutting across behind the stage when Michael came up beside me.

"I have to talk to you," he said. "Follow me."

I did. He strode a couple of yards ahead of me as we made our way through some trailers to the wardrobe/laundry room. He climbed up the steps, opened the door, looked in, and motioned me to follow. Once I was inside he locked the door.

"Don't worry. No one's going to be doing laundry. We're all alone."

So much for my plan not to be alone with any of the suspects. I couldn't see the target on my back but I sensed it turning into a blinking red warning light.

He came right up to me, well within my personal space, and said, "All right, you fucker. This needs to stop now."

Whatever it was, I was happy to stop it now as it seemed to have gotten him quite upset.

"Whatever you want."

"Fuck you. Don't give me any therapist crap. If you don't stop now, well, let's not have it come to that."

"Okay, but can you tell me what you want me to stop?"

"The pressure on me to confess."

"You think I'm pressuring you to confess?" I asked, using my best reflection technique.

"I don't know how you found out, but you're making things very difficult for me."

Not knowing what I'd found out nor what the difficulty was made it hard to take pleasure in my efforts. But I know one thing from doing so much therapy. When clients are agitated it's a good time to delve in and see what emotional material comes to light.

"Things are difficult for you?"

"Fuck, yes. Carol is all spiked up and ready to conquer the world. My world."

Oh. Spiked up. She'd definitely been more animated in the food tent.

"That doesn't sound good."

"I can handle her. She wants to be my agent. I don't need to be dealing with that on top of the shit you're throwing into the fan."

"The shit I'm throwing into the fan?" If nothing else I've mastered my reflective skills.

"Yeah, you fucker. What's with this Hunter Thompson bullshit. Did the doc talk to you?"

"No. Not about you. What would he tell me?"

"Nothing is what he should tell you."

"All I know is he practices the healing arts in creative ways."

"Stay away from him, and stay away from Carol. And while you're at it, stay away from me."

And with that he opened the door and left.

Michael was upset because he'd thought the doc had told me about his drug use, and that was putting pressure on him to confess. That made little sense to me. Confess what? His drug use? Why would I care about that? Unless he was using a drug that could cause paralysis if taken in certain dosages.

Michael was also upset that Carol was spiked up and trying to conquer his world. I don't know about you, but other people's wives don't usually want to conquer my world. But maybe I lead a sheltered life. He'd said she wanted to be his agent, but she might want more than that.

He'd also mentioned Hunter Thompson. Had he been referring to the ibogaine? I didn't think the doc had supplied the ibogaine. Johnny had. And he'd died for it. Unless the doc had gotten it and he would die for it, in which case Johnny died for something else.

I decided to go check on the doc. I could make a pitch for him surrendering his client's identity and telling me about Michael and his drug use. Perhaps having his life being in danger would make him bend the rules of patient confidentiality.

CHAPTER 40

"Doctor My Eyes"
Jackson Browne

THINGS WERE BASICALLY as they'd been before at the good doctor's trailer. People sat on beanbags, the examining table, and the massage table. All of them were pretty stoned. I stood inside the door and waited. If someone was out to kill the doc they weren't in a hurry. Of course, the killer could be in the room and I wouldn't know it.

We've all spent time waiting to see a doctor. While I don't like the waiting, I do like the doctor spending whatever amount of time is necessary with you before sending you on your way. We therapists tend to work by the clock, and if things are no better when time is up, well, we'll see you next week.

The space was too small for there to be much privacy, but when the doc saw me, he stepped to the edge of the examining table and pulled a curtain closed. I couldn't see beyond the curtain but I could hear... although I seemed to be the only one capable of paying attention. The doc was telling the person to take deep breaths and hold them. There were some more directives, then he came out, got a bottle of something, and went back. A few minutes later the patient was tentatively leaving and the doc came over to me.

"I remember you. What can I do for you?"

"Like everyone else here I'm hoping you can help me. I need to have a confidential conversation with you. Would it be okay to step outside for a moment?"

He assessed the room and nodded, and soon we were standing in front.

"You might remember I'm a therapist working with Magoo," I said, embellishing things somewhat. "Michael is very upset and while I know his particulars are confidential, I'm hoping you can provide me a professional courtesy and let me know a bit about how you've helped him."

"You'd have to ask him."

"I knew you'd say that, which is why I asked for the professional courtesy. I can't get him to sign a release right now."

"Is he OD'ing?"

"No, no. Not that bad. Just extremely agitated."

"Tell him to come here and I'll give him something for that."

"Yeah, I know you can do that. I don't think he's inclined to come now, which is why I wanted the information."

"I'm sorry. I can't give that to you."

Who knew a quack doctor would have so much integrity. "Okay, I get that. Let me just ask you a hypothetical question. If I wanted you to prescribe or give me some exotic drugs, would you do that?"

"If they would help you, sure. But hypothetically speaking, I wouldn't tell anyone what I gave you."

"That's reassuring. So hypothetically, if I wanted a drug that was used by tribes in Africa is that the kind of thing you could get for me?"

The question had startled him. He took a moment to think before replying. "Hypothetically speaking, I don't think your friend would have asked me for anything like that."

Wow, the doc had come through for me. Hypothetically speaking, whatever Michael had gotten from him wasn't ibogaine. Why

Michael would be upset I knew what medications he was taking I didn't know and wasn't likely to find out from the doctor.

"Anything else you think I ought to know?" I asked.

"While it's a large world, it's also a very small one."

And with that piece of vacuous philosophy he went back into the trailer.

Had he been trying to tell me something I ought to heed or distributing a medical thought for the day that I'd ignore? He'd given me a real answer, or so I believed, to a hypothetical question. It crossed Michael off the list of people who might have obtained the ibogaine from someone other than Johnny. I'd never really bought into the doc being the source of the drug so it wasn't like I was ahead of where I'd been before our chat. But I wasn't behind either. Was I?

All I knew was, Michael was upset the doc had told me about his drug use, even if he hadn't. You wouldn't like it either if your doctor spilled the beans. It was understandable he'd be upset, but not that upset. Therapists tend to go with the idea if something emotionally sparks you, there's something there.

It was mid-afternoon. While I wasn't completely feeling a time crunch, without any solid leads and the end of the festival in sight I wanted something to thread those loose ends together.

CHAPTER 41

"Throw That Beat in the Garbage Can"
B-52's

It was time to take stock. While there was more for me to find out, maybe I already knew more than I realized. If I had some comfort food and space to think, I might find my way to a solution.

The food pavilion wasn't quite so busy. I found a table to myself and sat down with a Coke and French fries. I asked one of the servers for a piece of paper and a pencil, and soon I was ready for inspiration. It didn't come so I listed the suspects I knew.

Timothy—controlled band, asshole, resented, OD'd/killed?

Aiden—ass-kisser, not liked, died in drug dealer's tent. Why?

Josie—slept with Timothy, Aiden, and possibly Drew. Now with Michael, who is jealous. Wants to go out on her own.

Michael—lots of issues, most likely candidate—that's never whodunit in a mystery, just real life.

Drew—wanted me here but for what reason? No old flames flaming up, but had flare-up with Carol. Seems least likely, might make him most likely.

CC—why kill unless in cahoots with Drew? Or some unknown angle.

Lilah—please don't be the killer. Not a good reason to keep her off the list. But why keep her on?

Ross—definite possibility, wife a handful who wants to be Michael's "agent." Lots of fires in the pot.

Carol—not nice, definite handful, has her own plans. Could have left her chill pills at home. Did she get meds from doc?

Sheridan—drug dealer, cynic, no obvious motive, but could have supplied the bad drugs.

Eve —rejected by many, wounded one too many times?

Writing the list gave me an opportunity to review the cast of characters but it hadn't tipped the scales. It was a bunch of generalities that didn't uncover much. I needed to listen to the taped replays of my conversations, but my brain wasn't playing ball. Something needed to stick out, make its presence felt.

Carol sat down next to me. I can't say I was happy to see her. I'd yet to see her happy about anything.

"Hi," I said.

She didn't respond to my greeting. I'd not had time to hide my list and didn't know how much she'd seen, though it was enough for her to say, "What've you got there?"

"I was making some notes to try and figure out what happened to Timothy and Aiden."

"It's a list of names with comments."

"You're very observant."

"You got me on the list?"

"As a matter of fact, I do."

"Will you read me what you wrote?"

"No, I don't think so," I said turning them over.

"How come?"

"They're my private notes. I didn't write them with the intent of sharing them."

"I do a lot of things with no intention of sharing them and then share them. That doesn't seem like a good reason."

"Yeah, but it's my reason."

"For a shrink that's awfully pig-headed."

"I certainly respect your opinion. I'll tell you what—how about I share some of what I wrote about you?"

"Why not all?"

"You're supposed to accept the compromise."

"Where is that written? You wrote something about me. I want to know what it is."

"I understand, but people like to retain the option of keeping some of their ideas to themselves. So how about I share some of what I wrote and you say, 'Okay, thanks.'"

"You can forget that. But let's hear it," she said waving me on.

"I wrote a note to find out whether you'd seen the doc since you've been here."

"That's what you want to know? What's that about? I don't like the inference there."

"Which is why I might have wanted to keep it to myself. But, come on, I told you what I wrote. Why don't you tell me if you've seen the doc?"

"Fuck you. I don't need to tell you that."

"I didn't need to tell you what I wrote, but you wanted to know so I shared some. That door ought to swing both ways."

"That's what you think. I think you can go fuck yourself."

"Well, that's an opinion I've heard before, and if I could I'd give it a try."

"You'd be a lousy fuck. Don't even bother."

"Anything else you'd like to share?"

"Yeah. So what if I saw the doc? He's good people and does right by me."

"That's good to know. You want your doctor to do right by you."

"Don't try kissing my ass."

"Okay. I'll remember that. Anything else?"

"Yes, there's something else but I'm not sure I want to share it now."

"I know the feeling. Suit yourself. You've already shared plenty."

"Don't be such a pussy. I have something to tell you, you're going to want to know. I figured out you were asking about Hunter Thompson because of the drugs. At first, I thought you were just afraid to ask who had drugs and where you could get some. But when I went to see the doc—yes, I went to see him—I realized you thought drugs had something to do with Timothy and Aiden's death. Something more than just OD'ing."

"That could be."

"Shut up and listen. I was sitting on the examination table with the curtain closed when the doc left me to talk with someone else. I overheard him mention Hunter Thompson. I couldn't hear what they were saying or who he was talking with, but I heard Thompson's name. I came over here to tell you that."

"Thanks. That's actually very helpful."

"I know. That's why I told you, asshole."

And with that she got up and left. I wasn't sad to have her go as she was combative and not prone to social niceties, which I don't mind skipping myself. But I like to limit the number of people who call me asshole to my face.

I could see how living with her could strain someone's tolerances. Her combativeness seemed to invigorate her, as if she welcomed and perpetuated it.

CHAPTER 42

"Healer"

Santana

HAVE YOU EVER done something because you believed it was the right thing to do, even if it wasn't? I knew the doc wouldn't tell me anything confidential about a patient. But I needed to see if I could, ahem, manipulate him into divulging information he wasn't supposed to let slip. They say there are no unintentional coincidences in mysteries. His mentioning Hunter Thompson was a coincidence I needed to probe. Maybe we could have a hypothetical conversation about Thompson and drugs.

I was neither licensed to speak about prescribed drugs nor informed enough to have something worth sharing that wouldn't be contradicted later. But I knew ibogaine wasn't on top of many people's drug-of-choice list. The doc clearly approached the healing arts in a creative fashion so maybe ibogaine had found its way onto his list. Maybe in small doses it was calming, or standing still for a few days was the latest pathway to higher consciousness. I didn't even know if it was available via prescription. What I did know was that, hypothetically, he hadn't given any to Michael. That wouldn't preclude him from giving it to anyone else.

Since I didn't know what the doc knew, and since he had a

license that allowed him to prescribe me drugs, I could request he write me one for ibogaine. Or if I didn't need a prescription maybe he'd say, "No problem. I've got some right here." Either way, I was curious.

I got to thinking about how people react to requests. I wasn't sure how the doc would respond to mine. If your boss says to do something, usually you do it. Someone else asks, maybe you do it, maybe you don't.

When I considered making a request, a strange idea came to me. What if I could persuade the group to volunteer for a few rounds of Simon Says? Remember that game? It's all about requests. Most of us have played it at one time or another. Simon says you do this, you do this. Simon says do that, you do that. Do something without Simon saying so and you lose.

Maybe I could use Simon to find out who'd killed Timothy, Aiden, and Johnny.

Things at doc's trailer were much the same. There was someone sound asleep on one of the beanbags who likely hadn't changed his clothes since he arrived. Either he'd lost his footwear or hadn't brought any.

The doc came out from behind the curtain and gave me a not-so-happy smirk. With certain people, the more time I spend with them, the more often I get that response. I guess I'm an acquired taste.

He sat down at his desk and I walked over. "When you have a moment, I have a question to ask you."

"I'm sure you do. You'll have to wait your turn."

"Sure."

I nodded toward a couple of people who, like the sleeper, were on a downward spiral. One gave me a weak nod, which cemented our relationship. We all took our own counsel and silently waited.

When my turn came, the doc gave me a pained expressed and asked, "What's it about this time?"

"I want you to prescribe me something, or give me some if you have it on hand."

"Before you tell me what you want, why don't you tell me about your symptoms?"

Just like a doctor to ask a doctor question. Where was the quack when I needed him? I'd have to guess what symptoms would make me want to freeze up. I figured if it worked for African hunters, it would work for me.

"Remember how I told you I'm investigating what happened to Timothy and Aiden? Perhaps they both OD'd, but maybe something else was at play. Either way, I need to conduct a stakeout that'll have me standing still for long periods of time. Do you have anything that would help me do that?"

Sometimes people give me a look, like they think I'm full of shit but not entirely sure. Maybe only eighty to ninety percent. I've seen that look often enough to know I can play it one of two ways—either admit to the bullshit, play to their ego about their lie-detecting skills, then tell them another more believable lie, or double down.

The doc didn't seem shocked or perplexed. He might know the drug but was wary of me. Of course, I had no idea what he was thinking, but I needed to keep him off balance enough to spill some beans.

"Doc, everyone says how good you are, and I could really use some help with this. I've heard there's a drug African tribes use to help them when they go hunting and need to be still for long periods. I could use some of that."

"You'll be fine with some muscle relaxants."

"Fine is fine, but I need more than fine here. Are you familiar with this stuff? Do I need a prescription? Can I get this over the counter at a pharmacy? Help me, Doc."

"Ibogaine is a root found in Africa and South America, but it's not readily available here."

"So you're familiar with it? Is it something you've given to patients? Is there someone I could speak with who might have used it so I can get a sense of what I'm in for?"

"You know I can't answer those questions. If you really want me to help you out, I can give you some muscle relaxants."

"Okay, I'll take the relaxants, but I want to run another hypothetical by you. Let's say someone had a drug that a doctor gave them, but they used it nefariously. And let's say that person didn't want anyone knowing where they'd gotten that drug. Do you think that person might kill the person they'd gotten the drug from?"

He stared at me like I was crazy. Maybe I was, but I felt it necessary to warn him, just in case. If he was going to be ethical so was I.

I took the meds—why not?—and left.

So Johnny or the doc could have gotten someone the ibogaine. The doc was still alive, so the odds were still in Johnny's favor, in an unfavorable way. But I couldn't rule out the doc.

CHAPTER 43

"Private Life"

Oingo Boingo

I WAS READY to pin the tail on the donkey and play Simon Says.

First, I'd need to call a meeting after Fleetwood Mac closed the show. I didn't think I'd be the best host for the event, but knew who would.

I didn't knock on Eve's tepee, just asked if anyone was there. I heard something indistinguishable. It wasn't a groan but it wasn't a "Come on in" either. More of an *Unnn*. I opened the flap and went in anyway. Eve was lying on her sleeping bag.

"Oh, hi," she said. "You woke me up."

"I'm sorry. I can come back later."

"No, don't do that. I was just taking a power nap. Want to replenish my energies for the night ahead."

It did sound like her energies could use a little replenishing, though I'm not the spunkiest when I wake up from a nap either.

Eve stretched, sat up, opened a canteen, and poured some water into her hand and dabbed her face.

"Ah, that feels better. Add a cup of coffee and a few lines and I'll be as good as new."

"That ought to do the trick. Once you're up and about I have a favor to ask."

"What's that?"

"I was hoping after Fleetwood Mac you could hold another gathering of your tribe."

"You don't have to ask. We always have an aftershow party. We do a gratitude round and then party it up."

"Perfect. Is it okay if I join in?"

"I would hope so. You're part of the family now."

"Thanks. I also want to facilitate a little something with the group that I hope will reveal the truth. Do you think that's okay?"

"Sure, why not?"

"Great," I said, turning to leave.

"Before you go, though," she said standing up. "I want to ask you something."

"Sure, what is it?"

"Do you think Ross killed them? I think so. Sheridan and I have been doing some of our own detecting and we've got the goods on him."

"Really? What've you got?"

"We know he and Timothy got into a big fight right before the show. Josie told Sheridan she overheard them yelling at each other."

"I kinda think Ross is a yeller at many people. Did she tell you if she heard anything specifically?"

"A lot of *fuck-yous*. She thinks Ross got wind of Timothy wanting to get a new manager and they had it out. I understand why he'd be upset. He discovered Timothy and helped him grow to where he is now. Or was now."

"I'm sure Ross was instrumental in the band's growth and would be upset if Timothy dumped him."

"You bet. Ross thinks of the band as his family. He was always the father confessor and ran the show."

"Maybe that's what Timothy didn't like. From what I gather, he liked to run the show."

"You're right about that, but Timothy wanted Ross to take care of the nuts and bolts so he could be free to create."

"Makes sense."

"Yeah, but Timothy felt that while Ross helped get them to where they were, he hadn't taken them to where they ought to be. Timothy wanted to be the show, and maybe being here and feeling the big time got him thinking Ross was small time."

"That often happens in relationships. One person feels they've outgrown the other."

"It was that, but also Timothy wanted to be in the mix with Dylan, Jackson Browne, Joni Mitchell, and Van Morrison."

"That's good company. Do you think he deserved to be in it?"

Eve gave it a moment. "Timothy said more than once that Ross and Magoo were holding him back. Dylan, Jackson Browne, Joni Mitchell, and Van Morrison play with a band but they go out under their own name. He wanted to dump the band and be the star."

"That makes sense. Do you think he had the firepower to do it?"

"Not really. He had the ego and he was a captivating performer, but not that good a songwriter. Maybe he could've earned his way to that level if he'd had a real breakout album. Magoo has a new album coming out. If it hits big, they'll move up to arena headliners. If it slumps, they'll be off the record label and playing at your local bar."

"Ow. That's harsh."

"Maybe a little, but the glory days would be over."

"So here's the million-dollar question. Was the next album going to make or break them?"

"I heard a tape of three songs. This could be the album that takes them to the top of the ladder."

"You heard three songs? That's cool."

"Timothy let me and Sheridan listen to them."

CHAPTER 44

"When the World is Running Down, You Make the Best of What's Still Around"
The Police

I LEFT EVE's tepee and got to thinking about murder. Most of us don't have real murderous thoughts. We might wish someone were dead or bad things happened to them, but we don't put our wishes into direct action. We're more passive-aggressive. But that's just most of us.

If someone had gotten Timothy and Aiden to take ibogaine, then shot them up with bad dope, they had to have hatched a careful plan. They say revenge is sweet and best served cold. If someone was extremely upset with Timothy and Aiden, they'd have had time to dwell on their anger, let it percolate while they planned the whole thing out. That required a certain mindset. Whether you're training for the Olympics or plotting a murder, you need to be able to put other life concerns aside and focus on your priority.

We all need to closely focus on something from time to time. Erick Fromm wrote that the art and practice of love requires your love to be "a matter of ultimate concern." The more concern you have, the more time, energy, money, and other resources you're going to put into it.

Usually, the people who gain our attention through music, politics, sports, or other endeavors have had the utmost concern to make their dreams come true.

Someone had that utmost concern.

I either had to find proof or get them to reveal themselves. I didn't hold much hope for the former. My Simon Says trick might not get anyone to pin the tail on the donkey but I had something up my sleeve that might take the game to a new level. Perhaps I could trigger the person with that utmost concern into blowing off some excess steam for us all to see. But to do that I needed to build up the steam. That could be dangerous.

Drew, CC, and Lilah were sitting at a table. I wasted no time joining them. I wasn't quite ready for dinner as it was more cocktail hour than suppertime. I opted for some Danish pastry left over from the morning and a cup of coffee.

"You having breakfast?" Lilah asked.

"It looks like it but, unlike many of our rock-and-roll counterparts, this isn't the start of my day."

"Hey," Drew said. "We've been up hours. Had to catch the Dead and then we had a little band meeting."

"How was that?" I asked.

"Grim, but helpful."

"How so?"

"We decided to finish up the tour."

"That's good news. Or at least I think it's good news. Is it?"

"We all have ideas about what we want to do next, but aren't really ready to take our next steps. It's easier to just finish the tour and go from there."

"Drew's going to put out his own album when the tour's over," CC said.

"That's great news," Lilah said, and I nodded my agreement.

"Yeah. It's a good thing. Just not sure what songs to put on there."

"But that's a good problem, isn't it? You have your own songs Magoo hasn't covered."

"He most assuredly does," CC said with some attitude. "Songs they should have covered, but now will be entirely his."

"I imagine having the sole rights does wonders for your bank account. And there's the pride and self-satisfaction."

"We hope to find out," Drew said.

"Do I tell you to break a leg or wish you luck?"

"Right now, you just help me keep things afloat."

"I'll do my best, but it seems like you're holding up well."

"So, Sherlock," Lilah said, "how's the sleuthing going?"

"The pieces are starting to come together," I said with a bit too much Danish in my mouth. "I gather there's an all-hands-on-deck gathering at Eve's tepee after the last song. I think, well, I hope we'll be able to get to the bottom of things then."

"You know whodunit?" she asked.

"Well, let's just say, when we're all together truths will be revealed."

"You sound like a New Age Magic 8 Ball," Lilah said, and I couldn't tell if that was a positive or negative thing.

"Right now, it says Ask Again Later. And hopefully later it will say Guilty As Charged."

"Come on," Drew said eyeing my Danish. "Tell us who's guilty."

"It's a fair request, but things are still a little cloudy with the Magic 8 Ball."

"You said, 'We'll be able to get to the bottom of things,'" Lilah said. "Why did you say we?"

"Very observant of you," I said poised to take a bite before Drew decided to rip off a piece. "Actually, we'll all know at the same time."

"What?" CC said.

"Drew may have told you that along with teaching and seeing people in therapy I also run a therapy and a supervision group. I'm a big believer in the power of groups. When we're all together we'll be able to discern the truth."

"How is that possible?" Lilah asked.

"I've learned groups can facilitate the unraveling of bullshit. I don't want to talk too much about it, but I want us to play a game we've all played. It will point us toward the truth."

"We're going to play Spin the Bottle?" Lilah asked.

"We can do that later. I have something else in mind for the whole group."

"We're going to play a game?" CC asked.

"Of a sort. I want it to be a surprise. In the meantime, I've got some sleuthing to do but am very much looking forward to seeing Jackson."

"We all are," said Lilah. "Why don't you meet us in front of Magoo's trailer in an hour or so?"

I'd have preferred to have Lilah to myself and Jackson but I couldn't complain. When Drew first asked me to attend the festival, we'd agreed I'd have time off when Jackson was on stage. It wasn't ideal to be watching Jackson standing next to my client, but Lilah's presence would more than compensate. Or so I thought.

CHAPTER 45

"Cheeseburger in Paradise"
Jimmy Buffett

I WAS NERVOUS because of what I needed to do next. When you confront a potential killer about their deeds there's always that possibility they'll add you to the list.

I went to find Michael.

The hints I'd put out about what I knew had so far been met with inaction. I'd hoped my hint of a big reveal at the end of the night would prompt someone to make sure I wouldn't do any unveiling. That hadn't netted any results. I was either teasing the wrong people or employing a questionable strategy.

I know my weakness—I bypass foreplay too often. My abruptness can move things backward. On this occasion, I'd tried to tease people—teasing was foreplay after all—but it didn't seem to be promoting any follow-up action.

I'd been trying to lay the groundwork for someone showing their hand, but maybe I wasn't very good at it. Either I needed to upgrade my foreplay skills, which was a good idea, or just jump in.

Be myself.

Be the cheeseburger in paradise.

I made my way over to the bus and stepped in. I started toward the back when I heard a gasp. I froze. A moment later I heard another. Then another. Then I knew what was happening. Someone was fucking. Well, someones.

Etiquette and my mother's voice told me to leave. Curiosity and my investigator's voice told me to stay. I wasn't sure how far along they were. The gear sounded high, and while I don't want to generalize from my own experience, usually the higher the gear, the closer to the end.

I could interrupt them right on the verge of climaxing, but why not show some common decency and wait until they'd finished?

"Hi," I called out. "Anybody in the bus?"

Okay, I'm inconsiderate. Not all the time. But some.

The gasping stopped.

If it were me, I'd have lain low and pretended I wasn't there so whoever was interrupting the proceedings would leave.

"Sorry if I woke anybody up. Is Michael here?"

I didn't make a move to leave. They didn't make a move to acknowledge their presence.

We were at a standoff. A sudden wave of competitiveness overcame me. I didn't want to give in and lose the moment. If you're going to be inconsiderate you might as well play it out.

I did the only thing I knew how to do.

I spoke the truth.

"I'm sorry if I interrupted you but if one of you is Michael, I'd really like to speak with you."

Still no sound.

When there still was no response I left. If my goal was to get Michael worrying about whether I had the goods on him, I might have achieved that goal.

Of course, if it wasn't Michael, I had no idea who was getting what message.

Someone was in there fucking and didn't want me knowing who

they were. It could have been a couple of teenagers who'd slipped into a band's bus to add a notch to their belt. Or it could have been Michael and Carol. Michael and Josie. Josie and Carol, and Ted and Alice as well.

I waited outside the bus to see if I could spot my muted lovers. I had a good thirty minutes to fill before I met Lilah. I took in the spectacle before me. While the heat and the murders had added an unwelcome aspect to the festival, it seemed most everyone was having a good time. A community had been built and there was a sense of camaraderie. People were happy to be here. This was a once-in-a-lifetime event that would imprint itself on everyone. And in the morning, everything would get torn down and the desert would go back to being a desert.

My reverie was interrupted by Ross rushing by. We caught each other's eye. Even though he'd been intent on going somewhere to do something, he came over to say hello.

"How are you doing, Doc? Anyone ever ask you that?"

"I'm happy to see you. Yeah. Occasionally people are interested and want to know. Usually people just say, 'How you doing,' and don't break stride. It's more a greeting than a question."

"I don't like that. If they want to know how you're doing, ask. If they're not, say something else."

"I'm with you on that. So, since you asked, I was just taking in the wonder of this whole thing. Woz built a city here so he could have people come and listen to music. He could have just had all these bands come and play in his backyard and saved a lot of money. But he wanted to share the music. That's cool in my book."

"Yeah. He's a saint. Well, you know, not really. I hear he can be a prick. But putting this event on, well, that's phenomenal. I've heard complaints about the toilets and showers, and the lack of water, but to have so many people in one place for such a short time, he's done well. Real well. And don't worry, he'll make more money."

"We'll see. So how about you? How are you doing?"

"That's very slick, Doc. You say very little and then you pass the buck."

"Guilty as charged. We therapists take the ball, run a little, then pass it right back."

"I'll have to remember that."

"I'm sure you have your own ways of taking and passing the ball."

"Doc, are you fucking with me?"

"No, I'm just curious about you. I'm very close to figuring out what happened with Timothy and Aiden and I overheard someone say there's been a third death. Have you heard anything about that?"

"A third? Another one of the band? What happened? What did you hear?"

"Not one of the band but maybe someone directly related to them. I don't know. It could be something else entirely. That's why I was so happy to see you. Well, that and I like you."

"Thanks, Doc. That's nice of you. I like you too. But we have to find out what happened."

"I was told to keep it private so best not to tell anyone yet. I just told you because I was relieved to see you."

With that he rushed away. I wasn't sure he would keep it to himself or sure I wanted him to. Sometimes saying something without much forethought isn't the wisest thing. Aside from wanting to kick things up a notch, I wasn't entirely sure why I'd told Ross about a possible third death. He hadn't blanched or been surprised or upset. But he had said all the right things, and, having said them, taken off.

I knew the killer was highly capable of controlling their responses and could put on a good game face. Yet, the killer was also ultimately incapable of controlling their anger. It wouldn't be easy to break through the veneer, but with the group's help I had a good chance.

I didn't want to leave my stakeout, but it was time to meet Lilah.

CHAPTER 46

"Hold On Hold Out"
Jackson Browne

I TOOK IT as a good sign Lilah had changed her clothes since I'd last seen her. The temperature was still hovering too close to a hundred degrees at 7:00 p.m. and there wasn't a lot of dressing up to be had. She'd put on a T-shirt that was a cross between a French stripe and a Venetian gondolier's. And with her beige shorts and long legs, I only wished I could have been in a gondola with her. Of course, we wouldn't have had Jackson to serenade us, but you can't have everything.

Drew and CC looked the same as when I'd last seen them, but smelled like they'd been toking up. I'd have liked to join them but I had work to do and wanted to keep my focus.

"How's everybody doing?" I asked.

"We're great," said CC, taking Lilah aside to talk privately with her.

"So, Dave," Drew said, "want to give me a status report? You know I'm paying you to be here and do your thing, and so far you haven't exactly been wowing me."

"I'm sorry. I tend to be a late bloomer in the wowing department. But I guess we're lucky the concerns that brought me here haven't materialized."

"Yeah. I've been lucky. Maybe I'm not the draw I hoped I was."

"Maybe. Could also be the way you ended those relationships was good enough not to compel them to come back into your life."

"I don't know if I'd say I ended those relationships per se."

"What did you do?"

"Mostly I slipped out the back, Jack."

"Well, whatever you did, it seems to have kept them away."

"Did I just throw away my money?"

"I hope you don't think the money's wasted. Think of it as insurance. You pay for it, hoping you don't need to use it. But if the shit hits the fan, you've got backup."

"That's a self-serving way to hold it. And who knows? I might still need to cash in my policy. In the meantime, any updates worth mentioning?"

"I do have a plan that I hope will make you think I earned my keep."

"Want to share?"

"Let's just say all will be revealed at Eve's tent after Fleetwood Mac closes the show."

"Okay, but come on. Don't I get any insider info?"

"Here's something to chew on. There's another body."

"What?"

"Another murder."

"What are you talking about? I haven't heard anything about this."

"You said you wanted some insider info. That's it."

"Whoa. Who, what, where, and when?"

"Those are the questions. I know who. I know where. I have a hunch when. A good bet about what, but I can't tell you if it was Colonel Mustard or Miss Scarlett. But do me a favor. Keep it to yourself. I'll let you know when you can share it."

"Okay, but that's a hard secret to keep. Just tell me who."

"Let's just say I don't think you'll be overly upset. I don't mean to tease you, but you wanted insider info and there it is. Let's just keep it between us a little longer."

"If you say so. But that's some heavy shit."

"I know. Sorry."

With that, CC and Lilah came over.

Lilah said, "If we're going to see Jackson, we ought to go stake out a place. I imagine we won't be the only ones."

She was right. By the time we got to the backstage area it was already crowded. Lilah slipped her way to the front. A few people seemed a little irked but she managed to find a space where we had a good side view of the stage.

She had a certain skill set. I wasn't sure how it would transfer into daily life, but she knew how to take care of herself. And, in this case, she brought along CC, Drew, and me.

I tend not to like it when people ask me what my favorite anything is. Narrowing things down is tricky. I have many favorite ice cream flavors, books, places, and things. That said, Jackson has been my favorite musician ever since I heard "Fountain of Sorrow." I was hoping he'd play that along with some of my other favorites.

He started with "Hold On Hold Out." It had never made it to my favorites list, but it was doing the trick today. Standing next to Lilah and watching her sway as she sang along got me a little weak in the knees.

I didn't love Lilah. But maybe I could. I didn't know much about her, but everything I'd encountered so far only made me want more. I split my time watching Lilah and listening to Jackson sing his profound songs of love, loss, life, and the values we share.

Between songs I asked CC where Drew was. She shrugged. I'd been lost in the moment and had no idea how long he'd been gone. Maybe he'd gone to the bathroom. I found myself torn between Jackson, Lilah, and my curiosity.

Goddammit, Drew. He'd given me this time off and then gone and taken it away.

CHAPTER 47

"Take Me to the River"
Talking Heads

THERE HAVE TO be people who make a living following others who'd do a much better job of it than I do. Having a visual on a person makes it easier. With no visual and limited skills, I felt like a rat in a maze.

Where's Drue?

I went to the bus. No luck. The trailer. Likewise. The food pavilion. Nada. As my strikeouts built I started to swing wildly. I checked out Eve's tepee. Empty. I checked where Johnny was resting. Things were much the same. The lake was still picturesque but no Drew. There were still a few thousand other places I could check out but I was running out of degrees of separation.

All else having failed, I went for the air-conditioning. Bingo. Drew was talking with Hale, the guy who'd spoken with Ross. While Jackson might not have been Drew's favorite, it seemed strange he'd leave our little group and head over here, mid-set, without at least saying something. Unless he was counting on me being unlikely to follow him.

While Ross's conversation had been animated, this one was

more conspiratorial. That might be an exaggeration, but they were off in a corner and seemed to be talking in hushed tones.

I could go outside the tent and try to eavesdrop on what they were saying, but why be covert when you can be overt?

"Hey," I said, surprising them. "What's going on?"

They looked like they'd been caught with their hands in the cookie jar. Well, Drew looked that way. Hale seemed confused.

"Hi," Drew said. "What are you doing here?"

"When I noticed you took off, I wondered where you'd gone."

"Must be awfully important for you to follow me since Jackson was the one person you wanted to see."

"You tell me. Is it important that I follow you?"

"I don't think so."

"You should," said Carol. I didn't know how I'd missed her but now she was standing right beside Drew and Hale.

"Oh, hi. I didn't see you."

"That's because you weren't looking."

"Sometimes I have tunnel vision. So, what are you all doing here?"

"I'm not sure that's any of your business," said Carol.

"You're right about that. But Drew asked me to help out with something and this might be a good time for that."

"What's he talking about?" Carol asked Drew.

"It's nothing. This isn't one of those things I told you I might need some help managing."

"That's good to hear."

Good to hear, especially since Michael told me Drew and Carol had a falling out. Evidently they'd patched things up.

"What do you mean, help managing? What's that about?"

I could see Carol was annoying Drew.

"Dave's here to help me deal with some issues, which fortunately haven't materialized, so he's been able to do other things, which is, I suspect, why he was following me. Right?"

"I'm just trying to put the pieces together."

"What does that mean?"

Now she was annoying me. I decided to ignore her and focus on my own agenda.

"So, what's going on here?" I asked. "Anything I should know about?"

"Not really," Carol said quickly.

"Drew?"

"We're just talking about some tech stuff."

"Related to the band?"

"Related to music," Hale said.

"Oh. How so?"

"We were talking about CDs," Hale said.

"CDs—what are those?"

"Compact discs," said Hale making a circle with his hands. "Billy Joel's next album is coming out in October and it'll be the first one produced on CD as well as an album and tape."

"I heard about that. Are you thinking of releasing a Magoo album on CD?"

"Not really," said Carol. Always a bright spot.

"That's Ross's call. I'm just trying to get an education."

"I believe in education. What are we learning today?"

"We're learning," Hale said, "that CDs are the future."

"Hard to conceive I'll ever not have tapes. Although my reel-to-reel is now asleep in the garage, but the tape player in my car is in heavy use."

"Dave may be right," said Drew. "I'm partial to albums but in my car, tapes rule. I can't see any CD taking the place of that."

"You'll see," said Hale, who was also starting to bug me.

"If you don't mind," Carol said, "we need to have a private conversation and would very much appreciate it if you'd leave us alone."

"Okay. I'll save the rest of my learning for later."

After a few quick goodbyes I left. I could hear Jackson singing a song I didn't recognize. It was unlikely to be his closer; if I hurried I'd be able to get back to Lilah and listen to the end of the set with her.

I wasn't sure what to make of the conversation. They'd been talking about cutting-edge technology but didn't want me included. Was Carol just being her less-than-pleasing self or was their talk really private? And if it was so private, what was the connection between Drew and Carol? Did she also want to be his agent? His lover?

I wasn't going to buy the Billy Joel album let alone the CD. Would others? I wouldn't know a CD if I saw one or how to even play one. If you had to buy a whole new delivery system just to listen to it, why bother? Technology might be the wave of the future, but I had yet to see the swell.

I'd just left the comfort of the air-conditioning when I bumped into Ross.

"Hey," he said. "Did you see Carol in there?"

"As a matter of fact, I was just talking with her."

"Was she alone?"

"Not really. She was with Drew and Hale."

"Shit," he said, and hurried past me.

I could have kept on walking toward Lilah, but I was on the case so I turned and followed Ross. It didn't sound like he was happy Carol was talking with Drew and Hale. Was he jealous? He didn't strike me as the type but I didn't really know enough to know. Plus, wasn't Carol interested in Michael? Was there something brewing between Drew and Carol or was it some other concern? Maybe their flare up indicated more was afoot with them than Ross or CC would want to know. I hadn't seen any displays of affection between them; but if there was something afoot, they wouldn't want to be overt.

I couldn't see Ross in the tent but I knew where he'd end up so I hurried over to the far side. There was enough of a crowd that I could keep people between us. I tried to angle my path so he couldn't have a direct view of me. Of course, I couldn't get a direct view of him either.

As I made my way to the corner, I spotted them. Ross was screaming. I couldn't hear what he was saying, but from the way passersby were reacting, it was clear he wasn't keeping the conversation private. He was gesticulating with his arms and making threatening gestures. He tried to grab Carol's hand and pull her away but she was having none of that.

There was a lot of back-and-forth, and then Hale said something that got them all to shut up. Impressive. Patiently, he explained something, and I could see it had calmed the waters. Carol and Ross stormed off and Drew followed.

I could have followed them, but why not take a chance and do something out of the box? I went over to Hale. I didn't know what his relationship was with them, but maybe he didn't know much about my relationship with them either.

"Say," I said, "I was coming back to ask Drew something and saw you in a heated discussion with Carol, Drew, and Ross. Everything okay?"

"Yeah, sure. They're just hyped up."

"About what?"

"You know, the music."

"Yeah. The music. Any distinct part of the music got them hyped up now?"

"Well, you know, the CDs."

"Yeah. But it's hard to think about anyone being hyped up about that."

"Some people are. Wait and see."

"So that's it? That's what got them so riled?"

"Well, that and the videos."

"The videos?"

"Yeah, you know, videos."

"Oh, videos. Right. Help me, will you? I can't remember why they're so riled about that."

"If you don't know, I can't tell you. And I'm not sure they will either. But you'll find out soon enough."

Great. Now I had a mystery on top of a mystery and no idea if one thing had anything to do with the other. I wasn't sure what videos had to do with anything. Within the last year a new TV channel showing music videos had launched—MTV—but I'd yet to see it and figured by the time I went to check it out, it would be gone, along with the CDs and computers.

If Drew, Carol, and Ross were banking on videos to win their day, they either knew something I didn't or they were jumping on the latest thing in hopes the gold rush would follow.

A lot to consider, but if I hurried, I might be able to catch the end of Jackson's set. I could hear him singing "Somebody's Baby," which had been featured in *Fast Times at Ridgemont High*, a movie that had come out last month and I'd yet to see.

I hurried but the song ended before I got there. So did his set. By the time I got back to where we'd been, Lilah was gone, along with everyone else. She hadn't held out.

CHAPTER 48

"Dance This Mess Around"

B-52's

IT WOULD BE a little while before Fleetwood Mac closed down the festival. It was a good time to eat and try to get my act together.

The food pavilion was full, but I didn't see anyone I knew so I found a table with a group of long-haired college-age boys who may have started tripping with the Dead in the morning and hadn't stopped. They all wore tie-dye shirts and seemed to have discovered Jell-O. After some hello nods they settled back into their desserts and I ate my spaghetti with garlic bread. The garlic wouldn't serve me well with Lilah, but I figured it would have receded into the background by the time the opportunity presented itself. It wasn't a smart romance move, but I'm partial to garlic bread.

I hadn't been able to put two and two together and come up with anything other than playing Simon Says and hoping I could trip up the killer. It was wishful thinking to hope my game playing would do the trick. My therapeutic razzle-dazzle could very well fall on its face just like CDs, music videos, and computers.

As I was visualizing playing the game when something my table-mates were saying caught my attention.

"Dude, he blew my fucking mind."

"Yeah, dude. I told you."

"What was that shit he gave us?"

"The truth, man. It was the truth."

As a therapist and teacher, I do my best to live within the truth. Still, I also know one person's truth may not be another's. I was going to have to take people on a bit of a therapy journey to deeper levels of truth. We therapists do like to mine for psychic gold. Maybe if I dug deep enough I could strike ore.

I was pumping myself up—probably a good thing as I didn't have much of a plan and needed as much confidence as I could muster. Therapists will tell you that sometimes the sessions in which the client comes in with nothing to talk about are the most productive. I wondered if that held true for mystery reveals.

CHAPTER 49

"Sugar Magnolia"
Grateful Dead

FLEETWOOD MAC WERE playing "Second Hand News" and I figured it was time to see if I could make some front-page news. To pull it off I'd need an ally, and if I didn't find one now I'd have to go it alone.

The problem was, I didn't trust anyone. But I needed to. I didn't want to put Lilah in jeopardy, but of all the people I'd met she was the one I trusted most. Well, maybe I trusted Bill Graham and Sully more, but they weren't invited to Eve's tepee.

I went back to where I'd last seen Lilah in hopes she'd try to find the same viewing spot. Luckily, she had. She was doing her smooth cruising along to a song I didn't know. CC was with her. Drew was nowhere to be seen.

"Hey," I said. "It's good to see you."

CC smiled at me and said, "We missed you at Jackson. You said you were a big fan."

"I am. And I wanted to be with you, but there was something I had to do."

"I hope it was worth it," said Lilah.

"Well, yes and no. I really missed not seeing Jackson with you, so that's disappointing. Whether it was worth it, I don't know. I hope so, but it remains to be seen."

"You a Fleetwood Mac fan?" CC asked.

"Not really. I know their hits but I don't have any of their albums. How about you two?"

"Me maybe more than Lilah. We both have the *Rumours* album and I have the live one as well. You don't have that, Lilah, do you?"

"No. Just *Rumours*. It's enough."

"I'm sure they'll play a lot from those albums. Before they get too into it, would it be okay with you both if I had a private word with Lilah?"

"Sure," CC said, and turned to face the band. I couldn't tell if she was fine with it or miffed, and I didn't really care.

Lilah and stepped a few yards away. I liked watching her move. She didn't glide, but she was casually graceful.

"What's up?" she asked.

"I need your help. I have a favor to ask."

"Let's hear it."

"I don't know how things are going to go down at the aftershow party in Eve's tepee, but at some point I'm going to ask for everyone's attention. I'm going to say if we all work together for a few minutes we'll know who killed Timothy and Aiden."

"You know who killed them?"

"Not entirely. But I know what we can do as a group to get the killer to reveal themselves."

"You do? That would be magic."

"That's one way to see it. And I'll need a little magic. Therapy magic. I don't think I can make anyone disappear."

"You're going to reveal whodunit? That's a cut above pulling a rabbit out of a hat."

"Thanks. I'm going for a little therapy playground razzle-dazzle. But I'm going to need your help."

"Sure. What do you want me to do?

"I want you to be open and enthusiastic."

"More so than I'm being now?"

"No, this is great. I'm going to have us play a game and, you know, not everyone may want to join in. So I need a ringer, someone to say, 'This sounds great. Let's do it.'"

"Don't you think you should have someone who has more credibility with the group?"

"Yes, but I don't trust any of them. I trust you."

"That's very kind."

"It's true. I sure hope you don't turn out to be the killer. I'm rooting for a happy ending."

"Keep rooting. Anything else you want me to do?"

"Yes. I'm going to have us play a version of Simon Says. Don't look like that. I know, it sounds weird, but that's part of the razzle. I'm going to ask questions and have people step forward while we're in a circle. It would be best if you stood opposite me, because it's difficult for me to see the faces of the people right next to me. But you could. I don't need you to say or do anything about what you see per se because, hopefully, if you see something so will the people next to you. And that's what I'm counting on."

"What are you counting on?"

"I'm counting on people answering my questions honestly. Well, mostly honestly. For others to be honest you'll need to be too. I'm not sure what I'm going to say, but I'll ask some general personal things that might be embarrassing to admit. Sort of to make it a fun and adult-game-like. If I ask those kinds of questions to warm everyone up, I want you to be honest and step forward. And even if it's a lie, I want you to step forward as if it's the truth."

"That last part was confusing. Can you give me an example?"

"How about I say, 'Everyone who thinks they're a better artist than Timothy step forward.' I want you to step forward. I don't care if you think you are or aren't. I want you to show everyone you're not afraid to be honest. Even if you're lying."

"I get it. I'm the enthusiastic honest lying participant. I can do it."

"Good. Of course, not everyone will be honest, but I'm hoping when I ask the big-money questions we'll be able to spot the truth. At least, that's the plan."

CHAPTER 50

"Searchin'"

Santana

THERE WAS ONE more thing I needed to do before we all met up at Eve's. If Lilah helped me reveal the killer, there would be aftereffects to deal with. The killer would likely not take kindly to the experience. Maybe it would be one of those moments when, overcome by guilt, the killer revealed themselves and was grateful to have the burden released. That kind of tent revival conversion could happen, but I knew I didn't have the chops for it. I needed a different kind of backup.

There are solid, law-abiding citizens who feel only gratitude toward the police. I sometimes have those thoughts. But I also have fear and dread. The police can put you in jail. Until this weekend, I'd limited my lawbreaking to going over the speed limit, jaywalking like a New Yorker, smoking a joint, and driving under the influence. Well, that's not entirely true. If you've read *A Lesson in Sex and Murder*, you know I've also stepped out of bounds a time or two.

Even if I handed in a donation to the Police Benevolent Society, I'd still have a degree of anxiety in their presence.

But I needed help.

Bill Graham was somewhere else. Sully was reading something on his desk. I waited till he paused.

"Hi, remember me? I'm the shrink with Magoo."

"Yeah, the would-be detective shrink. I remember you. What are you going to annoy me about now?"

"That's the attitude I like from those who are in charge of my security."

"You get what you deserve. So, what do you deserve?"

"How about a little time and maybe a favor. A favor that might turn out very well for you."

"What are you selling this time?"

"After the final show, Magoo and some of its significant others are having an aftershow party. Timothy and Aiden's murderer is going to be there."

"What makes you so sure of that?"

"That's a fair question and one I'd rather you hadn't asked. But since you did, I'll just say we haven't come this far for this not to pan out."

"What does that mean?"

"You ask a lot of questions. Why don't you just let me make my pitch and then you can ask questions. You're interrupting my flow."

"Oh, I'm so sorry about that. I don't want to interrupt your flow."

"Okay, bust me for that. I apologize to you and me for that. But let me just repeat: the killer will be there and I'm hoping to get them to reveal themselves."

"You don't know who did it?"

"If I did I wouldn't need the favor."

"The favor isn't sitting here, listening to this?"

"Yes. That is, of course, a favor. And thank you for giving me the gift of your attention. Yes, I do plan—well, hope—to get the killer to reveal themselves. And when they do, it would be great if you could swoop in and arrest them. That's the real favor I want. I want you to be close at hand when needed. Is that something you'd be willing to do?"

"You don't seem to understand a few things. I'm not your personal security guard. If you provoke someone and they decide to kill you, I'm not going to be there to rescue you."

"I hadn't really worried I'd be at risk since there will be others there. But you're right. The killer might not be happy with me for outing them. I could be at greater risk than the others. But, come on, how come if a festival-goer is at risk of being killed you wouldn't want to be there?"

"Half the people here have been tripping out, thinking someone is out to kill them, or the world wants to make love to them. I can't chase after everyone's fantasy life."

"Trust me. This isn't my fantasy life. Or my real life. We've been thrown into extraordinary circumstances and it would be comforting to know I could count on you."

"It would be comforting to know I could count on you as well. Comforting to know you won't bother me anymore. Do you know what happens after the last act? Chaos. We have over a hundred thousand people, most of whom are loaded and about to drive out of here. They'll be exhausted and jacked up. They'll be puking, crying, looting, and floundering, and you want me to not deal with that but come find you and be ready should you need me?"

"You got it. You don't have to do it all night. We'll convene approximately fifteen minutes after the last number. I'm not entirely sure how things will proceed, but I'm guessing between fifteen and forty-five minutes after that we'll have our killer. So come by thirty minutes after the last number and stay thirty minutes. Smoke a cigarette. Take in the scene. And while you're at it, try to stand close enough to the tepee to hear any loud noises."

"And, once again, the reason you think the killer will be there and you can out them is..."

"What we're talking about."

By the time I left, Sully knew the location of Eve's tepee and seemed interested enough to make me think there was a chance he'd show up. It would likely depend on the degree of floundering going on. I just hoped that wouldn't include someone finding Johnny Romano and causing a whole other scene.

It wouldn't be too long before everyone knew about Johnny. I'd already let it slip to Ross and Drew that someone was dead, but I wasn't sure whether anyone else aside from the killer knew who. I was banking on that rather private piece of knowledge to help me out.

Even though I might earn some points with Lilah if I circled back and finished out the Fleetwood Mac set with her, I needed some alone time. I heard them playing "Go Your Own Way" and I did. I figured it was their last song, though they'd play an encore.

It was down to the last scene before the big scene. I went down to the lake. The place was mostly deserted. I took some time and had a talk with myself.

David, take this in. Breathe. Be here now.

In that moment, right there, with music blaring in the background and the desert stretching out past this small lake, life was good. My romantic interests were sparked, I was getting paid for being at this event, and I was about to do something I'd never done before—play Simon Says with adults. It was a crazy idea, which was why it might work. It was likely no one in the group had played Simon Says in years, and never the way I'd play it. I just needed their buy-in. That meant enough peer pressure to make everyone feel compelled to play. I wished myself good luck.

CHAPTER 51

"Hit Me with Your Best Shot"

Pat Benatar

RESEARCH SHOWS OUR bodies basically react the same way when we're nervous or excited. I was getting a double dose as I lifted the flap and made my way into the tepee. Evidently, the aftershow party was in full swing. The smudging and incense-burning was partnering up with the pungency of cannabis, and Eve's boom box was playing *Greetings from Asbury Park*.

Almost everyone was there. Lilah and CC were chatting away. Drew, Carol, and Ross were passing a joint with Sheridan. Eve was searching for something in her belongings. Michael and Josie were missing; I wondered if they were going to pass.

I walked over to Lilah and winked. I'd have liked to have gotten a wink back but she wasn't really the winking type. She did, however, give a slight nod of the head, which I took as sign enough, even though it could just as easily have been her agreeing with CC about something. Thankfully, Josie and Michael joined the group.

People milled around for a few minutes, then Eve banged a drum.

"Everyone, please join me in a circle."

Once assembled she said, "This has been a challenging festival for us. We've lost two of our own. Our family, while it is ever strong, has been hurt. Not only are we mourning the loss of our brothers, we're also needing to find closure. Tomorrow morning, we'll wake up and go back to our lives, but they'll be forever altered. We will have emptiness where there was fullness, sorrow where there was joy. We cannot bring back our brothers, but we can honor them as we go forward. We can take the love they created and add to it, build from it, and grow with it. I know the future is uncertain. I hope that, whatever transpires, we continue to be a family for one another. We've been here for each other before and we can again."

There were some *Amens*, an *Ahos*, and a *Hear hear!* and everyone looked into each other's eyes. I could feel the shared care and connection in the room. It felt good to be a part of it. I didn't want to spoil it, but sometimes you need to tear something down before you can rebuild. Fortunately, Eve made it easier.

"I know we're all deeply troubled by these horrible losses," she continued. "We have no closure in part because we don't know how or why this happened to Aiden and Timothy. But I have a feeling we may find out tonight. David has asked me if we could use this sacred place to come together to find the truth. I'm not sure what he has in mind, but I'd like us to listen to him."

All eyes came my way. Time to fire away with my best shot.

"Thank you, Eve. And thank you all for bringing me into your family. I can see and feel the love you share with one another. It's in the spirit of that bond that I believe we can leave here tonight knowing what happened to Timothy and Aiden."

"You know what happened?" Ross asked.

"No, I don't know for sure, but I have a pretty good idea. And, more importantly, if we all put our energies together, we'll know for sure."

"Let's do it," Lilah said.

"Sure," Eve said. "What do you want us to do?"

Not everyone was as eager to join in, but I knew enough about building a ground swell not to dwell on the maybes but to join with the yesses.

"I actually have a game we can play, one we all know and one which will help us solve the mystery. I know it might seem strange to play a game, but remember when you were a kid you played games all the time. Games tell us a lot about ourselves and others. It's with the intent of finding the truth that I'd like you all to join in. We can do this."

I paused. I wanted to make it hard for anyone to bow out. At one time or another, peer pressure has gotten us all to do things we'd have been better off not doing. I was hoping the killer would feel that way soon.

"It's a game we all know—Simon Says with a little Ouija thrown in. What I'd like to do is have everyone stay in the circle, and when I say Simon Says you take a small step toward the center. You'll find as the circle closes, truths will be revealed."

"This sounds like a lot of bullshit," Michael said.

"You're right about that. It is a lot of bullshit. But, you know, sometimes you have to go through shit to get to the other side."

"Let's do it," said Lilah.

"Fine," said Michael.

"Great. Thanks. Then let's stay in the circle but move it as far out as we can so we have room to move forward."

Once everyone had spread out, I said, "Simon says, every time Simon says something that's true for you, take a very short but noticeable step forward. If you understand that, Simon says, take a step forward."

They all did that. Not without some chuckles and sneers.

"Simon says he's going to ask a lot of questions, some of which are going to sound irrelevant and unnecessary, but he wants you to fully participate. Simon says, if you agree take another step forward."

Once again chuckles and sneers as everyone moved in.

"Simon says, everyone who thinks they're a better artist than Timothy, please take a step forward."

More chuckles, more sneers, one "Really?"

Surprisingly, one by one everyone moved in. More chuckles.

"Simon says, we need more room so everyone step back to where you started and take slightly smaller steps going forward."

Everyone did so.

"Simon says, anyone who has had their feelings hurt, been upset by, and wished harm on Timothy, please step forward."

Bit by bit, everyone but Eve came forward. Then she said, "All right," and joined the group.

"Simon says, anyone who has ever had their feelings hurt, been upset by, and wished harm on Aiden, please step forward."

Eve said, "All right," and came forward. Lilah followed. Then so did everyone else.

"Simon says, anyone who ever got drugs for Timothy, step forward."

Sheridan stepped up. Then Drew.

"Simon says, anyone who ever got drugs for Aiden, step forward."

Sheridan came alone.

"Simon says, anyone who ever bought drugs from Aiden, step forward."

Josie, Drew, and Michael did. Then Ross.

"Simon says, anyone who has ever written a song or part of a song that Timothy stole and gave them no credit, please step forward."

No one moved.

I hadn't thought anyone would tip their hand that easily but I'd hoped.

"Simon says he knows when you're lying. Simon says, if you ever wrote a song or a part of a song Timothy stole without giving you credit, please step forward."

Reluctantly, Drew came forward. Then Josie and Michael. Then Sheridan.

Everyone started to examine each other more earnestly.

"Simon says, thank you for being honest. Simon also says anyone who had plans for a solo career should step forward."

Drew, Michael, and Josie moved.

"Simon says, anyone who heard some of the new songs Timothy intended to put on the upcoming album, please step forward."

Eve and Sheridan.

That got a raised eyebrow from Josie, a frown from Drew, and disgust from Michael.

The circle was closing and I could see people reacting to who was and wasn't coming forward. There was still enough room for everyone to see each other's faces. I was counting on us all being able to catch the moment when the guard went down and the truth came out.

"Simon says, anyone who knew a significant amount of their lyrics were copied on the new album please step forward."

I could tell right away.

I hoped others had seen it as well, but I needed some help.

"Sheridan!" Lilah blurted out.

"What?"

"You flinched. Did Timothy steal your lyrics?"

"Huh?" Drew said. "Why did he use yours?"

"Yeah, what the fuck?" said Michael.

I kept my eyes on Sheridan. He wasn't crumbling but he wasn't standing tall. He needed a push.

"I don't think Timothy asked you. He stole them from you and planned to claim them as his own. Is that right?"

Silence.

"Tell us," Michael yelled.

Silence.

"Honey, you're okay," Eve said, and put her hand on his arm to console him. He gave her an obligatory smile, but not much else. He didn't look very okay.

"Come on," said Michael. "We all know what it's like to be fucked over by him. He stole our stuff too, but he'd alter it just enough so he could claim it as his own. It's no surprise he fucked you too."

"He stole your music?" Lilah asked.

"Just the lyrics," Sheridan said.

There was an unnerving silence.

"Before he was very sneaky about it. I suspected he'd done it but I was never sure. He'd take bits and pieces of things so I could never really say the words were mine. But, this time the son of a bitch gave Eve a tape with exact passages. Such an asshole thing to do. I confronted him and we had it out. He told me no one would ever believe me. I asked him to give me writing credits, but he told me I didn't know what I was talking about."

Michael chimed in. "Yeah. I know that story. He never gave any of us credit for shit. Our words and chords are all over the music. But if we pushed back he told us he would leave or fire us."

"So, Sheridan, can you tell us what happened?" I asked.

"Dave, you're not saying I killed him, are you? I admit I wanted to. And I might have. It was just so disgusting to hear my words coming out of his mouth. But someone else beat me to it."

"When did you hear the songs?" Michael asked.

"Timothy gave a tape to Eve a couple of hours before their set. He said they might play one. We smoked some shit and listened to it."

"And then what?" Drew asked.

"I rushed over and found him alone in the trailer. I was as mad as I've ever been. It was all I could do not to kill him right then and there. He was so arrogant and said I should be honored he'd used some of my 'ideas.' Some of my ideas? I laughed in his face. He'd stolen the soul of my poetry. Lines and images straight out of my poems. He told me I was exaggerating and nobody would believe me. He was the poet. I was a hack. That's what he said.

To my face. I almost strangled him. I possibly would have but we got interrupted."

"You got interrupted?"

"Yeah. CC came in. I don't remember why, but when she came into the trailer I stormed out."

"When was this?"

"Right before we all gathered. Maybe an hour and half before their show. I wanted to expose the whole sham before they went on, but Eve calmed me down and told me to wait till after the show and not ruin it for everyone."

"Well," said Ross, "someone ruined it for everyone."

"Yeah," I said. "Simon says, if Timothy and Aiden's death ruined it for you, step forward."

No one stepped forward. Then, acknowledging the probable spiral ahead, Ross took a step.

"Hmm," I said. "Evidently not everyone thinks the deaths ruined things for them. In fact, I'd venture to say some think they'll profit. At least from Timothy's. Only one person profits from Aiden's."

"Who's that?" Lilah asked.

"The person who Aiden confronted about killing Timothy."

"What?" Lilah said. "Aiden knew who killed Timothy?"

"Yes. From what I've learned about Aiden, I imagine he tried to get the person to come forward. He might have been an asshole to some, but Timothy's death put an end to his hopes of riding the coattails. He may have wanted to blackmail the killer or just get them to step forward and do the right thing. I don't know what motivated him. Maybe he was trying to be a good friend to the killer."

"How did Aiden know?" Lilah asked.

"When Timothy didn't come join the rest of the band, Aiden went to find out what was keeping him. He either saw someone else leaving or Timothy told him something before he died. Either way, Aiden suspected someone, and when he confronted that person they probably said they'd do the right thing. Then later on, they killed him."

"But the police said both were overdoses. What makes you so sure they were killed?" asked Carol.

"The police may be right. We won't really know until they've had time to do the autopsies. But I don't really think they both OD'd. Do you?"

Silence.

"Let's find out. Simon says, all those who think Timothy and Aiden mistakenly overdosed, please raise your hand." We were running out of room so I wanted to save stepping forward for my big-ticket questions.

No hands.

"Okay, so we all think they were killed. But the question is how. I know how, but I'm guessing only one other person in here knows how. But since I'm a teacher as well as a therapist, let me ask the class: How do you get someone to tie themselves off and stick a needle into their arm if they don't want to? Any guesses?"

"You could hypnotize them," Eve suggested.

"That's crazy," said Michael.

"Anyone here know how to do that?" I asked.

No volunteers.

"You could put a gun to their head and force them to do it. That's what I'd do," said Ross. Everyone turned to him. "I'm just saying."

"I get it. That could work. In which case, anyone with a gun could have done that. But it's a bit risky. The intended victim might fight back. The gun might go off. You might draw undue attention to yourself. There was a quieter, more effective way."

Silence.

"I've spoken to all of you about Hunter Thompson. We've all read *Fear and Loathing in Las Vegas*. But he wrote another excellent book that provided the inspiration for how to get Timothy and Aiden to appear as if they'd chosen to shoot up. I don't expect anyone to volunteer they read the book so let's try put that aside for the moment and take a pop quiz. If anyone here wanted to get some drugs, who's the first person you'd ask?"

All eyes focused on Sheridan.

"Okay, that was obvious. But who else might you go to?"

"The quack," CC said.

"Right," said a few others.

"Sheridan, want to tell us who else you'd go to?"

"Johnny Romano."

"Right, Johnny Romano. Anybody know why he'd go to Johnny?"

"Johnny could always hooked you up with whatever we wanted," Michael said.

"Yeah. Dope, hookers, Mallomars, you name it," said Drew.

"So if someone read that Hunter Thompson—a certain authority on drugs—knew about an exotic drug that caused paralysis, they might go to Sheridan, the quack, or Johnny."

Silence.

"I'm going to say they went to Johnny," I continued. "The doc certainly has a ready supply of various salves and lotions, but I don't think he'd have this drug handy. You'd need to order this drug ahead of time and Johnny ran a national delivery service. But maybe someone sees the good doctor outside of festival hours?"

More silence.

"I'm not hearing anyone owning up to being a 'patient' of the good doctor. Of course, someone might want to maintain doctor/patient confidentiality. That's entirely possible. But Johnny was our supplier."

"How come?" asked Lilah.

"Upon Sheridan's recommendation, I went and talked to Johnny. We got off to a bumpy start, but we were able to develop a level of trust and swapped information. He was very concerned I wouldn't squeal him out. That was very important to him."

While what I said was true, I was kinda spinning it so the killer would think Johnny told me who the killer was and not just that he'd gotten the ibogaine.

"Squealing isn't something Johnny's family takes a liking to," Sheridan said.

"He told you he got the drugs, but felt honor bound not to tell you who he got them for? Is that what you're saying?" asked Carol.

"Not really," I said. "Johnny told me something, but even though he was concerned about squealing, Johnny no longer cares. He's also been killed."

"What?" cried Eve.

"No way," said Carol.

"That's horrible," cried out Sheridan as everyone was taken aback. Emotions started to flow.

Before anyone could say anything more, Michael demanded, "Tell us what he said. Who did he get the drugs for?"

"In a moment," I said. "But, first, I want to say something to that person. It would be to your advantage to explain yourself than to have me out you. I don't think my explanation is going to be as charitable as yours."

A long shot. And the accompanying silence didn't help. I gave it an extra moment, just to allow the pressure to build, but nothing happened.

"All right. Simon says, will the person who killed Johnny Romano please step forward?"

"He did it," said Lilah, pointing.

And I agreed.

Then Ross broke out of the circle and ran from the tent.

CHAPTER 52

"The Pretender"

Jackson Browne

THERE WAS A lot of commotion.

"What the fuck."

"The bastard."

"I don't get it."

Some started crying and moaning but no one ran after him. I wasn't sure why.

Lilah came over to me and gave me a well-received hug. "You okay?"

"Yeah, I'm good. A little surprised because I hadn't pegged him for the deed, but I'm really glad he showed his hand."

"You were right. When you asked who'd killed Johnny, he reacted way differently than the rest of us. He had a different kind of shock on his face, like when you realize your parents found your hidden bong. A guilty-as-charged look."

"It was a good thing we both got a clear view of him. I wonder if others saw it too. He really did flinch."

"It's too bad he got away. But now we know whodunit, the police will be able to find him."

Not long after, Sully opened the flap and brought a handcuffed Ross back in. Everyone turned towards him. He looked defeated.

"This the guy you were telling me about?" Sully asked.

"That's him all right."

"I don't know what you're talking about," Ross said. "I didn't kill anyone. Why would I do that? Timothy was like a son to me. So was Aiden. Johnny I barely knew. I had no reason to kill any of them."

"Then why did you run?" Josie said.

"Yeah," said Michael. "What the fuck? Why did you kill them?"

"I didn't fucking kill them. You've got this whole thing wrong."

"I don't think so," said Michael. "You knew Timothy wanted new management and was going to leave you. You're past your prime. He was your golden goose and if he wasn't going to lay eggs for you, he wasn't going to for anyone else."

"That's such bullshit. Sure, there were rumors. There are always rumors. But even if he'd left me, the rest of you would carry on with me. I've got lots of irons in the fire."

"Like CDs and videos? How are those fires going?" I asked.

"That's nothing," Josie said.

"I know it's nothing but Ross thinks they're the next big thing," I said.

"Fuck you," said Carol. She obviously didn't like my opinion, but when I'm right I'm right.

Unfortunately, I wasn't feeling so right about Ross. I'd definitely seen him flinch and so had Lilah, but something didn't fit. I know there are no guilty people in prison and everyone protests their innocence, but I believed Ross. Yes, he could be a bull in a china shop and had some side deals going on, but I couldn't see him as the killer.

Which meant somebody else was. Someone who had their act so together, they could hide their sustained anger and plot Timothy's murder. Someone who could get close to the victims and get them to do drugs with them. Or someone who could slip the drug into a drink and have each of the victims share a toast with them.

But who?

"Hold on," Ross said on the verge of breaking down. "I'm sorry. You're my family and it's not good for me to bullshit you. I'm not proud of it, but you're right. I killed them."

"You asshole," Michael shouted. "Why did you have to do that? Just so you don't lose money? That's such a fucked thing to do."

"I know. I'm sorry."

"You should be," said Eve. "And to kill poor Johnny. All he did was help you out and you fucked him over."

"I just can't understand it, man," Drew said. "Timothy fucked us all over and we all wanted to throttle him a time or two, but was it really necessary to kill him, then Aiden, and Johnny? I guess we're lucky you got caught before you killed the rest of us."

They were starting to pour it on. Ross was having a hard time, but it was clear he felt it was his due.

Unfortunately, I didn't share that view.

"Ross, I want to ask you something. It's very brave of you to own up to the killings, and for that you ought to be commended. But I'm just not clear about one thing. Could you tell us about the drug you got from Johnny? What exactly was it and how did it work?"

"What? Oh, it was just some drug that paralyzes you. I don't know what it was called."

"Okay, I forget names too. But help me—when Thompson wrote about it, what did he say? Can you share that with us as some of us don't know."

"It was just some drug he took. I don't remember it very clearly."

"Yeah. I can tell. So just tell us in what context he wrote about the drug. Surely you remember that."

We could all see he was floundering. Time to bore in. "That was a memorable story he told. If you read it, you'd remember it."

"To tell you the truth, I can't remember. Someone probably just told me about it."

"Okay. So, what was it you told Johnny you wanted?"

"Some drug that would paralyze you. That's what I told him."

"And did he know what you were talking about? I didn't take Johnny as a big Hunter Thompson fan."

"Sure, he knew. He knew all about drugs."

"Okay. One more thing. How did you kill Johnny? The same way or differently?"

Silence.

"Okay, that's it," Carol said. "Quit browbeating the son of a bitch. He's just covering for me. He could never kill anybody. Timothy was fucking him over, sure. Just like he fucked everyone else over, but it was worse for Ross. Ross discovered him and made him what he was. Ross saw the writing on the wall months ago. He knew the time was coming. He's not stupid. His son was leaving him. Fucking him over. I had to do something. As much as I love you, you ain't no Bill Graham. If Timothy left there'd be nothing for him. The rest of you assholes would dump him too."

"But why kill him?" Drew asked. "With him dead there's no band. No more music. End of story."

"Not really," I said. "I imagine Ross wrote up Timothy's contract, and there's a clause in there about how if Timothy died, Ross would retain those rights. I'm sure Colonel Tom Parker, and whoever managed Jim Morrison, did just fine when Elvis and Morrison died."

"So, let me be clear here," Sully said. "I'm not arresting this guy. I'm arresting her."

"Unless someone else wants to volunteer."

Silence.

"You better drop by in the morning and tell me about this Johnny Romano."

CHAPTER 53

"I Wanna be Sedated"

The Ramones

It was a different scene in the tepee after Sully and Carol left. Ross was the only one sad to see her go. I imagine having someone willing to kill to help you out is an act of love few of us ever experience. That's just as well.

Everyone tried their hand at cheering Ross up and supporting him, but he was destined for some difficult days ahead. That said, he might very well be the recipient of a good percentage of the profits from Magoo's sales.

Eve tried to get the group together for one more round of kumbaya, but everyone seemed ready to call it a night.

I was hoping someone would ask me how I'd figured it out so I could kinda show off a little. But since Carol had confessed in front of us and we all understood her motive, there wasn't a lot of interest in how I'd put the pieces together. Maybe in the morning I could recount it, but it seemed my moment of glory had come and gone.

It reminded me of how, as a therapist, one day you'll tell your client something and then a few weeks later they'll say the same thing. Except they'll wonder why you didn't think of that. Since empowerment is the name of the therapy game, I just tell them I'm happy for them. The group felt empowered by being able to discern the bad apple. The hugs were heartfelt. The goodbyes sad.

Lilah asked me if I wanted to take a walk. I sure did. We left the tepee. There weren't a lot of people still up and about, just a few die-hards still partying strong. She guided us to where we'd had our first kiss and I was hoping we could add to it.

"Thank you for helping out tonight. You really did a great job of getting people into the whole thing."

"It was exciting. I didn't have to act. And I swear Ross flinched in some serious way."

"He did. But maybe that was a flinch of realization Carol had done it. He was protecting her like he protected the band. He was doing well enough until he wasn't, and she saw he couldn't pull it off. I guess she really loves him. She didn't have to confess. It was apparent he didn't know the details, and he'd have been set free and given whatever slap on the wrist they give people who falsely confess."

"What's that about? I never understood people doing that."

"In his case, I'm guessing it was about love. In other people's cases, well, let's save that discussion for another day."

"Speaking of which, there's something I want to tell you."

"You want to play Spin the Bottle?"

"That's not where I was going."

A sinking feeling started to come over me.

"It's not that bad."

"It isn't?"

"No, it isn't. But it's not that good either."

"Okay. What is it?"

"I'd be happy to go back to LA and get together and see what happens."

"That sounds good."

"But I'm not going back to LA. I have a teaching job at the Sorbonne in Paris. This weekend was my last fling with CC before I take off."

"Wait, you're going to teach at the Sorbonne? Don't you have to speak French to do that?"

"I do speak French. It was my college major. I got my PhD in sociology but French was my minor in undergrad."

"So are you going over there for the school year or what?"

"I don't know. I've already sent my stuff over and I'm going to see how it works out."

"Yikes. I wasn't expecting that. Just when I thought we might actually be able to make something of this."

"I hear you. I think so too. But we need to carry on with our lives. Let's be thankful for our time together and see what the future brings."

"That's very grown up of you. But I'm not feeling that mature about it. I'm sad, angry, disappointed, and confused all at once. I could get mad at you for not telling me sooner, but how would I justify that? It's not really something you needed to say when we met—'Hi, my name is Lilah. Just want you to know I'm about to take off to Paris so I won't be seeing you much after this weekend.'"

"Maybe I should have said something earlier. I'm sorry. It just never seemed like the right moment. I've really enjoyed our time together and I'm glad we had it."

"Yeah, me too. I just wanted more."

EPILOGUE

"Running on Empty"
Jackson Browne

THERE WASN'T MUCH more worth sharing after that. Lilah and I gave each other a long hug and headed back to our respective tents. Even though there were still thousands of people camping out for the last night before heading home, I felt very lonely. I wanted to be grateful for our time together, but mostly I felt like I'd been in the kitchen all day making dinner and hadn't gotten to eat it. I guess that's what chefs feel. I wasn't liking it.

Sleep didn't come easy. I kept replaying scenes from the tepee, juxtaposing them with ones by the lake. By the time I closed my eyes, the light was beginning to shift for sunrise.

I felt myself being shaken and it took me a moment to focus.

"Come on," Drew said. "Get up and come to the food pavilion. We're having breakfast and saying goodbye." Then he left.

By the time I got there most people had said their goodbyes and only Drew and CC remained. I loaded up on the coffee, eggs, bacon, and toast and joined them.

"So, Doctor, how are you feeling this morning?" CC said. "Pretty proud of yourself?"

"I was for a few moments last night, but that's come and gone.

Right now, I just want to get home and crawl under the covers, but I'm going to have to put together a little story for Sully about Johnny otherwise I might not be going home today."

"Good luck with that."

"Thanks. I'm hoping all's well that ends well, but not sure he'll feel that way. I'm sorry I didn't get over here soon enough to say goodbye to everyone."

"Everyone said to say goodbye to you," CC said.

"Like you said, all of us want to get home and they couldn't wait. But before they left, we were talking about last night and Simon Says. How did you come up with that?"

"Yeah, and how did you find out about Johnny and the drugs?" CC asked.

"I'm glad you asked. I was hoping somebody would. I'm not sure how I put it together, but Drew had faith in me and I didn't want to disappoint him."

"Bullshit. You wouldn't have minded disappointing me. Just as long as I paid you."

"That's partially true. I came here to help you out in one way, and it seems you've been able to take care of yourself fine without me. So it was good to help you out in another. I'm a curious guy anyway, so when Timothy died I wanted to know what had happened. You didn't think he'd done it himself and it turns out you were right."

"But you haven't answered my question."

"I don't know about Simon Says. It just came to me as a way to help figure things out. Everyone had motive and opportunity so I couldn't separate anyone out. I figured maybe if I asked some probing questions we all might be able to spot if something was off. We could have just sat talking, but playing the game sort of threw everyone off a bit."

"I get that," Drew said. "I was sure Ross did it there for a while, but glad he didn't."

"I get it. I kind of think he suspected Carol as well but didn't really want to admit it to himself. He did tell me he was with Carol when Timothy died, but I suspect he fudged a bit on how aware he was of her presence."

"He wanted to protect her, like he tried to do with the rest of us."

"Yeah," said CC. "He's the papa bear."

"If she killed Johnny because he might out her, how come she didn't kill you?"

"Yeah, I was wondering that myself. I think she felt she had things well enough in hand and if she killed me it would shine the light too brightly on our group. She knew I was on to the ibogaine, but also knew Johnny wouldn't out her, but she made sure. She was hoping to get away with the ODs and hope the police attributed Johnny's death to his other dealings."

"That makes sense. But it's fucked and weird at the same time. She wanted to be my agent but I wasn't sure. She was really into CDs and videos being the future and wanted me to get on board."

"You're better off without that distraction."

"I'm not so sure," CC said. "But how did she kill them. I don't get it?"

"Johnny she shot. I imagine she spiked some drink, had a toast with Timothy and then one with Aiden and the ibogaine paralyzed them. I don't know if it paralyzes you completely—probably depends on dosage—but it immobilized Timothy and Aiden enough that Carol could tie off their arms and stick in a needle. It's cold, but I don't think any of us ever experienced her any other way.

"I imagine there are other drugs she might have used, but since this one isn't your everyday one, she bet it would go undetected. When she heard me mention there was a connection with Thompson, she said she'd overheard the doc talking to someone about Thompson to throw me off."

"And Johnny Romano?"

"Sheridan told me Johnny was good for getting all manner of things. Since he traveled so much and was connected, he was able to score the drugs. I went and talked with him and then snuck back to search his truck. Unfortunately, he caught me and we had a little quality time together that allowed us to come to a mutual understanding. He suspected what the drug had been used for but was uncomfortable telling me. Being a snitch did not come naturally to him. He likely as not asked Carol to come and talk with him and she shut him up. She left him in his truck, which is why no one discovered him."

"But you said he'd told you who bought it," CC said.

"That may have been an exaggeration."

"Johnny didn't deserve to die. Well, none of them did. But why kill Aiden? He wasn't the problem."

"He was only a problem because he saw her leave the trailer right before he went in to get Timothy or Timothy told him before he died. I'm guessing he went to talk with her about it and she arranged to meet him later. Aiden told her he was going to see the drug dealer in tent city—and she met up with him there. When she got him alone, she gave him a peace offering and they had a toast from her handy thermos."

"So that's it? The end of the story?"

"Well, that, and Lilah's going to Paris, you're going to carry on, and I'm going to talk with Sully."

"I guess the show's mostly over."

"We'll see..."

Like most fiction, parts of this story are true. The US festival was in 1982. All the bands mentioned, with the exception of Magoo, played at that festival. The chapter titles are songs the various bands performed. Steve Wozniak was the visionary and pocketbook who paid the bill. Bill Graham was the producer who booked the acts and made Woz's dream come true. I never spoke to either of those men, although I'd have welcomed the opportunity. I also never met Christine Lund, a popular local newscaster. I wouldn't have minded meeting her as well. I took certain liberties with the backstage area but did my best to present the festival as it was.

If you'd like a peek into what the future holds for David, take a look at what comes after the Acknowledgments.

ACKNOWLEDGMENTS

First off, I want to thank Hale Milgrim. He told me he couldn't remember anything about the US festival aside from the fact he wore a Grateful Dead T-shirt and was asked to make a cassette of music to play before the Dead played on Sunday morning. He started the cassette with George Harrison's "Here Comes the Sun." As we talked, he began to recall bits and pieces that now are included throughout the book. Thanks, Hale. Everything about you I wrote in the book is fiction, but you were there and your contributions to music are worthy of their own book.

Hale introduced me to Bob Barsotti, who worked closely with Bill Graham on the US festival. Bob told me he'd fly down from the Bay Area every week for a few months before the show to help set things up. Then he'd fly back north to handle whatever concerts Bill Graham Productions were promoting that weekend. Bob gave me some behind-the-scenes stories that also made their way into the book. I mention an incident when Bill Graham had someone forklift the Kinks' manager's car to the farthest parking lot. Bob was leaving later that night on his motorcycle and saw the manager; he gave him a lift to his car. Bob was known for his kind hand.

On a side note, Bob now helps put together the Kate Wolf Music Festival, where he gets to work with Wavy Gravy—a sixties prankster if ever there was one, and is still at it.

I also want to thank Dr. Jill Stein, who advised me about what transpires backstage. She's had an insider's view and shared some of her knowledge with me as well as provided much needed editorial guidance. Some may notice the similarities between her and one of the characters in the book.

I need to apologize to my friends. Some of them might find facsimiles of themselves here. Indeed, I've used certain of their characteristics to inform some of the qualities of the characters in the book. The positive qualities of these characters are my tribute, the lesser my creative license.

I also need to thank my editors Lulu Swainston and Ursula @ Owl Pro Editing who took my rambling, grammatically challenged writing and rendered it digestible.

Perhaps the cover of the book beckoned you, in which case Chrissy and the artists at Damonza are responsible. Their work adorns all the mysteries for which I am very thankful.

More and more people are listening to books. If that's how you found this book, lucky you. I know I'm lucky for having found Jake Robertson to narrate the books.

Thank you for taking the time to read or listen to the book and read the acknowledgements. Hopefully you'll carry on with *A Lesson in Therapy and Murder.*

David

A LESSON IN THERAPY AND MURDER

DAVID UNGER, PHD

A LESSON IN THERAPY AND MURDER

David Unger, PhD

PROLOGUE

"The best I ever had? That's tough."

"Come on. I'm sure you've had plenty."

"Well, I've certainly had more than my share. But picking the best, that's not easy."

"Okay, how about you pick the best 'aha' moment? You know, a time when the light went on and the world lined up just right."

"I haven't had many of those, but there's one that stands out."

"Come on. Let's hear it."

"I was sitting naked in one of the hot tubs at Esalen, looking out at the Pacific Ocean after a blissful massage, and suddenly realized my life was crap."

"What? That was a peak moment?"

"Well, not in a kumbaya way. But, right then I knew I needed to feel more like I did in that moment. My life, which looked good enough on the outside, wasn't going the way I'd hoped it would."

"Yeah. I know that feeling."

"So what about you? What's the best therapy–kumbaya–'aha' moment you've ever had?"

I was kind of curious to hear it for myself. Eavesdropping on these women while they stood in the reception line, I hadn't been surprised by what the first had said. We can all relate in some way. Maybe not in the naked-Esalen-tub way, but in the way of our lives not being all we'd like them to be. Sometimes it becomes abundantly clear that if we don't do something, nothing is going to change. That realization is terrifying, liberating, empowering, and life-altering all at once.

So, yeah, I was curious what her friend had to say.

"I'm gonna go another way. I can relate to the realization that your life needs some upgrading, but the moment I'm thinking about is when I was lost in bliss."

"How's that?"

"You know that moment right after you have a really good climax and all the tension leaves your body and you feel light and carefree?"

"Boy, do I. I wouldn't mind some more of that this week."

"I'm with you on that."

Me too.

"I was in the midst of one of those glorious moments. I had nothing to do but languish in it. It was serene. I was lost in space, just floating aimlessly with no cares, when I heard my husband yell out from downstairs, 'Where the hell is dinner?'"

"What? No, you're kidding."

"Bless the man. I knew right then and there I couldn't live with him another day. That was one of the best days of my life, right there."

I don't know if it was one of her husband's best days, but maybe. If that relationship wasn't right for her, it wasn't right for him. But that's easy for me to say as I didn't have to go through that upheaval.

I was enjoying listening to these women swap stories about impactful moments in their lives. I suppose this was as good a place as any to be having those discussions. We were checking in to the American Association of Humanistic Psychology's 1983 annual conference in Santa Barbara, California. Most of the attendees were therapists, graduate students, or educators, here for a ten-day conference dedicated to learning and experiencing the latest theories and practices.

It wasn't long ago that I'd been to the Annual Conference of Sex Therapists and Surrogates and got caught up in a murder mystery. I'd stood in that reception line and overheard a couple of women talking about the best sex of their lives. Soon thereafter, the keynote speaker had been kidnapped, then murdered. I got swept up in the action—it was a sex conference, after all—and ended up solving the mystery. Here I was, back in the reception line of another annual conference, overhearing two women talk about peak therapeutic experiences.

Go figure.